HEAT LIGHTNING

LEAH HAGER COHEN

HEAT
LIGHTNING

AVON BOOKS  NEW YORK

I'm grateful to Kate Sullivan for teaching me about marshes.

AVON BOOKS
A division of
The Hearst Corporation
1350 Avenue of the Americas
New York, New York 10019   AUG 1 1 '97

Copyright © 1997 by Leah Hager Cohen
Excerpt from *The Crofter and the Laird* by John McPhee. Copyright © 1969, 1970 by John McPhee. Reprinted by permission of Farrar, Straus & Giroux, Inc.
Interior design by Jean Cohn
Visit our website at **http://AvonBooks.com**
ISBN: 0-380-97468-1

Library of Congress Cataloging in Publication Data:

Cohen, Leah Hager.
  Heat lightning / Leah Hager Cohen.
     p.   cm.
  I. Title.
PS3553.042445H43   1997   96-47656
813'.54—dc21   CIP

First Avon Books Printing: July 1997

✦ To My Mother ✦

HEAT LIGHTNING

◆

OUR MOTHER AND father drowned in the Kittiwake River when Tilly and I were babies. This is the story Tilly said Hy told us before I could even talk:

A storm came and our mother climbed to the top of the hill to watch it come. She had loved storms (Tilly said Hy said). She would listen to news of one's approach on the black transistor radio she kept over the kitchen sink but often carried with her from room to room, diligently monitoring the predictions of radio meteorologists, delivered in that dislocated drone that got people comparing aches in their knuckles and knees, got them noting aloud the peculiar behavior of house pets. I'd imagine our mother bending her ear toward the metal grille of the speaker, listening to the forecast, following the storm's course.

This particular storm had been a little storm. It had no name. But the sky grew dark just the same, and when the wind picked up toward evening, our mother stepped out into it.

She climbed the hill and walked the path that trimmed the edge of the ridge, high above the wide river. From there she spied a rowboat in which she counted several passengers, first hooting and tossing bottles into the water, then, as the wind slapped up bigger waves, struggling to row ashore. She watched for a quarter of an hour before it became apparent that the boaters, on their own, would not manage to reach land.

She ran then, back down the dark, wet hill in order to call the police station. But the telephone on the kitchen wall would only crackle and spit. So she and our father climbed back up and over the hill themselves. Their bodies washed ashore the following afternoon.

"But where were me and Mole?" Tilly thought to ask when she was about six.

The three of us had been making Kool-Aid pops at the kitchen table. Hy, our mother's older sister, had brought home the popsicle kit from Coffey's Hardware, where she worked. It came with six plastic molds, red and yellow, and its own yellow plastic rack that slid into the freezer. Tilly and I each took a turn with the wooden spoon, dissolving the pink powder in a heavy glass bowl of steaming water. Artificial cherry vapor rose thickly around our faces. We all had bare arms: Hy's sturdy and tufted with straw-colored hair, Tilly's ravaged with mosquito bites she'd clawed, mine tan and plump as fried chicken drumsticks. I remember this afternoon in detail; it is the only time I can recall Hy telling us the story in any fullness.

"Well, you were fast asleep in your cribs," she replied. "Before they left, your parents got me to come over and sit with you." She took a final stir with the spoon, set it on the table with the muted rap of wood on wood.

I wanted to ask a question, too. "What happened to the people throwing bottles?"

"They all stayed in the boat," came the answer, smooth and neat as hospital corners. "It never did capsize. Later in the night, after the storm passed, they rowed themselves in."

"But . . ." I croaked, and trailed off.

Tilly tried for us once more: "Was there lightning?" But that wasn't what she meant, I knew; neither of us was able to frame a question that could get at the information we might need.

"I don't remember," said Hy. She tipped up the bowl, poured warm liquid into the neat plastic molds. "Some."

That, as we knew it, was the tale in its entirety. For years I had no memory that did not include this story, etched spare and exact in my mind. I would tell it to myself in bed at night, constant as an old newspaper clipping that has been creased and smoothed, creased and smoothed, beyond legibility—nothing ever altered, nothing further explained.

To whatever other questions Tilly and I had once thought to pose, Hy supplied such disappointing answers that we eventually stopped asking. We knew that our mother had been born twelve years after Hy, that our parents had gotten married at eighteen, that what family our father had (Hy had never met any of them) lived in Maine, that our father had worked on a road crew, pouring asphalt. Later in life Tilly and I would be able to make surmises from such facts about our parents' lives, to interpret them in ways that led to at least probable textures, partial elucidation— but for us as children, they existed simply as bricks of information, perfectly literal and frustratingly opaque. And even such bricks were sparse; Hy demonstrated a limited ability to describe anything of her younger sister and brother-in-law beyond the most meager and impractical scraps of information.

"Violet liked peanuts and pretzels and ham," she once told us. "Anything with salt."

And: "David was handy. He built those shelves in the front hall."

And: "Violet had an inborn sense of direction. You could plunk her down blindfolded somewhere and she'd tell you which way was north."

Such details fell randomly and infrequently from her lips. Tilly and I were hoarders, jealously storing them, much as we did the particular shells and stones and bits of soft-edged glass we had been inspired to collect from the lake and keep on beds of cotton in old cardboard gift boxes: undisputed treasures whose usefulness, we felt certain, we had only to decipher. Here, Hy was no help. When milked for further details, she would only shrug and clamp her lips; when pressed she would say, "I don't know, *you* have the cookie tin."

She meant the old butter-cookie tin filled with snapshots, which she had given us to keep. Tilly kept the tin beneath her bed. Its lid was awful to pry off, especially in humidity; an array of dents along the rim betrayed my various efforts with a spoon, a barrette, and once a pair of nail scissors (the results of which attempt had led to four stitches across the heel of my left hand).

When the lid finally popped free, the contents would release a dense, pointed scent. Twelve photographs, all of them black-and-white with scalloped borders, showed the same young man and woman engaged in a variety of activities. The man lay in high grass, shirtless, reading a newspaper; the woman, eyes shut as the picture was taken, grinningly displayed a lopsided loaf of bread on the flat of her palm; the man pushed a frilled baby carriage down a partly sunlit lane; one of them (it was impossible to say which; Tilly and I had debated the matter more than once), face obscured by a hooded parka, tobogganed down a snowy hill.

The picture I liked best must have been taken by a third party. It showed both the woman and the man sitting on a woodpile. It might have been early morning. She had eyeglasses on and a thick braid coming out in wisps; he had what looked like a trace of shaving cream on his ear and wore a plaid jacket; they both held cups of something hot. They looked as if they didn't realize anyone was taking their picture—her staring heavily into the steam from her cup, him watching as though waiting for her to speak. This was our mother and father.

For years, one of Tilly's and my favorite games involved arranging these snapshots on her bedroom floor and making up stories and dialogue to animate the images, the way other children might have done with dolls. These twelve pictures afforded us such latitude in constructing an idea of our parents that we learned not to mind the paucity of Hy's reminiscences; her story we appropriated as well, and privately embellished. Thus the storm, in my mind, comprised hail, gales of wind, thunder, and lightning. The sky was gray-green, the color of the place between yolk and albumen in a hard-boiled egg. The rowboat was red. Our parents wore rain slickers: hers yellow, his navy blue. They washed up on the sand clean and pale, their mouths and eyes closed, their fingers interlaced.

As we got older, our need to flesh out the story grew—not

just the costumes and props and blocking, but things we couldn't name, temperament and motivation and, in a way, a moral—and bit by bit, we supplied these elements, too, so seamlessly that they appeared to have been spawned by the story itself: thus Violet's passion for storms bordered on madness, but a kind of magical, fairy-tale madness; she could not help herself; she was some kind of water sprite; she was enchanted. The woman holding the lopsided bread and the woman staring into the steam in her cup became, in another picture, a woman running through trees and running through rain, followed into the stormy Kittiwake by a man who loved her enough to join her there. That was how we worked it out; if they were heroes for risking their lives to save the people in the boat, they were even more heroic for the qualities of magic and loyalty with which we endowed them. We did not articulate it as we did the rest, but it was there between us, this part of the story, unspeakably frightening and glorious; it bound Tilly and me with its shameful beauty.

Eventually all the details we contrived, singly or jointly, mundane or ethereal, combined in a sort of life-giving alchemical reaction, so that as the story increased in size it increased in legitimacy. Our own contributions took on such steadfast authority that they melded with fact. It became our own private gospel. So seriously did we take it, that any time Tilly's idea of the story and mine happened to clash, we fought bitterly—one time in particular I remember disagreeing over how many people had been in the rowboat: four or seven. I had ended up knocking Tilly into the corner of her dresser; she'd had to go downstairs and have her temple iced.

It is difficult now, looking back, to be sure how much we

really came to confuse our own version of the story with Hy's lean account. What is certain is that we found it far preferable to hers, which gaped ominously full of holes; we felt the cold shudder and rush of things pressing to inhabit them. Or did we wish the danger, wish the holes, which we then so meticulously filled in ourselves, on endless afternoons on the floor of Tilly's room, the snapshots laid out on her braided rug, her and my fingers colliding as we moved the images around and made up sentences for our dead parents to speak? When I think of our story and of all the years Tilly and I spent telling it back and forth, stroking and shining it like a secret inheritance between us, what I wonder is not how we came to make it up in the first place, but why we ever let it get away from us one summer, let it grow so recklessly large and poorly tended that it had no chance but to hatch shatteringly, falsely apart.

I imagine Tilly correcting me: "You do know why."

She would hate for me to say that she has become like Hy, equating the baldest facts with the purest explanation, but she did grow more Hy-like every year, cloaking herself in formidable plainness, excluding all that was not obvious and useful and daily. For my part, I remained unconvinced that explanations did not lie low between the facts, emerging only with their retelling, with their manipulation. Even all these years later I can't keep from going back and worrying the events of that summer like a scab, chipping and prying that I might understand what exactly we surrendered that summer, and why.

But "You already know," Tilly insists in my mind in her cool, impatient way, so sure of being right—and in a way, she is right. "That was the summer the Rouens came."

JULY

CHAPTER ✦ ONE

WE GREW UP at Pillow Lake—the name of both a lake and a town. The lake, two miles around and shaped like an egg on its side, separates our house from the town. On our side of the lake rises the hill, which is wooded and sparsely populated, but long ago it had been the reverse: where the shops and buildings now stand had been only farmland, while the hill had teemed with activity. All of this we got from Hy, but Tilly and I could see for ourselves it was true. Back in the woods we had found the mossy stone foundations of several houses, and at the top of the hill a graveyard lay webbed in weeds and ivy, its field rock markers cracked and fallen.

We had lived with our aunt nearly ever since our memories began. Tilly had been three, and I not quite two, when our parents drowned. Hy had told us she'd always wanted children but never cared to marry; as children we did not find this odd and naturally considered her lucky to have us. Hy was tall, near six feet, with big hands and crinkly brown hair, which she usually wore in a print kerchief, knotted either at her nape or up across the top of her head. She had an oblique smile, which is to say a dimple in only one cheek; it showed when she was fretful as well as when she was glad, and it made her pretty in a way that she otherwise was not. She had the awkward grace of a large-boned animal— many, many years later I came to think of her as having possessed a kind of loneliness that gave her dignity. She must have been in her forties the summer the Rouens came.

Our house stood three-quarters of the way up the hill. It had been built by our great-grandfather late in the last century, before Ice Cart Road even had a name. The road wound behind Pillow Lake, past our house, to the top of the hill. Here it branched, with one tongue continuing around the lake, the other snaking sharply down a rocky drop. Below this drop flowed the Kittiwake.

Long ago, before refrigerators, people used to harvest giant blocks of ice from Pillow Lake. Our own grandfather and his father as well had worked winters on the lake. Operating a horse-drawn ice plow, they'd carved fault lines across the frozen surface. Once the blocks of ice were cut loose from their grid, they got carted up the hill on a little custom-built railroad, pulled across the flat top by horse, lowered on cables over the ridge, and sent on steamboats twenty-seven miles down to the city, where people purchased pieces to stick in their iceboxes. Hy told us this was how people had kept their meat and milk and vegetables cold.

"Why didn't they just cut the ice out of the river instead of lugging it from way up here?" Tilly had asked.

Hy said Pillow Lake was famous for the purity of its ice. "And in any case," she added, "the Kittiwake is brackish."

"Brackish?" I said.

"Salty," said Hy. "Backwash from the ocean."

"*Brackish, brackish,*" I whispered, charmed, and for the next

"You don't own it."

"Well, yes." Hy corrected her almost modestly. "I do."

I think it was in the moment just before she said it that I realized, with a funny smashy feeling deep inside, that it was true, that I had dimly known it all along, this fact, however buried it had been. As if, in the same instant that her words came forth, released by her breath and floating independently now across the tabletop, my own knowledge jogged loose and rose up in unwitting fellowship.

Over the stillness I could hear something electric—the light fixture or the fridge: an obvious, edgy sound. The whole room seemed to grow very large in it, every object to swell in it, become mockingly conspicuous: the grease-dulled toaster, the yard-sale paper napkin holder, the salt and pepper shakers in the shape of cocker spaniels, the volunteer firemen's calendar thumbtacked to the side of the dish cupboard.

I looked across at Tilly. Her eyes had gone watery and she had red patches on her cheeks. She looked as if she had just bitten into a sour pickle. She looked as if she had just been caught in a lie. We all might have been embarrassed for a moment.

Then Hy's fork skreaked against her plate; Tilly winced; Hy took a bite and spoke mildly around it.

"It goes with the property." Some muscles tightened, the dimple showed. "You remember." She looked at Tilly's face, then mine, then Tilly's again, then down. She poked at some baked macaronis. The tines of her fork scraped at bits of oily potato chip topping. I felt in a minute someone's glass of milk would topple, could see it, almost, in advance: a white flood across the table, soaking napkins, seeping under plates.

"We remember what?" I said, and at the same time Tilly said, "Can you please not make that sound?" Hy lifted her fork.

"I spoke with a real estate agent in town who said it would be easy to rent out for just the summer," she continued conversationally. "So no fussing with radiators or anything. So."

"We remember what?" I repeated.

"Hm?"

"We remember what, you were going to say."

"You remember . . ." But she drew the phrase into a singsong and changed her mind midstream. "I was going to say you remember it's part of this property. I thought."

Tilly slid her chair back, making (I might have pointed out to her at another time) a far harsher grate than fork on plate. "I'm done may I be excused," she said, words all run together and toneless like the pledge, and she brought her plate and glass to the sink, banged them there, and slapped straight out through the pantry. The storm door moaned shut on its spring.

"Can I go—?"

Hy nodded.

I took my windbreaker from the peg.

April at Pillow Lake never signified much in the way of spring. The air hung raw and damp; the evening looked made of glass. I tried to keep my chin tucked inside the collar of my jacket as I scudded down the footpath. At the bottom I saw Tilly facing the lake, which, still choked in parts with soft hunks of ice, lapped sluggishly at the rocks. She stood, coatless and unflinching, her toes at the precise line where the water's tongue ran out and met a crust of dry sand. I came up beside her.

"It'll ruin all our privacy," she said without looking around.

She bit a draggling tail of thread from her cuff and spat it neatly into the water.

Tilly had become a great enthusiast of privacy during the past year. Despite being her closest relative, I no longer qualified for automatic access to my sister's company. Lately she had seemed even to be rationing the amount of time that I was permitted, literally, to see her; while getting ready for school in the morning, if I went down the hall to her room with the aim of borrowing a belt or a hairband, she would crack her door only a few inches, and through this slot a single hand would emerge, briefly, dangling the desired object. Or worse, she'd pretend not to know what I meant: "What belt?" She'd make me describe it.

So when she called it "our privacy" I felt a warm, liquid hope, and was glad I'd come after her to the lake instead of staying in the kitchen to cheer Hy; already I see I was taking sides, forming allegiances in preparation for what was to be the most difficult summer of my childhood. Hy had betrayed us somehow; that much I read in Tilly's posture, and anyone who moved into the dead house would be complicit in that betrayal.

"I love how she doesn't ask us," Tilly went on, still staring straight across the lake, where the sky, watery pink, was now hardening into ribbons of sunset. Her nose had started to run, but she didn't take her fists from her jeans pockets to wipe it.

"I didn't know the dead house was hers," I offered. It was the best thing I could think of to say.

"Yes, you did," said Tilly. "Don't call it that anymore."

So maybe, really, it was Tilly, back on that raw evening, who first allowed the story to begin to crack.

*   *   *

All that spring Hy worked at transforming the dead house. She hired a carpenter to repair the rotted porch steps, and painters to brush on a fresh exterior coat the color of sweet corn. On weekends she tackled the interior herself. She brought home paper sacks from Coffey's Hardware, a steady stream of them, filled with little tubs of spackle and switch plates and packages of screws and things, all purchased with her employee discount. She traveled to and fro along Ice Cart Road, toting scrapers and rollers and rags and buckets, evacuating the house, I imagined, of years of dust, droppings, webs.

She had managed to rent the house to one family for the entire summer. The parents were scientists, she told us, marine biologists. They wanted to come up and study the river, or the lake; she couldn't remember which.

This news elicited further distress from Tilly. "They'll probably dig up the whole beach," she predicted, triggering in my mind, a quick, vivid image of scientists in white lab coats steering forklifts and dredging great scoops of sandy bottom from Pillow Lake.

They had some kids about our age, Hy also informed us.

"Boys or girls?" I asked, and, "How many?" but this she didn't know.

Tilly and I did not offer to help with fixing up the dead house. To our initial relief (and, I think, subsequent vexation), Hy never asked. She left the house each Saturday and Sunday after breakfast, dimple etched deep, whistling as she walked down the road, and although she looked neither angry nor sad, something in her manner precluded offers of accompaniment.

Our aunt's face was capable of great shifts, and although I suppose she had a whole range of expressions, reflecting a complete range of moods, as a child I divided them all into two slots, which I thought of as the berry-plate face and the walnut face, and one was good and one was not. The berry-plate face was warm and pliant, lit by silver-capped molars that glinted when she smiled wide, lit, also, by green eyes that scrunched narrow at the outer corners like apple seeds. The intricate, rosy veinwork that laced across her cheeks always put me in mind of what Hy called the good china, which had belonged to her mother and was patterned with wild strawberries and all the fine, cream-colored cracks that years of washing had wrought in the glaze.

But other times her face went dark and knotty, as if carved of walnut, and everything about it then—the vertical creases around her lips, the length and curve of her nose, the shelf of bone beneath her eyes—looked set, like a mask. Even the dimple became forbidding.

Tilly called it "going off" whenever she got this way: "Hy's gone off," she'd mutter, in hurt or disgust. As children we thought this phenomenon was peculiar to Hy; I don't know why, except that we didn't know any other grown-ups really well. I remember the hot, pricking disappointment I felt years later when I realized virtually everyone has a version of "going off"—it was not so much disappointment at the fault itself, but at its *commonness*. In Hy it manifested itself as snappish remoteness; she'd be cross and impersonal at once. If we tried to carry on a normal conversation with her when she got this way, she wouldn't answer properly. If we remarked on her odd behavior, she would recede even further, becoming standoffish and vague, as if we were strangers trying to strike up conversation in a public space.

Because we thought such behavior was peculiar to Hy, we

associated times when Hy went off with our own unusual history. It frightened us and angered us—frightened because it evoked images of our mother going off in the rain in the night; angered because it was Hy's responsibility as a grown-up not to frighten us. But that spring I almost came to look forward to those times, delivering as they did a certain benefit: Tilly. They prompted in her an ever-rarer cordiality; she would invite me to her room, where we'd lie on the braided rug and pore through the stacks of magazines and catalogs that Tilly had begun keeping under her bed. They were neither secret nor illicit, all of them having been either purchased from Conklin Stationers in town or sent through the mail addressed to Hy, but because of the way Tilly stored them, and because of the special circumstances under which I'd be invited to peruse them with her, to me they reeked of contraband. We lay on our stomachs, pretending to smoke pieces of chalk we'd scammed from blackboard ledges at school, and flipped through images of lipsticked mouths and diamond pendants, nail-polished fingers holding lean cigarettes, ladies dressed in nothing but bras and girdles.

"I never could be a model because of all these bruises," Tilly would observe without rue as she appraised her shins; the seventh-graders were playing field hockey that spring. "And you"—turning to me, searching, frowning, her gaze tripping up and down my body—"you don't have the bone structure," she would pronounce, not unkindly. Far from being crushed, I thrilled to her scrutiny.

Or, "No, Mole, not like that; relax your other fingers," she'd admonish, adjusting my grip on the stick of chalk.

"How do you know?"

"I just do."

Under her bed I could see the cookie tin, its royal blue dully gleaming from the dark recesses where it had been pushed by piles of magazines, supplanted by glossy pictures of ladies in their underwear, perfume ads with men's sad faces and peel-strips we'd exhausted against the insides of our wrists. We had not had it out in years, the cookie tin. The last time I had suggested playing with it, Tilly had demurred in such a way that I was put off from doing so again.

Similarly, never did we mention, Tilly and I, during all those weekends when Hy went off (literally and figuratively), the hammer we could sometimes hear ring smackingly in the distance: Hy pounding something, Hy driving nails. Nor did we allude to the family whose advent they signaled. I suppose to discuss it would have constituted an admission of interest.

I thought about the scientist family all the time.

I could feel myself waiting for them, could feel myself being patient for their arrival, and I daydreamed about them with faithful expectation. Often my fantasies were quite specific: there would be a daughter my age, with ash-blond hair (I could see it exactly: earlobe-length, a bit lank), a scientists' daughter with her own microscope; we would prick our thumbs and examine drops of our own blood, mix potions with pilfered household items: olive oil, paprika, moth powder. Other times my fantasies translated into more general longings, a romantic feeling about the arrival of strangers, the idea of them being drawn behind Pillow Lake, where our lives would intersect in inexplicably significant ways. I anticipated their coming all through the spring, desired them in a sense both material and mystical, the way I might a beautifully iced miniature cake, or a pair of velvet shoes in a dusty shop window.

Tilly did not confess to any similar feelings, but I knew that her curiosity was aroused. Sometimes after supper (never when Hy was there), as the afternoon light began extending into the early evenings, she and I would stroll down to the house, examine it from the road. As gradual and discreet as the swelling of blurry green buds in the woods around it, the house emerged from its own dormancy that spring, appeared sensate. We inferred the changes even when we couldn't identify them.

"It's the windows," I would declare one evening, shading my eyes as I looked up. "She's washed them."

"No," Tilly would contradict, fingers clasped behind her waist. "It's the weeds. The walkway is much clearer."

We'd stand there scrutinizing windows and walkway, the rose-blue dusk slipping down around us, roof shingles glowing in the last reach of light, a sudden breeze riffling through the ivy on the side of the house: a little less sure of ourselves than the moment before.

It was the last Saturday in June when the Rouens finally arrived, pulling into our drive at midday in a decidedly corporeal scramble of limbs and noise and dust. All the doors of their squarish black car seemed to spring perpendicular at once, and even before anyone emerged we could hear the general sounds of squabbling. Tilly, her body stiff with disapproval, watched from the doorway that led from the pantry into the yard. I stood just behind her on tiptoe, being careful not to breathe on her neck.

Hy was in the kitchen, where she had been fixing lunch half

the morning, cooking things—deviled eggs and hermits—in spite of the heat. Even now, from where we stood in the pantry, Tilly and I could hear the oven door creaking open behind us: one more reason for us to be against her. Our house, located in the woods and near the top of the hill, caught a cross section of shade and river breeze that usually ensured a pleasant sharpness in the air. But that day it was hot. Wisteria and trumpet vine crept purple and orange from the eaves of the stable (which we used as a garage); the drive had been baked to loose ocher dust; the crickets chirring in the grass had taken on their parched summer sound. Ordinarily, in summer Hy hated to turn on the stove for anything besides tea. She made two exceptions: boiling jam at the end of August, when Coffey's closed for a week, and baking a cake in mid-August, for Tilly's birthday.

We tried to count the children as they disentangled themselves from the car. I glanced at Tilly sideways and saw her mouth puckered as though she tasted lemon. *"Five?"* she whispered, then, "No, the littlest's a doll."

Across the dry yard, grainy with particles of agitated dust, they stood out against the white of the stable like a magazine family, all rumpled khaki shorts and vivid ankle socks. The kids blinked and shook themselves in the brightness, then went about hitching themselves up to their respective belongings: a fishing rod, a plaid knapsack, a gray stuffed something for the smaller girl. And talking all the while:

"I want a drink."

"Should I put on my bathing suit right away?"

"Cut it out, jerk!"

"A horse lives in this barn?"

"Daddy said it's my turn to wear the sunglasses now."

"Are we staying here? Is this our house?"

At that, Tilly made a little sound in the back of her throat as if it itched. Then Hy's shoes clucked across the tile floor and our aunt came up behind us, smelling of hot raisins and sweat. She rested her left hand lightly across my back. The father must have heard her or spotted the movement, because he looked up then from the jumble of kids and possessions, and shaded his eyes in our direction.

"Hello there!" he called out, and Hy lifted her right arm at a slant. "I'm Bill Rouen!"

All spring long, whenever we had referred to them at all, it had been as "the people coming this summer," or "the renters," or "the scientist family." Until that day, I had seen their name only on paper, and as the father pronounced it that first time, sending his voice to us across the yard, I was struck by the sound of it: exactly like *ruin*.

The father wore a brass belt buckle. Sunlight smacked off it blindingly as he approached the pantry door, and when he came near enough, I saw it was in the shape of a scorpion. It didn't seem like a belt buckle for a father to wear.

Just before he reached us, Tilly slipped behind Hy, giving a light jerk to the waist of my T-shirt. I followed her into the kitchen. She dragged a stool from under the counter and perched. I did, too.

"Leave your things right in the driveway," we heard Hy call out in her deep voice. "I'll take you down to the house after you've eaten."

The pan of hermits cooled on the stove. The table had not been set, but a stack of plates and forks had been laid out. The elephant pitcher and a can of frozen lemonade sat on the cutting board. Lots of feet clopped across the drive, and all the sounds of greeting simmered and multiplied: there was a large and jovial bark of adult laughter, and we heard the screen door strain open as wide as it would go.

"Come on," hissed Tilly, her mouth all drawn and white. She slid from her stool and retreated farther into the house, all the way through the dim hall to the front door.

I envied the severity of her anger, and marveled at it. My own overriding state was an unwieldy, heady agitation, and it made me stall in the doorway and ask, "Where are we going?"

"You don't have to come if you don't want to," she said, and went down the porch steps.

She had gotten very quick, Tilly had, become maddeningly, determinedly ephemeral. She would stiffen her lips into a bloodless stripe and let her gaze turn gelid—she had developed a trick of making her eyes seem to recline, to tilt back, like the eyes of a model in a cosmetic ad. And she never seemed to allow herself to waver anymore, just decided and vanished.

I peeled a splinter of wood from the doorframe and rolled it between my fingers, listening to her clamber down the shortcut even after the trees had swallowed her from sight, thinking, *Will I follow her?* From inside the house came another merry hoot, and the sound of chairs being pulled out. The porch trembled under my feet. I waited a long time, maybe a minute—a mosquito came and landed on my arm and I let it begin to drink before I blew it off—and then went back inside.

Everyone in the kitchen seemed to be generating noise. Two little girls were arguing over who could sit in our rocking chair. A woman, crouched next to a small, slight boy, was picking magnets up from the floor and sticking them back on the fridge. The man was already refilling a glass of water at our sink and talking over his shoulder with Hy, who was removing jars from the cupboard and thunking them down on the counter. A tall boy standing by the garbage said something I couldn't hear to the little girls; one jumped down from the rocker, went around back, and began to push.

"Mole!" Hy spotted me and smiled. "Come in from the doorway there." I took a step into the kitchen. "This is my niece Mole," said Hy, and everybody looked.

"Hi," I said.

The father smiled. "Hi," he agreed, and stuck out his hand. "I'm Bill Rouen." I shook his hand, which was wet from filling up his glass, and then we both wiped our hands on our pants, and he laughed.

"I'm Delia," said the woman, still squatting in front of the fridge, "and this is Gus," hooking her thumb at the little boy, "and Isobel, Norah, and Walter." In the rocker, behind the rocker, by the garbage.

"Where's Tilly?"

"I think she's at the lake." I answered in a low voice, with a grim look sent just to Hy, but she turned to the company and announced, as if it were amusing, "Well, I've got another niece around here someplace," and then briskly to me, "Would you help with the sandwiches?"

I dragged the red step stool to the counter and began unscrewing lids: peanut butter and two kinds of jam. "How do you want me to make them?"

"Just do some of each."

The jams were store-bought grape and homemade choke-cherry (which I always liked because it sounded so deadly). The homemade wore a thick rind of paraffin under the lid and Hy's blocky signature on the label. It was one of the last jams left over from the previous August; every year she gave some away to friends and sold some on commission at The Sleeping Dog in town, and some she kept for our pantry. The jams were Hy's pride; she rationed us to make them last through the year.

A window of leaded glass over the counter cut the backyard into diamonds and hexagons, and I peered through these shapes, framing empty bits of view. I thought Tilly might have come back from the lake or wherever she'd gone, might have nipped around behind the stable and was signaling me. I tried to conjure a vision of her arm, a flash of gingham shorts, behind the dense hydrangeas that bordered the stable. Or maybe she had gone to the top of the hill, and I was supposed to guess that and meet her—it would certainly be cooler there, with river breezes skimming through the crabapple trees in the old graveyard. Hy used to make preserves from the fruit of those trees, she once told me, until they had been stricken with blight.

"What's blight?"

"Disease. Makes plants wither."

"Does blight hurt people?" I didn't tell her that Tilly and I had tasted those apples on our wanderings. Shrunken and lumpy, with blackish boils on their skins—we used them mostly for throwing practice, tossing them over the ridge into the Kittiwake far below. But once, when thirsty, we had tested the fruit with gingerly, feral nibbles and found it mealy and bitter.

"Only plants," Hy had replied. "But it can ruin whole orchards."

"Blight" and "ruin" were the words that came to me now, while standing on the step stool spreading jam across sandwich halves. The syllables rolled silently around my mouth like lozenges; I sucked them carefully, nursing their juice, and the sounds twisted themselves into rhyme:

Blight and ruin all my life,
Stuck in the kitchen with a butter knife.
Tilly gone, won't come back soon:
Stuck in the kitchen with blight and Rouen.

This pleased me; later I would copy it down on one of my recipe cards.

The Rouens' voices crisscrossed behind me, an intricate field of foreign sounds. I concentrated on my own thoughts to keep from tuning in to their words, to keep from turning around and seeing them. After months of fantasizing, the robust physical presence of the Rouens came as a shock.

Quietly, then, in an imagined cube of solitude, I took my time with the sandwiches, cutting them diagonally into long triangles, which I fanned around the lip of the platter. Outside the window, branches dipped and shadows skittered across the counter like a school of guppies.

I used my annoyance with Hy, and my sense that really I belonged out hiding with Tilly, as dual barriers, twining these thoughts pettily around me, knotting them to make them stay. They would not stay. More than being annoyed with Hy, I longed for her. More than wanting to dodge the Rouens, I was drawn to them. I built the sandwich halves round and round in a spiral fan. A hand on my back made me jump.

"Thanks, Mole," said Hy, and she lifted the platter over my head before I had quite finished the pattern.

Down at the lake after lunch, I gathered mussel half shells.

I did not go as far as the public beach, although it lay within view down the shore a slice, two hundred yards or so, sectioned off by a rope and powder blue buoys. I could make out there a few family picnics, kids leaping from the end of the dock, the fierce glint of windshields on station wagons parked above the slope. Sounds of splashing and voices carried indistinctly to where I crouched in private, picking shells from the pebbly shallows.

I had left the house right before Hy served the hermits. I had intended to leave before lunch, but Hy had patted a chair for me at the table. "Come, Mole," she'd appealed with her berry-plate face, and in spite of myself, I had accepted the seat.

The Rouens plus Hy and me made eight: a tight fit around our table. The grown-ups sat at one end and talked the way grown-ups do, managing to render every subject odd and distant. The most ordinary subjects grew bloated and complex in their mouths, phrases and pauses measured in a manner at once formal and abbreviated, like Morse code.

"They've lived with me since their parents passed away ten years ago," I overheard at one point, Hy's voice pitched deeply across the table, the statement as informative and accurate as any sample sentence in an English primer. I could picture Tilly and me as stick figures, in triangle skirts to show we were girls, and our mother and father drawn horizontal, X's where their eyes should be. And I gathered that the Rouens were telling Hy about their work. They used language too stilted for me to follow, although certain words and phrases caught indecipherably in my mind: *private grant monies, freshwater adhesive properties, lifelong attachment.*

I stole occasional glances down that end of the table. The Rouen parents looked nothing like what I'd expected (that is, thin and grayish, with identical horn-rimmed glasses and lab coats). They were smashing. The mother's skin was nearly caramel, and she had dark curly hair caught up in a high ponytail, and a magenta sundress with smocking at the shoulders over a neat, stalwart frame. The father had pale marmalade hair and skin so white it looked as if it would spoil like milk in the sun. Besides the scorpion belt buckle, he wore just jeans and sneakers and a white T-shirt with some paint splatters on it. He chewed his food with strong, ardent bites that made his cheeks bulge, and when he smiled his gums showed.

I spent lunch wedged between the little boy (atop both the local and the county phone books) and the bigger girl, my elbows necessarily pinned at my sides while I ate, and listened to the kids, who, with their own equally codified language, marked off distinct territory at our end of the table. It started with Isobel, the littler girl across from me. She held up her sandwich and whispered, "The peanut butter is dog doo."

"The bread is filthy sponges," Norah, the bigger girl, answered back. "No, dead mummy wrappings." She let some chokecherry jam plop onto her plate. "What's this, Gus?" She pointed to it, a thread of grime showing under her nail.

"Blood!" shrilled the little boy, so readily and positively I was sure he had been coached.

"Shhh," hissed Norah, reaching across me to press her hand against his mouth, while Isobel bit her paper napkin in a futile attempt to squash giggles. I could smell Norah's arm, feel my own breath ricochet off it.

Their mother glanced in our direction, ascertained a reassuring absence of actual blood, and said, "Hey, hey."

I spoke once, when Norah asked, "What grade are you going into? I'm going into fourth."

"Seventh."

"Do you have pierced ears?"

"Not yet."

Otherwise I just watched and listened, pretending to be shy.

The tall boy, Walter, did not speak at all, except when his mother handed him the pitcher, and then he said, "Give me your cups," to the little children, and I could hear his voice had changed. He poured them all drinks through the elephant's trunk. He reminded me, in a way, of me. I stared, but he didn't look up, only to see if I wanted milk, too, and then it was as though he had an invisible drape across his face. I handed him my cup. He wore wire-rimmed glasses and had freckles all over himself.

Now Hy would be helping the Rouens move into the dead house.

I squatted alone on the beach. My scalp itched; scratching it, I found the crown of my head already hot to the touch. Sand caked hard and white in patches along my body. I rinsed the shells in warm water and lined six halves, insides up, on the ground. I had come in a T-shirt and shorts, but now I stripped to my bathing suit, slinging my clothes onto dry ground behind me.

At this part of the lake there was almost no beach: a few yards back from the water, stiff, low blueberry bushes started, and bony tree roots, and shade. I crept back here until I found a good bed of moss, stretched like downy webbing between two roots. Gently, I pulled up a patch and brought it down to the row of mussel shells. Wavelets lapped the sides of the old aluminum rowboat, half afloat and half beached, tethered to the silver trunk of a scrawny tree. I knelt over the shells, my back to the woods. A motorcycle droned distantly, tiny in the background.

I had not really expected to find Tilly here.

The moss broke apart easily in little furred cakes. I lined four of the shells with plush green carpet. The other two would be kitchen and bathroom; their own pearly bottoms would do nicely as linoleum.

A branch cracked behind me. I started but did not turn, only uncurled my spine slightly, listening.

What did I think I was listening for? Did I envision Tilly coming down beside me, finding me at the lake; asking what I was making? Was it a Rouen I envisioned, one of the family exploring, discovering me already, already knowing how to locate our secret spot? Was it a stranger, a high school kid with a pack of cigarettes, a one-eyed man with a sack of gold and a knife, a scientists' daughter with ash-blond hair, a fawn that would not bolt but look me in the eyes and say, in eye-language, something powerful and sweet? I would not be scared. "This is a mussel house," I would say. "This is going to be the living room and this is going to be the kitchen." I would tell it what I was doing.

I listened, attentive to the play of light on water and the curly smell of cedar and the faint reek of warm lake, the back of my neck very alert. At no time did I turn to look behind me, to search the shady growth at my back. At any rate, the sound did not repeat itself; after a bit I relaxed my spine, and curled back over my shells.

Why, all these years later, have I bothered to recall that occurrence? Not an occurrence at all, really: an empty moment in time. It insists itself upon my memory—so compellingly that I think if I were to select the single telling event of that whole charged day when the Rouens arrived at Pillow Lake, it would be that moment at the cove when nothing happened, when I only heard a sound behind me and did not turn.

It seems to me now that this was no small fault, this quiet stillness with which I met the possibility of an intrusion. In some ways I think every wrong turn I was to make that summer could be traced to similar moments of inaction, moments when I noticed things unfolding wrongly and failed to query or object.

CHAPTER ✦ TWO

IN THE MORNINGS they would go past our house, the Rouen parents, and I would wonder then about the kids, about that toddler, who didn't seem old enough to be left at home, and the others, whether they were fixing themselves breakfast and finding their socks and that, but especially I would wonder about the parents and what they might be telling each other as they walked beneath my window. Although they never touched hands or made eye contact, I could tell they were in conversation: their heads inclined almost imperceptibly toward each other, their feet in rhythm, or, if not the actual tempo of their steps, then something about the swing of their gait, something understood and constant in the space between their bodies. (Once Hy and I, driving through rain to pick Tilly up from recorder club, had each begun humming separately against the metronome of the wipers, and startled ourselves by dovetailing into serendipitous duet, a chance harmony both interesting and pleasing; we were never able to sing it again.)

The Rouens walked in the cool hour of the morning, when the sun was first hoisting itself over the ridge so that light stung through the trees, and each pebble cast its own fleck of a shadow; when mist hovered over low patches of road, and spiderwebs glistened in daunting perfection, still poised intact on bushes and branches or spanned the openings between trees. It was cool enough for the mother to wear a cardigan—white, buttoned once, at the middle—and for the father to wear a khaki vest, the many pockets of which (I could tell even from my window, whose screen imposed a kind of mesh static over the whole picture) bulged: I imagined them filled with beakers and test tubes, perhaps a collapsible microscope, and pointy metal tools, each with a specific function. I could see the father's belt, too, I mean the buckle, when occasionally the brass scorpion caught the light and spat it back in a brassy flash: like someone signaling with a pocket mirror.

I noticed them by accident the first day, waking just before they came into view around the bend, and then by design on succeeding mornings from the foot of my bed, where I sat with my legs crossed, nightgown stretched over my knees and wrapped securely under my toes. My bedroom was at the front of the house, shady at that hour and somehow lively with the invisible nip of summer morning. My nightgown was very thin flannel, faded the color of raspberry yogurt, the plastic button at the neck cracked and split from my habit of sucking on it. Hy and I had picked out the pattern, the fabric, and the single button together nearly two years earlier, and although the gown fit me that summer such that my shins showed long and stark beyond the hem, and the armpits chafed up high against my skin, I had not allowed Hy to interest me in a new store-bought one that spring.

I sat there in the bland chill of the morning shade, watching them that whole first week. I studied them each morning until they dipped below the rise that began the descent to the Kittiwake. Every morning I pretended it was me conjuring up their image, that by imagining it, I brought their daily passage into being. I sat in my window and breathed life, and the mother and the father came walking up Ice Cart Road. *Now*, I'd think, and through a nimbus of pale orange, from around the bend they'd emerge.

"What are you staring at?" asked Tilly on the sixth morning, pausing outside my door on her way back from the bathroom. She had remained true to the pointed lack of interest in the Rouens she had demonstrated on the day of their arrival, and asked the question now with a kind of critical detachment. The belt of her short robe was tied smartly over one hip: new for her this summer, hips. This, at least, according to Tilly; I was unable or unwilling to perceive any development.

"Mr. and Mrs. Rouen," I told her.

"Dr. and Dr."

"Well, them."

"Why, what are they doing?"

"Walking."

"Gee."

"No, every morning they go by our house. They go down to the river. Every morning, this early."

Tilly didn't respond, but neither did she leave. She yawned gigantically, remembering to cover her mouth halfway through, and leaned against the doorframe.

"Come look." I patted the bed.

"That's okay, I believe you."

"I don't get what they're supposed to be doing."

"Ask Hy. Studying the fish or something." Tilly straightened herself and smoothed her lapels. The robe was new, too. She had told Hy she needed a cover-up for summer, and they'd gone shopping for it: blue-and-white-striped cotton, with modest vents up either side.

"But what do you think they actually *do?*"

"Ask Hy."

"Do you want to spy?" This was a mistake, I realized instantly; spying was a child's game.

"You can if you want to," she said coolly, and glided past the threshold, back into the hall.

"Tilly?"

"What? I want to get dressed now." She spoke through a sigh and her moon face grew dull, as if a scrim had dropped across it.

"How come you're talking that way?" She had that spring affected an almost lisp, a soft slurring of her *s*'s, as though she held a hard candy in her mouth. And her *l*'s, she was doing something to put them all the way in front of her mouth, right behind her teeth, so they sounded loose and slippy. I had been noticing it for weeks and weeks.

"What way?"

"That way, that—can't you hear it? You sound different, the way you pronounce things, like an accent."

"Accent?"

"Not an accent, but—you know, just not like you."

"I don't know what you mean."

"Yeah, you do. Like on certain words . . . you must."

She lifted her eyebrows and shook her head in a demonstration of how only too willing she'd be to admit it, if there were any truth in what I was saying. "I really don't, Mole. I'm sorry, but I don't." She even said this kindly, albeit dismissively.

Cut it out, Tilly, I wanted to say, wanted to snap her into admitting she knew what I meant. A dangerous lesson she was giving me that morning with her round, placid face—that if I wanted us to be in agreement, I would have to pretend I didn't notice what I noticed. Tilly, holding her lapels together with one hand, removed herself down the hall. I heard her bare feet recede, and in a moment her bedroom door shut with the smallest clack.

I looked back out the window. The road lay bare. There was nothing now to suggest whether the Rouens had been gone for minutes, or for hours, or had even been there at all.

It's hard to imagine how we missed crossing paths with the children all that first week, but we managed, whether by dint or by chance I'm not sure, to see them only once before the Fourth of July, and then we did not talk. I don't think they saw us. It was the same day Tilly declined my invitation to spy. She and I were riding our bikes back from Coffey's, where we'd met Hy for lunch: egg salad sandwiches and oranges toted from home in Tilly's bike basket, and Mountain Dews from the machine outside the gas station.

In the summers we often ate lunch with Hy in the garden behind the hardware store. Not a real garden, it wasn't, but my favorite kind of garden: a brief, untended plot, with hairy weeds all tilting into one another and flopped against the high wooden fence. We would sit out back under the fringed and listing red umbrella on the lawn table, tall grass pricking our calves as we ate sandwiches and talked with Hy. If the day were dry and not too bright, just before we left, Hy would bring her adding machine, ledgers and files, and electric fan (its heavy yellow extension cord snaking under the screen window) from the tiny rear office and spend the rest of the afternoon working out back.

What she did was a mystery to me: the darkly inked columns of numbers she recorded; the airy pink sales slips that ruffled like tissue in the garden breeze; her long, blunt fingers jabbing at the buttons on her adding machine, which produced printed tabulations with the imperious, flat *grrr* of a mechanical rodent. The inscrutability of her job sometimes caused me a niggling unease— to think Hy had such a foreign realm. But her physical environment I knew intimately, had memorized.

I looked up from my sandwich that day to ask Hy about the Rouens, asked her to explain what exactly they did down at the Kittiwake every morning.

"I don't know exactly," she said.

"Tilly said you did."

"No, I didn't." Tilly pinched a piece of bread from her sandwich and put it in her mouth.

"You said ask Hy."

"Yeah."

"So that makes it sound like she would know."

"So I didn't say she did know." Tilly looked down under the table. "Please don't kick my chair, Mole."

"I wasn't." I ceased.

"You could ask them yourself," she suggested. I started to retort, but her tone had not been nasty. I looked to gauge her meaning; she lifted her eyebrows at me in straightforward encouragement, then reached blithely for the paper sack in the middle of the table, from which she pulled an orange.

"I do know," offered Hy slowly, "that they're working on a grant to study mussels, but—"

I sat forward in my chair and interrupted. "Muscles as in strength or mussels like the shell?"

Tilly drove her thumbnail into the thick orange peel and spray burst from the fruit; it dotted the back of my hand like miniature rain.

"The shell, the animal," said Hy.

I felt my heart stiffen with coincidence.

As Hy spoke, Tilly glanced sideways from her orange and shot me a smile rich with complicity. She had seen my mussels at the rocky cove, seen where I kept them under a blueberry bush at the foot of the zigzag path, seen the small rooms I was making, the moss rugs nestled in the dips of the shells, the tiny table I'd made of birch bark and twig, the easy chair that was a perfectly scoop-shaped yellow pebble. I had revealed these things to her this week, afternoons while we played cards at the cove and pretended indifference to our new neighbors. I knew she liked this about me.

"Why did they come specifically to study mussels here?" I asked softly, but Hy said she really did not know a thing more.

"Not what it is about mussels they're studying, or what it is you do to study them. Or," she added, with no trace of derision, "why anyone would want to study them."

Half closing my eyes and playing my tongue along the rim of the Mountain Dew can, gathering up the sweet trail of liquid retained there as if I were a wasp or a hummingbird, I thought of them: Dr. and Dr. Rouen, their daily journey to the Kittiwake, their daily conversation. My own mussel project now leapt in significance; it seemed to me suddenly that I might have something to say to them, a place in their mysterious conversation.

Before we left, Hy gave us quarters so we could split another drink on the ride home; the day had grown wretchedly muggy. We passed back through the dim, sawdust-smelling aisles of the hardware store, calling bye to Cal, who was waiting on a customer. In front of the gas station, Tilly fed coins into the slot and let me choose. I punched the button for Yoo-hoo, and we rode home relay-fashion, passing each other and the can at intervals. You never could predict when Tilly was going to turn sweet.

We were nearly home, walking our bikes past the turnoff for Short Clove Lane, up the steep part of Ice Cart Road where it passes above the public beach, when we spotted the Rouen children. Actually, Tilly was still on her bike, pumping hard and slow and weaving her front wheel in spasms to stay balanced, when I said, "Is that them?" and she gave up her struggle with an irritated sigh, as if to make the point that it was me and not the incline that had forced her, finally, to halt.

"Where?" She touched her toe to asphalt.

I pointed. They were all four at the edge of the water, building a sand castle. The two littler ones were digging a wide moat, and the older girl was dribbling wet sand over one of the turrets to make pointy shingles, and the tall boy was standing a few paces off, arms akimbo, a bright orange bucket suspended from one hand, gravely appraising the construction like a kind of foreman. Even from where we stood, it was clear that it was a very good castle, large and solidly packed and elaborately festooned.

The tall boy knelt and began molding some new feature along the wall closest to us. Out on the lake, people dove off the aluminum raft and threw beach balls and churned up great sprays of white as they jousted in chicken fights, and I could hear the faint, gasping strains of "Marco! . . . Polo! . . . Marco! . . . Polo!" And down the beach a girl chased a dog around the lifeguard chair and people tossed a hot pink frisbee and a father dangled a little shrieking kid, upside down, over the shallows. But the Rouen children remained busily intent, all four working in concert without ever appearing to consult one another; it was as though they were all following a single, ingrained blueprint. Their sobriety, their separateness from the frivolity of the beach, seems strange, almost sad, to me now, but we looked on it then only with admiration, and with familiarity.

"Pretty good, huh?" I said, wiping a crescent of sweat from below each eye.

Tilly agreed without moving her lips.

"You want to go down there?"

She flexed her wrists on the handlebars and squinted. It was a moment before she said no.

"Are you still mad they're here?" The question was more direct than any I would have ventured all spring, but now that the Rouens had arrived (had been here nearly a week with no contact), their actual presence seemed so minor, and Tilly's fears of invasion so unwarranted, I thought it safe to ask.

"I don't know," she said, and paused long enough that I thought she had sealed off, fed me this terse little shrug of a reply as a rebuff, in order to avoid really answering. But in a moment she continued. "I guess they can't help it. It's not their fault. It's just, Hy gives the impression she expects us to act like it's some treat she arranged for us, when really it's because of the money."

"What do you mean?"

"She's making money off renting the house."

I thought this over. "Are we—do we not have enough money?"

Tilly shrugged. "You don't make that much keeping books for a hardware store."

I got my image then of Hy, just as if I'd snapped open a locket with her picture inside: her with her bare feet on a garden chair, tapping a pencil eraser against her chin while she did math in her head, dark spots spreading in the armpits of her blouse. I'd never thought of what she did as earning a lot of money or a little money. I'd never thought of it as connected to what we lived on, somehow. Hy went to work just as we went to school. We used money to buy groceries and clothes. I'd always thought of these facts as being separate and inevitable, without any one being contingent upon the other.

Coffey's was, after all, so familiar, everything: the metal pendant light fixtures, the green linoleum floors, the pegboard partitions with cellophane-wrapped packages dangling from looped metal arms. Tilly and I had always treated the shop with a kind of proprietary license born of years of meeting Hy there after school and in the summers; helping, for fun, to unpack new stock and arrange displays; bringing home paint chips to make collages; playing hide-and-seek among the aisles when we were small. It was jarring to think of it differently, to think of Hy as depending on her employment there in order to support us. And to think of Cal Coffey as anything but Cal—so big across the chest and soft-spoken, smelling of turpentine and tobacco and bringing Hy tea—to think of him as her boss and not our friend was odd and disturbing, and I was all the more disturbed because I recognized that these facts were ordinary and obvious.

And of course I had known the Rouens were paying rent, but I'd thought of that as only incidental, not as the basis for their being here, certainly not as the reason Hy would have them. Hadn't she made it seem like a treat, a caper? Hadn't she delivered the news as though presenting us with a gift: this family, these children, to live behind Pillow Lake with us for the summer? The details had all fallen into place like glass bits in a kaleidoscope, arranged themselves into a charmed design: the Rouens were drawn here, to Pillow Lake and the Kittiwake, and to the dead house, the mother and the father and children all drawn here, to this place, and we would know them and they would know us, and they would study the mussels and the river and tell us what they found there, reveal to us something important about where we lived.

But in fact, it was only for money. That's why Hy had gone into the dead house, opened it up and washed it out and brought strangers in. The kaleidoscope tilted; bits of glass swam and locked into a new pattern. I looked down at them now, the Rouen kids, very bright and busy in the sun, crafting their castle on our beach, and I felt a rotten flush of disappointment, a hot visceral sheepishness, creep down my neck. It was all spoiled. Tilly held out the can of Yoo-hoo, but I shook my head and started pushing my bike again, up the climb into the shade of the woods.

Hy had a way of sometimes not knowing things, and it scared me in the loneliest way, made me feel homesick in the deep bottom of my stomach. I would explain something and she wouldn't get it, or she would finally get it but without the sudden melting pleasure of certain recognition; she would appear, instead, to comprehend it as a new thought, one that had never occurred to her, one that belonged entirely to me. "Uh-huh, Mole," she'd say, with an almost tauntingly gentle smile.

It was something like Tilly with her new style of speaking that she was supposedly unaware of, only with Tilly I consoled myself that she did know what I meant, that the change in her pronunciation was deliberate. I recognized it as the way some of the older girls talked, those eighth-graders who had charm bracelets and boyfriends and lockers in the basement, and I forgave Tilly for pretending that she wasn't conscious of adopting it herself. Far worse than her lying would be if she really didn't know what I meant. To be alone in knowing, to be unable to explain—that would be worse.

For this reason I decided not to raise with Hy the subject of why she'd let the dead house to the Rouens. I could imagine her response if I did broach it, could hear her logically explain, without assuming any responsibility for my sense of disappointment, "Of course it's normal to charge them rent, and sure, we can always use the money. But I did think it would be nice to have people back here, and especially other kids for you and Tilly." I wouldn't be able to articulate why she was at fault, how she'd robbed me of my pleasure in the morning walks and the mussel connection, made my excitement something foolish and false.

By evening I had worked myself into a sour bulb of resentment. Hy came home from work with a carton of ice cream, and after supper we all took bowls in front of the television. We had no lights on, it was so hot. We watched a show about insects. A man's voice, faintly British, told about cicadas, said they hatched only every seventeen years—not yet during Tilly's and my lifetime. We watched them perch on slender stalks, watched their humorless chewing jaws.

I sat on the floor, leaning back against the couch, and lifted my T-shirt in order to set the bowl of ice cream against my bare stomach. I had been dour through dinner and no one had noticed. The thin paddles of the ceiling fan revolved and the light of the television flickered across my legs and the rug and the coffee table; the whole room seemed to be under water. Tilly sat next to me and ground fierce X's into her mosquito bites with her thumbnail. Hy sat behind us on the couch. She had gotten peach melba, her favorite, not mine. I could hear her breathing above and behind me, could hear her spoon against the bowl and her breath as she took a bite. I was angry that Hy didn't know I was angry with her.

As twilight shuffled into darkness, we saw, through the high windows on either side of the television set, heat lightning—dumb, silvery flashes leaping just above the horizon—and a second later the picture would buzz as if in sympathy. But no rain fell; outside, the insects, after a moment of hush, would resume; and inside, the scientist's voice carried on and on, explaining everything magnificently, while we three sat silent in the hot, dark room. It didn't become cooler with the onset of night; the air only pressed heavier and shaggier, weighing against my lungs. Even later, when I was in bed, no breeze came through the screen, only dampness, and the metallic ripplings of mute lightning. It did not rain. I woke in the night and lay awake, heard Tilly cough twice in her sleep down the hall, and the sound of Hy turning on her mattress. I remember that night as being swollen with a queer heaviness, an anticipation—possibly an effect only of the lightning, or hindsight—but it is true that that night was the last we were really together, intact, as the three of us; I mean, the last night before Tilly met the Rouens.

Then morning came and it was Saturday, the Fourth of July, and Hy had the oven on again.

Tilly and I, coming down to the kitchen in the morning, could feel the heat from the other side of the door, and by the time we swung it open to the sight of tarts, pear and peach—some finished ones already bubbling on the cooling rack and some raw ones waiting to be put in—and Hy—bent over the counter in the brown gingham apron she never normally bothered to wear, humming—we were already united in irritation.

"Who're those for?" I asked.

Tilly, looking wonderfully blasé with her eyes still puffy from sleep, simply cut a wide path around the whole baking area and took the box of cornflakes from its shelf in the pantry, her bare feet slapping the tile in a way that almost didn't steer clear of insolence.

Hy had her hair in a green kerchief tied on top of her head. Her big, floury hands looked exotic with the creases of each knuckle sharply defined in white, and she wore thin gold hoops in her ears. Tilly and I used to have arguments (discussions, Tilly would say) about whether Hy was beautiful. It seemed to me that all the reasons she shouldn't be (the silver in her molars, the crinkles at her eyes, the bigness of her hands) were precisely what did make her beautiful. She swiveled toward me now, flushed and dimpled. I felt suddenly, dangerously hopeful.

"For us," she answered, "and the Rouens. We're having a picnic."

"We are?" A little prickle surged up the back of my scalp. "Where?"

"Bluefields." An hour up the Kittiwake. We had hiked along the cliffs there.

"Do we have any say in this?" Tilly, from the table, asked with something like annoyance, but it was funny how she said it, the words lumped around an exaggerated mouthful of milk and cereal, so that it was comical as well as insolent, and plain to everyone that she was just keeping up appearances.

Hy played along. "Absolutely no say."

"Gee, how ironic," Tilly cracked, "this being Independence Day."

All week long I would've been glad to hear we had plans with the Rouens, but now I checked myself. Why should we let Hy force us into a friendship they probably didn't even want?

"Whose idea was it to get together?" I asked, leaning against the counter.

"Bill Rouen called early this morning, wanting to know what people did around here for the Fourth. We wound up deciding to all picnic together."

"But who suggested it?"

"It really—" Hy brushed past me with the last tart, her elbow narrowly missing my ear, and set it on the cookie sheet on top of the stove. "The idea just grew out of the conversation."

I trailed close behind her. "But I'm asking—"

"I don't know, Mole. We were both talking about what we might do."

"You don't even know whose idea it was?"

She opened the oven door to slide in the pan and a wave of heat rolled over her shoulder, hit me full in the face like a humid breath. I recoiled with a furious, indignant jerk, unsubtle enough so that although Hy's back had been to me, she wheeled around and stared, her eyes cold and hard as marbles. She looked from me to Tilly and back again, and when she spoke, her voice was lowered severely in pitch. "Cut this out."

"What?" cried Tilly, shocked and innocent behind her cereal bowl.

"I am sick of the way you two have been carrying on."

"What am I doing?" she protested, turning both palms up. Hy looked at her. Tilly still gripped her spoon; I saw milk drip from it onto the table.

"You're not doing anything right now," Hy said, her voice still hard and quiet. "But I think you know the kind of behavior I mean. If you have a problem, then you talk about it."

I could smell fruit and sugar baking. There must have been a breeze, because the stained-glass rooster clicked against the window, but the air seemed as viscid, as stifling, as it had the night before, and the sky, low and hazy out the window, had a greenish cast. I saw a bead of sweat trail down the flushed curve behind Hy's ear and get trapped in a web of hair. All at once I felt abashed, sorry for Hy, who'd been up early peeling peaches and pears alone in the kitchen, who'd been up early with her apron on.

"This is ridiculous," pronounced Tilly, and she rose brusquely, took her bowl and spoon, and headed toward the living room, turning once in the doorway to look back flatly at Hy and add, the words scraping with sudden bitterness from her mouth, "As if you ever talk about anything."

For a moment there was just the rooster-click. Then Hy brushed past me again, undoing her apron and looking out the window as she spoke: "Why don't you eat your breakfast in the other room, too."

Tilly was right. This was the way we fought: all feint and swift departure. We pretended not to understand what was really at issue. We circled the heart of it, sometimes on wide orbits, sometimes skimming closer, but always pretending innocence of the shape and nature of whatever it was that exerted such a pull on us.

We took one car.

Hy and Tilly and I walked down Ice Cart Road a little after noon. Hy carried the tarts, layered in wax paper in a red cardboard box from last Christmas; between us, Tilly and I carried the cooler, loaded with fruit and ginger ale. Tilly, to my great surprise and vague chagrin, right before we left, had changed into her culottes and fastened a bracelet of tiny red beads around her wrist—I debated changing then, too, but didn't have the nerve. We both wore bathing suits under our clothes; I could see the lime-green strings of Tilly's poking out of the collar of her shirt. Hy walked just ahead of us, her sandals beating a soft tattoo on the hot pavement, her breath knocking audibly out of her nose with each step. We didn't talk.

As we approached the dead house we heard someone intoning, in a high, plaintive voice, "Corn on the co-ob . . . corn on the co-ob," over and over. When we got closer we saw it was the youngest Rouen, sitting on a towel on the hood of the black car. He spotted us, broke off, and regarded us austerely.

"Hello," said Hy.

He blinked once, then directed his attention back over the treetops and recommenced his song, now pitched slightly higher, the tempo slightly increased.

"Put it down," directed Tilly, lowering her side of the cooler to the ground. We stood by the car, at the edge of the haggard, weedy lawn, and watched Hy cross it. Before she reached the steps, Bill Rouen came out onto the porch.

"Hi!" he greeted her. He peered across the lawn and nodded at me and Tilly. "Hello!" He grinned as if there were something amusing about us, something witty that we were doing and he was just clever enough to appreciate. And then, back to Hy, "My brood's about ready."

They crossed the lawn. "You've already met Mole," said Hy. "This is my other niece, Tilly."

"The disappearing niece." He grinned again and stuck out his hand. "Bill Rouen."

Tilly slid her bracelet up her arm and shook with him.

"And this is Gus," he said, turning to the boy, who only then stopped his chant, breaking off mid-cycle, and stood up on the fender, clutching his father's sleeve for balance. "Something you're trying to tell us, Gus?"

Gus surveyed Tilly, Hy, and me with the coolness of someone whose privacy has been grievously breached. Then he put his lips to his father's ear and said in a loud-to-normal voice, "I wanted some corn!"

"Well," said Bill Rouen in a confidential tone, placing his hand full across the top of his son's head, "corn on the cob's a pretty difficult thing to take on a picnic. Because you have to cook it. But I think we may be able to have some later this week." He opened up his smile and I noticed that one of his top front teeth overlapped the other; it looked winsome and careless—again, I thought, not the way a father ought to look.

"The week's over," said Tilly.

Bill Rouen raised his eyebrows. Gus looked at her.

"It's Saturday," she said.

Bill Rouen looked at Hy, and jerked his head once toward Tilly. "A pragmatist," he said.

I didn't know what "pragmatist" meant, and doubted whether Tilly did either, but I knew his remark would nettle her. I stole a look beside me: he had made her blush. Bill Rouen laughed then, a sudden, delighted bark, and Hy, to my outrage, joined in and then Gus, with the forced hilarity of a child trying to keep pace with adult humor. I saw Tilly's eyes recede; she lifted her chin and became lofty; I was proud.

Then I saw Bill Rouen, his eyes still narrowed with mirth, turn a slow look on Tilly, a slow, canny look with his lips still parted and she responded to it—broke out of her vacuous composure to glare at him, her nostrils arched, her jaw extra sharp. And I saw that he had meant to rile her, had said it for exactly that purpose.

It had been understood, I thought, between Tilly and me that I was the one of us who cared about the Rouens being here: that they were, in a sense, *my* Rouens, if I should so choose. Partly as a courtesy to Tilly, I had been refraining from overture, but she knew how I sat up in my bedroom window each morning and watched for them; she had seen me take special note of the fact that their study involved mussels. Now, for the second time in twenty-four hours, my grasp on them had been loosened. In that conversation the previous afternoon, while standing over the beach looking down on the children's castle, and now in this gaze sent and returned between Bill Rouen and Tilly, I felt my private hold evaporate.

CHAPTER ✦ THREE

AT BLUEFIELDS THERE were people flying. The strangeness of it—of the whole hour driving north squashed into the Rouens' car (the adults up front, their long busts silhouetted against the bright windshield; Walter, Tilly, me, and the food all relatively quiet in the middle; the three youngest very chatty and upright on a nest of blankets in the back-back, transmitting frequent high-pitched questions and observations up to the forward regions of the car); of finally disembarking in the gravel lot high above the river and finding the air mysteriously cool, almost minty, sharp as thistles; of traipsing up the short knoll that separated the lot from the succession of bowl-shaped meadows that formed Blue-fields (already a kind of rearranging under way, so that I found myself carrying a canvas bag of Rouen sandwiches, while Tilly shared the cooler with Walter); and then of finding, as we climbed over the top of the knoll, a hang glider, resting like a giant orange-and-scarlet insect across the high bearded grass, and two more poised at the top of a slope at the distant end of the meadow—the strangeness of all this seemed to me fitting.

We rose over the knoll one by one, each of us halting as we

came upon the scene, then fanned out into a staggered line on the cusp of the meadow. Talking, joking flickered out. Damp wind blew through the grass, a warm breath singing round my ears. We all just stopped and watched. The figure (male or female, we could not tell) attached to the frontmost glider on the slope took a few running steps, causing the wide single wing to tremble and teeter, then pitched its body forward and out.

For several seconds there was flight: a hushed arc of airborne propulsion so low to the meadow that it might have been illusory, except that then the pilot landed, took crazy headlong gallops to keep from tumbling, and the fluidity was broken. The wing tips jerked and dipped recklessly, but the pilot managed to keep them from snagging in the high grass, and finally came to a stop. Someone far across the meadow let out a cheer.

The crown of my head hummed. It had been a beautiful thing to see, all the more marvelous for the fact that it had barely occurred (the glider flying so low to the meadow); it made my heart feel light and loose in my chest. But I was shy to see such a sight with the Rouens right there—not my Rouens any longer, only them, those people paying rent in the dead house, not friends to us but strangers only. Who knew if they'd understand that this was beautiful? I was afraid one of them would make a joke.

All during the car ride up I had sat silently, my temple against the lower portion of the windowpane, the bones of my face absorbing the vibrations of the car, and tried to rework my idea of the Rouens. I tried to work out a new way to feel, to determine: *how shall I be with them?* And then to arrive at Bluefields and encounter this specter, before we had eaten our picnic together, before we had found a blanket spot, before we had a chance to warm up to each other—it seemed an impropriety.

"Parachutes!" breathed Isobel at my side. The top of her sorrel mop came to just below my shoulder. She had dropped her hands, palms forward, in a silent-movie gesture of wonder.

"No," Norah said without taking her eyes from the meadow, and she, too, sounded solemn and awed. "They're . . . what're they called, Mommy, those things?"

"Hang gliders," Dr. Rouen replied in her voice with its accent of the city. "It looks like they're beginners. Practicing. From such a little hill." And then she started to explain everything.

Everyone drifted a few steps toward her: the little kids clustered by me, Tilly and Walter on her other side, Bill Rouen and Hy behind. She talked of hang point and trailing edge, king post and rigging wire. She talked of air currents and gravity. She used her hands as she spoke, pointing across the field, sketching a shape in the air, once steering Gus forward so he could see past his sisters.

I listened, only half believing. Under the flat spell of her words and gestures, all sense of the miraculous threatened to fall away. And yet there was something compelling in the way she spoke, the grain of her voice, a rich, staccato energy packed into every syllable. There was something in it of the television voice from the night before. Its very banality seemed promising: that voice could explain anything.

Each of her kids, her husband, Hy and me, we all watched her as she spoke. Even Tilly, from whom I might have expected a subtle show of disdain, or at least boredom, appeared attentive. Her head tipped to one side, she fiddled her bracelet up and down her forearm in an absentminded massage, and regarded Dr. Rouen with open interest. Dr. Rouen wore a dress similar to the one she'd worn the day of their arrival, only turquoise this time; it hung straight on her short, solid frame and flapped a little in the wind. She passed her gaze over each of us evenly as she spoke, children and grown-ups alike. I saw that the whites of her eyes were not clean white, but slightly discolored, faint pink in regions, yellow-gray in others, with a brownish speckle on one, and it made her eyes unpretty. But there was something appealing about them still, so round and bright, like a bird's, and keen with a kind of practical intelligence. The father we were already on the verge of calling Bill, but her we would never think of as anything but Dr. Rouen.

"Have you glided yourself, then?" asked Hy. She stood nearly a foot taller than Dr. Rouen. She still held the red box carefully at waist level.

Dr. Rouen directed a smile, warm and brief, at her. "My brother."

"Uncle Frank?" asked Walter.

"Uncle John."

"I didn't know about that." He sounded mildly indignant, and frowned. I saw a row of freckles knit into a line above his lip, a pale precursor to a mustache. In the car he had told Tilly that he was fourteen and would be a freshman in September. He was thin, rawboned, with his father's coloring; when he spoke, his skin passed bluish, almost translucent, over his jaw.

"Yeah, how come I never knew Uncle John could fly a hang glider?" This from Norah, fists on hips in an effort to match her brother's indignation. Her mouth was near my shoulder, and her breath traveled across my face: some sweet chemical smell—gum? toothpaste? sugar cereal? It occurred to me we were all standing very close together.

"No special reason," said Dr. Rouen.

"I thought you guys knew that," said Bill Rouen.

Their kids all shot them shrewd, pitying looks, and in that brief familial exchange a recognizable division established itself; the grown-ups on one side, not even realizing what vast stores of information they controlled; the kids on the other, keeping vigilant watch, scavenging for data at every casual opportunity. A hang-gliding uncle is no trifling fact. I felt a charge of brilliant, involuntary camaraderie.

The single glider that remained on the slope now shifted; its zebra-striped wing lifted and maneuvered, again with that curious jerkiness that did not correspond to the gracefulness of flight. We all looked. The sky had grown more thickly overcast as we'd driven up the Kittiwake. What had been haze at Pillow Lake turned into a filmy, cheesecloth dampness here at Bluefields. The wing, this one yellow and black, looked brilliant under the sky's dull lid. My skin felt slick, basted with sweat and humidity. Instinctively, we all spread back out, away from each other, in order to see.

On the slope, the glider paused and wobbled and paused. The pilot seemed to consult with two other figures. "Do it," someone whispered near me, one of the kids, with fervor, as if reciting magic. Finally, with purposeful runs and a leap, the glider took off. It rose and dipped and then lifted again, actually soared a bit higher as if kept afloat by a giant hidden in the grass, puffing at the sky. I could see the pilot, a narrow dark insect body suspended horizontally beneath the florid wing. The arc this time was clearer, longer; there was no doubting aviation.

My forehead was taut, tingling, my heart again airy as a cork. Then I slid my hand up a cluster of tall strands and got a fine, light grass cut between my thumb and first finger. I looked down. A filament of red sprang across my palm, not enough to ask a grown-up for comfort. I pressed the web of skin to my mouth; it tasted of metal and salt.

I looked up again in time to see this glider landing farther across the meadow than the first. It was a sloppier landing and more abrupt ("Easy tiger," said Bill Rouen), with pounding legs, a terrible scramble for equilibrium ("You're weaving, Buddy"), and then the nose of the glider slammed fast into the earth.

"Oof," said Bill Rouen.

"Is he all right, Dad?" asked Norah.

He did not answer, and in the wake of his jokey commentary it seemed a negative response. Dr. Rouen took one quick step forward in the high grass and stood there, turquoise cloth blowing around her strong calves. I looked behind me and saw Bill Rouen and Hy also looking ready to move, toward glider or car I wasn't sure; perhaps they were weighing that very decision, calculating the surest way to offer help, to attend the emergency—and a thrill of gladness poured over me like a third flight, my heart going to cork once more, to see them all so serious and able.

In the distance, the other figures jogged over to the crumpled glider. I was almost disappointed to see the pilot get out of the harness, stand, and, limping a little, walk away from the striped wings. Someone laughed roughly; the sound carried, disembodied and oddly intimate, spooned into our ears on a warm gust. We began to walk.

Past a copse of stubby trees ("Are these quince?" mused Dr. Rouen aloud, and Hy seemed quick to say, "Crabapple"), we came into the next meadow and there found a spot. Hy and I shook out and laid down two scratchy smoke-blue woolen blankets. Bill Rouen pulled things out of a canvas bag and handed them, assembly-line-style, to Norah and Isobel. Tilly and Walter pried the lid off the cooler and started fishing cans of ginger ale from the ice. Dr. Rouen took off Gus's shoes. Certain clouds shredded away from the sun, for a moment jeweling the grass a hazy yellow-green.

We barely chatted while we ate; what conversation there was consisted mostly of a kind of practical shorthand: "The cherries?" "Watch her cuff." "Napkin, please." We reminded me of mechanical dolls in a storefront display—all handing each other sandwiches and chicken wings, the older kids snapping back the flip tops on soda cans before distributing them to the younger ones. A single knife, wiped clean at intervals on a paper bag, spread both mayonnaise and mustard. It was too breezy for bees, but ants kept crawling onto the blanket. We flicked them away.

Once Gus, reaching across my lap for a tart, dug his elbow into my thigh. A jolt went through the muscle; I sucked air between my teeth. Gus remained oblivious, intent only on the tart. The back of his head hovered right beneath my face. I could see a soft hollow between two cords at the base of his neck. With a

little grunt, he got his tart and removed his elbow. I exhaled and
rubbed my thigh, strangely flattered.

I trained my eyes on the distance, the other side of the wide
river. From where we sat I could make out a strip of Kittiwake at
the opposite bank. It looked fake today, the river. White sails
flecked it. Wind gouged silver streaks through its surface. Something about the moisture that hung between our picnic and the
far shore made it look like an artist's idea of a river, painted,
dreamed up.

Beside me on the blanket, while Hy sucked a chicken bone too
loudly and Walter tried to teach Isobel how to burp on purpose
and Norah gathered cherry pits people had spit into the grass and
Gus and Dr. Rouen sang, "Row, row, row your boat," Bill Rouen
slipped off his shoes. He slipped off his socks. He stretched out his
legs and one foot touched Tilly on her hip, barely.

Tilly sat still. I knew his foot was definitely touching her because I could see his toes dimpling the red cotton of her culottes,
making a slight impression. Walter burped expertly, a sustained,
froggy sound, and Isobel laughed. I kept on watching Tilly sitting
unnaturally still.

"I have a stomachache," I said to Hy.

"Maybe you ate too fast." Grease shone on her lips. "Why
don't you lie down on your side."

After a moment I did curl up, feeling snubbed (by Tilly in a
way as well as Hy), and rested my cheek against the scratchy,
smoke-colored wool. I didn't close my eyes. I saw the corner of
the tart box and Isobel's bare knee and the dirty knife resting on
the mustard lid, all of it magnified, exaggerated, as though I had
lowered myself into a miniature city.

Far above me I heard, from a different place, Norah stand and rattle the contents of a cherry-stained paper bag. "Mommy, can we throw the pits over the cliff?"

Her mother's voice: "Go with them, please, Walter."

And Tilly offering: "I'll watch them."

From far away: "Does Mole want to come?"

A pause.

A vibration closer by: "She isn't feeling well."

And then pieces of the miniature city shifting, breaking off: a commotion of ankles and sneakers, enlarged and fragmented, great geometric slices of body and clothing crossing my field of vision and disappearing; then their whole frames reemerging, but little now, with receding backs, Tilly and Walter and Norah and Isobel and Gus all dwindling to figurines at the edge of the meadow.

I understood perfectly well that I could not have joined them and noticed them both. I wondered which I would have preferred. I closed my eyes.

Colors and shapes I could not quite name presented themselves inside my lids. Little sounds got big. I heard crickets in the grass and thought of the cicadas from the night before, their mouths huge on the television screen. Hy picked up a section of my hair and began working her fingers through the knots. We had not spoken easily to each other since our clash in the kitchen that morning. I closed my fingers around a piece of her skirt, a little bunch of hem.

Then Hy asked the Rouens about their work, and I knew she was asking for me. She didn't say, "Mole's been wondering," or "Mole wanted to know." She just said, "Will you tell about your work?" She said, "You're looking at mussels now, is that right?" And moved her fingers through my hair.

I opened my eyes a sliver and caught the wavering iridescent fringe of my own lashes, the coarse fibers of the blanket, the milling disks of pixie light that I thought must be molecules.

"Yes," said Bill Rouen. I heard his voice and at the same time felt its deep timbre. He cleared his throat, shifted on the blanket. "We're interested in the way mussels adhere—they attach themselves to rocks, or piers or whatever, and they remain there for life, you see. Very strong grippers."

"Byssal threads, explain," said Dr. Rouen.

"Yes, they have—do you know about byssal threads?"

Hy must have shaken her head.

"Well, that's what they attach with, byssal threads. Kind of like whiskers, a little beard of these threads they extend from one end of their shell, and they just clamp on, with these very, these incredibly tenacious fibers."

I opened my eyes all the way. The voice seemed to come from a different person than the one who'd called Tilly a pragmatist, who'd put his toes against her hip. This person sounded serious, wholly engrossed, and I could feel myself bask a little in the easy authority of his voice.

"So one thing we're interested to know," he went on, "is how they attach so well; what, biochemically, is it that makes them stick, that makes them just—stay, hold fast." He paced his speech without real pauses, but by drawing out certain word endings instead, elongating the vowels in his rumbly voice, almost purring their final sounds.

"Dentists, for one. They're especially interested." That was Dr.

Rouen's voice, choppy, matter-of-fact. "If we can figure out the chemical formula, there could be terrific applications. For, you know, caps, bridgework."

"How about that," said Hy, and the foothills stirred. "Now, how do you do that, figure out the formula?"

I pushed myself up. Hair stuck to the side of my face and I was thirsty, my mouth pasty.

"Well, that's not actually our, our end of things, so to speak," answered Dr. Rouen (with a curt, friendly nod to acknowledge my having sat up). "When I say 'we,' I mean the scientific community."

That was lovely, I thought: to have a "we" like that, to be able to use the term so casually about a group so encompassing. For me, "we" generally included only Tilly, sometimes Hy.

"I mention the dentistry because so much of the funding is that," Dr. Rouen went on, and again I was oddly mesmerized by the lack of mystery in her speech, the unadorned ease of her narration. "The drug companies. Because of the potential applications to dentistry. But that's lab scientists, chemical engineers. Bill and I do field work."

"We look for patterns," he said, and it came out less in agreement than as an amendment to her way of putting it.

She shot him a fast, irritated look, and with her tongue, wryly stroked a rear tooth.

He did not notice; he was looking into the distance with a squinting intensity, as though discerning patterns in the haze even as he spoke.

"Anyway. What's really interesting," said Dr. Rouen after a moment, "is that while the drug companies are courting mussels in hopes of profit, at the same time we have other companies complaining that mussels are hurting their profits."

"How so?" asked Hy.

"Well, the zebra mussel—which has just in the past few years been spreading through North American water systems—the Great Lakes, the Mississippi—anyway, it can clog up intake and waste pipes. So say you've got Smith's Shoe Factory down the river, trying to dump its garbage in the water, and instead it's all backing up inside the plant."

"Smith's Shoe Factory?" I asked.

"Fred's Fork Factory. A biotech operation. Whatever. At any rate, production gets messed up, zebra mussels get blamed, and bam: you have a team of scientists working on how to get *rid* of them."

"Which side are you on?"

Dr. Rouen's eyebrows flashed up and she nodded vigorously before any words came out, as if her mouth could just barely keep up with what she meant to say. "Neither; our funding comes through the university, which makes it theoretically ideologically neutral. We're just gathering data. Which in itself is pretty fascinating: data has no bias, no agenda. It just is." Her lips moved with great precision and energy.

I couldn't follow all that she was saying, but I almost thought I could. *Theoretically ideologically* sounded like water moving over rocks; saying it over again and again in my head, I could make the stream run faster or slower.

Hy took up the dirty knife and sliced herself a square of cheese. "But people have biases; people have opinions," she said, putting the cheese in her mouth.

"I don't get it." I turned to Dr. Rouen. "Are mussels good, then, or bad?"

She looked at me and beamed. "Exactly!"

I didn't know what she meant but felt praised by her snapping smile, felt welcomed near the threshold of her "we," and I smiled back as if I did.

Bill Rouen jerked out of his reverie. "That's not necessarily our concern. Good or bad. Not, at any rate, for us to say."

"Your concern is . . . ?" Hy prompted, but then yawned with her lips shut, nostrils flared, and I was sorry that she was continuing this for my sake. I wondered what the Rouens must think of her.

"We're looking at the population of mussels within one given area in the Kittiwake." He was addressing the sky. "Determining patterns in density that could be compared with data taken over a period of years, or from other similar regions. Theoretically, certain conditions would affect the mussels' ability to adhere—"

"Essentially, we monitor variables," Dr. Rouen cut in with her rapid, neat syllables. She raised a hand as if to place it on her husband's forearm, but didn't, only let it hover there, interrupting without touching him. "Such as wave frequency, pollutants, salinity—"

"And each piece of data is a clue." Bill Rouen cut back in. "As we monitor variables and look for patterns"—he stressed this last phrase as if to wrest it back, reinsert it—"we're constantly recording our data." Now he did look at me and Hy. "And each piece of data is a clue."

He winked then, quickly, the quickest wink I had ever seen, and lifted a dark brown bottle to his mouth, and I saw for the first time that he was drinking beer. The Rouens must have brought it. He tilted his neck back to drink. I heard teeth clink against glass, saw his Adam's apple chug twice.

I felt my chance to ask a question. I wanted badly to think of one, to think of something that would reveal my worthiness to them, something that might make them guess that I, too, had knowledge of mussels. What could I say that would clue them in to me? But then Bill Rouen burped, almost silently, his chest heaving with the effort to suppress it, and Dr. Rouen turned her head and looked at him without a single thing in her eyes, and the moment drained of possibility.

"Do we have anything left to drink?" was all I managed to say.

"You can check the cooler," said Hy.

"It's empty."

"That's all we brought, Mole."

Bill Rouen, taking another swig, lowered the bottle, his lips gleaming wet, his eyes meeting mine over the sweating brown glass, and half extended it, grinning. I shook my head and breathed a little laugh to show that I understood him to be joking. I was pretty sure he was joking.

Years later I would come to understand, or at least to recognize, Bill Rouen's kind of charm; I would learn, when I encountered it in a person, to more or less gauge what it meant and what it wanted, how much weight it was capable of bearing, how much damage it was capable of doing. But that summer it was brand-new to me, disturbing and singular. Because I had not yet learned that there are men who flirt with girl children as a matter of course, I thought it was us, Tilly and me, something special about us he could see.

A distant bass that might have been thunder or early fireworks ripped low from the west. I brought my eyes away from Bill Rouen, made a visor of my hand. Across the meadow, right before it discontinued, five kids stood flinging cherry pits over the ridge. I couldn't see the pits, only the motion. They threw without abandon, hurling their whole arms forth. They were all in a line, very close to the edge, and I wondered why one of the grown-ups didn't notice, didn't yell at them to take a few steps back.

So many of the details of that day contributed to a sense of make-believe, everything gone askew, ungoverned. Like Gus's song, which he sang again and again, all afternoon. "Do merrily!" he'd command, and his mother would oblige, marking the tempo with her chin. "Merrily, merrily, merrily, merrily," hitting the *r*'s hard with her city voice, "life is but a dream."

After the food was gone, we covered the cooler and left the blankets and walked across the succession of fields. The hang gliders had departed, leaving behind no sign. We found rocks to climb on, and a big rock to wet behind; I went and squatted there with Norah and Isobel (Tilly said she didn't have to go). Our urine made a pattery sound hitting the earth, then broke up among the grass like mercury, trickling in fast rivulets and meandering around stones. We watched beneath us, peering, charmed, under our own bottoms till it soaked into the ground. We wiped ourselves with leaves and washed our fingers on wet grass and dried them on our shorts.

"Aao! Aao! Aao!" yelped Isobel for no reason, and Norah asked me, "Can you bark like a seal?" and I flattened my upper lip against my teeth and made my gerbil noise instead. "Do her your ears," ordered Norah happily. She held back her sister's curls and Isobel pursed her lips and after a time grew very pink. "There, did you see them move?" cried Norah. I had not, but I did notice how fine and soft and curled they looked, like dried apricots. The sky grew darker, the ripe smell of mildew; "I felt a drop!" said Norah, and Isobel immediately stuck her tongue out to the sky, but nothing came.

We grew tired, punchy, chasing each other across the meadows, and the clouds rolled in heavily and a metallic taste came into the air, reminded me of licking my cut. The day seemed made-up, almost false, the kind of excitement and tension that would make me sick if I didn't seize it, leap into it head-on. It was Norah and Isobel and their seal-barking, guileless whimsy that swayed me, made me pitch myself forward, give up my watch, my noticing, to join the others in motion. We stamped and fell across the grass, all of the children plus Bill Rouen, played Living Statues and Mother, May I? and a wild, ruleless game of tag, shrieking in order to hear what the wind would do to our voices, sweating under the dense, ash-colored canopy of sky.

After being chased and tagged a final time (the sting of Walter's fingertips, slapped lightly against the back of my neck as he tore by on long legs, in pursuit of his father), I let myself tumble and roll, shoulders crushing into soil, grass streaking my elbows and knees, smearing every angular joint a deep, concentrated green, and there I lay, panting in the tall grass. Above my face, a tiny bug, translucent and frail, clung to the underside of a curved blade. When it does start to rain, I thought, this bug will stay dry.

Still on my back, I propped myself up on both elbows and spotted Hy and Dr. Rouen standing by the rocks: Hy tall, Dr.

Rouen short, each with her arms folded round her middle. They weren't watching us play, but faced the tree line beyond the meadow and moved their lips and bent their torsos, rocked slowly in the postures of listening and agreement. Hy looked like a mother, I thought, like someone else's mother: possessed of her own history, great impervious vaults of knowledge, as inscrutable as I'd ever seen her. It seemed dangerous and unthinkable that I could be angry with her. I wanted to charge over there now, wanted to uncup her big hand from around her hip, line up her long fingers with my own, hear what she was saying.

I let my head fall backward and looked upon the others in the field behind me: they appeared upside down and far away, as if glimpsed in the bowl of a spoon. Gus and Isobel each took shelter behind a leg of their father and Norah squawked and darted like a chicken out of Walter's path, but he was after Tilly, pursuing her to the outer reaches of the meadow, his legs churning up long, easy strides. Even so, Tilly outpaced him, so smooth along the horizon she might have been gliding above it. Bill Rouen, turning to watch, rubbed a palm slowly across his mouth, then absently unhooked his children's fingers from his legs.

The bugs had gotten quiet. The sky, as I watched, settled perceptibly even lower, sneaking itself down a silky notch upon us. I found myself wishing for an event, something to call us all in, distract Hy and Dr. Rouen from their place by the rock; and Tilly and Walter from what had become their own private chase, or race, along the rim of the meadow; and Bill Rouen from the way he seemed lost in observing them. I wished for a hang glider to crash over the hill, for one of us to break a leg, for rain to come.

Excitement and tension burned in my stomach, but I had grown silent and inert again, and only lay watchful in the grass.

After a bit, Tilly and Walter did return, flopping not far from me, and the other players followed suit, the game over. Isobel lay with her head in her father's lap. Walter took off his glasses to wipe his eyes; without them, he looked different, undone, like a cookie taken from the oven too soon. He put them quickly back on. He and Tilly breathed heavily in syncopation.

"A fast young lady," said Bill Rouen, dipping his head at Tilly. He spoke as if reading out a slogan, enunciating each word with an ironical edge.

Tilly did not know whether she was being mocked or not. She nodded back at him without smiling. Her bangs had clumped into damp spikes. Her hair looked very black; a piece of it stuck to her cheek. Walter sniffed loudly, a couple of times, and wiped his nose with his knuckles. I looked over toward Hy and Dr. Rouen, far across the meadow.

"You play a sport at school?" asked Bill Rouen.

Tilly picked a leaf off her knee. It left an impression. "Field hockey." She didn't really; she would go out for it in the fall.

"Ah." He turned to me. "And how about you?"

"No. Well, in gym."

Gus sang very softly, "Row, row, row your boat, row, row your boat. Merrily, merrily, merrily, merrily, row, row your boat." He hit his r's hard like his mother.

"Only Tilly plays," said Bill Rouen, looking at her.

"Hey, Dad, aren't we supposed to be going swimming?" asked Norah.

He squinted at the sky with his head tipped all the way back.

"Yeah, I don't know that that's going to happen today. Why don't you go consult with your mother," he told her.

So Norah brushed herself off and went toward the women. Walter rose, too—abruptly, I thought—and sort of moseyed after her, wordless, his hands sliding into his back pockets as he left us. Then Gus, with suddenness, scrambled after him. Blades of grass unflattened themselves in the three spots their bodies had vacated. I wondered whether I had missed the signal for a general exodus, but Isobel remained anchored across her father's lap; and neither did Tilly move.

After a minute, Tilly said, "You're a scientist, right?"

Bill Rouen looked back at her, still squinting. "That's right," he agreed, and his eyes were pale and watchful, as if he were trying to figure out what she meant by it. "In the area of inverte-brate zoology." Waiting to see what she would do with that.

"Mm," she said, the briefest of sounds, unmoved, polite, not even looking in his direction.

His smile came slowly then but spread. "My pet interest, how-ever, is chiromancy." He dragged out the syllables and continued to regard Tilly, whose dark eyes had gone to slits against the wind.

"What's that?" I asked, when she did not. "Something to do with shells?" My stomach was feeling so peculiar I thought I'd have to get up and move around. I looked again toward the rocks, marking the women and three children quite far from us there.

"Something to do with hands," he answered me, but looking at Tilly, waiting for her.

And she did turn to him, with narrowed, olive-pit eyes and her face swept bare and smooth. "Chiromancy?" She pronounced it the way he had, but in her new accent, a hint of a lisp softening the end. "What's that supposed to be?"

"I'll show you." Bill Rouen leaned forward and took Tilly's wrist from where it rested in her lap, turning her hand over so that her palm was open to him.

Tilly snatched it away. She did it reflexively, automatically, I could see that; yanked her hand into her chest. And then she gave a small cry and cupped her wrist with her other hand, and tiny red beads came flooding through her fingers and dripping off her elbow, scattering in the grass.

"Daddy, you broke it," said Isobel in high, distinct tones, picking her head up from his lap.

Bill Rouen didn't say anything but started parting the grass, searching with his fingers for fallen beads.

"It doesn't matter," said Tilly. She removed her hand from her wrist. All the rest of the beads spilled to the ground. "Anyway, it's raining."

It was true; a drizzle had finally begun.

By the time we reached the blankets and packed everything up, the rain was falling hard; by the time we pulled out of the parking lot, it had turned into hail, which for a few freakish minutes pelted the roof and hood with random fierce smacks before becoming rain again, large-dropped and steady, streaking down all the surfaces and encasing us in a kind of luminous din. The kids in the back-back fell asleep and the grown-ups up front fell into silence and Tilly and Walter played tick-tack-toe on a fogged-up window all the way back to Pillow Lake; I watched.

*   *   *

That night, with the rain still falling hard in the darkness, splashing from the gutters and beating at intervals against the panes, Hy came to the bathroom where Tilly and I were sharing the sink, brushing our teeth, and said, "I'm sorry we didn't get to see any fireworks this year."

She stood in the doorway, her head cocked a little uncertainly, and really, she was asking us something else. I thought of how I'd made her go off that morning in the kitchen, and then of how distant and unattainable she'd looked standing across the meadow that afternoon. In the light of the bathroom's naked bulb, fine lines showed all over her face. I took the brush from my mouth and spoke through lather. "That's okay!"

"I hope you girls weren't too disappointed," she said, and I thought of the rain, and how it forced us to run and climb together into the closed capsule of the car, and I shook my head again.

Hy smiled at me but stood there still.

Finally Tilly spat. "I wasn't," she said, bent over the white bowl of the sink, cupping rinsewater into her mouth.

After Hy left, I sat on the hamper, hunched a little under the ceiling that sloped with the eaves, and watched Tilly put cold cream on her face. She had recently learned to do this from a magazine. I watched her in the mirror; she clipped her bangs back to stroke the stuff across her brow, then stretched her top lip down to smear it below her nose.

"Did you really have a good time?" I asked.

"Sure." Her fingers dipped into the little blue pot and, working in circles across her cheeks, built a shiny white mask over her features.

"Are you upset about your bracelet?"

She shrugged. "It wasn't that nice."

She must have heard me take a breath in order to ask the next question, because she met my gaze just then in the mirror, and her dark eyes in the gobliny-white transmitted a brief, firm warning. I shut up then, and for that she let me watch her perform the rest of her rite in silence.

CHAPTER ✦ FOUR

IT WAS A fire (Hy said and Cal Coffey said, too) that had destroyed most of the old hamlet, the shops and houses that once decorated the hill on the east side of Pillow Lake. In August of 1926 it happened. The blaze swept right down Ice Cart Road and raged for three days, leaping from one side of the street to the other, outwitting men from fourteen fire departments that had been called in from surrounding towns, leaving in its wake only smoldering timbers where buildings had stood, their burned, blackened shells lining the road like a row of open mouths.

A handful of houses—those set back in the woods and around the south bend of Ice Cart Road—escaped the blaze, but most of the structures from the road right down to the edge of the lake did not. The fire consumed five huge icehouses along the shore; the blocks of ice they harbored proved no match for the heat, while the sawdust insulation packed between their inner walls provided excellent fodder for the flames. Also ruined were a church, two butcher shops, a post office, twelve summer bungalows, two saloons, two candy stores, a hotel, three boathouses, and a roadside stand that sold hot dogs, taffy, and live bait.

Hy, like us, knew the story only from being told, but Cal had been alive, a little boy, when it happened. After the fire, he and his family (like most everyone else who had lived along Ice Cart Road) moved to the west side of Pillow Lake. New edifices went up quickly; within twelve months of the disaster, practically the whole town had reappeared across the water, the shops arranged in their new locales with little deviation from their original positions—the grocer's next to the dry goods next to the funeral home next to the inn—almost as if the entire town had been preternaturally transported.

In fact, Cal said, the migration had been a long time coming. Artificial refrigeration had begun hurting the ice industry earlier that decade. The primary means of transportation had also changed; it was no longer by boat along the Kittiwake, but by automobile along the new thoroughfare that curved around the eastern shore of Pillow Lake. The town was already in decline; the fire was simply the last straw.

This story had always interested us, if not quite as much as the story of our parents' drowning, not very much less. It seemed equally a part of the insolvable past, equally a part of our own history. Threads of the fire had been woven into the lives that caused us to be born where we were, to live where we lived— our house had been one of the few left standing, unburned, at the end of it all; consequently, our grandparents had been some of the only ones to remain, to stay behind when the rest of town left. Occasionally I tried to imagine what it would be like to live on the town side of Pillow Lake, on a regular street with sidewalks and yards, fences and garages, and sprinklers and neighbors. But

I did not go so far as to wish it. We were rooted on the hill side, inalienably.

A history of ice, of fire, of drowning—these belonged to Tilly and me, and we to them. Cal was our great source on the fire, although he'd been so young and remembered, he said, only isolated scenes from the event, like snapshots without captions. We always pestered him anyway for stories about it, which he'd relate obligingly, often dishing up the same fragmented images: himself waking up among other evacuated children on a metal cot in the brick schoolhouse; a cluster of women in white shawls praying on a street corner—but occasionally dredging up some new item, as he did one night early that summer: a lady in a plumed hat passing out bananas to sooty-faced firemen.

"But is that true?" he said.

We were sitting in the Lefferts Engine Company, the fire station over in town. Pillow Lake had no cinema, but on Monday nights from June through August, old movies were shown in the firehouse. One week it would be a World War Two picture; the next, a Hollywood musical; the next, the life of the grizzly bear, and so on. Tickets cost a dollar. Under-twelve went free. The tickets came off a great green roll that sat next to a gray metal lockbox on a card table outside the entrance. I didn't yet qualify for a ticket, but Tilly, for all her publicized contempt for sentimentality, had been saving all of hers since she turned twelve last August; she kept them, I happened to know, along with some thumbtacks and baby teeth, in a little pewter box shaped like a pig on top of her dresser.

Inside the fire station, on large folding tables, were plastic baggies of heavily salted popcorn, free, and paper cups of grape soda, seventy-five cents apiece. The women who sold the tickets and soda, all of them wives or girlfriends of the volunteer firemen, treated one another as if they were members of an extended family or secret club. They would call snippets of conversation through the open doorway, volleying highly inflected, cryptic messages from refreshment table to ticket table—odd, dislocated phrases, like, "Donna says try shoes next time," and, "Not *too* little," and once just a number, "Seven and a half!"—and invariably one of the women would go pink and the others would roar.

In past the free popcorn, the meeting room was appointed with rows of rickety wooden folding chairs. In front of these, foam rubber cushions provided additional, juvenile seating. And in front of these, flanked by an American flag and a filing cabinet with a toy fire helmet on top, stood the portable movie screen, hitched open on its metal tripod. Always, before the movie began—as people gathered and greeted one another, scraping back chairs and weighing creakily into them, kids kneeling backward in theirs to carry on with schoolmates in posterior rows, parents dispatching their children, equipped with dollar bills, to the soda table, and firemen's wives moving along the west wall, pulling shut the orange drapes against the last stinging light of sunset—it was hard to believe that this small, bland screen would become the sole object of our attention for the next few hours, that it would be able not only to command our interest, but to ferry us, in unison, out of the Lefferts Engine Company and the town of Pillow Lake. Like the ersatz society of firemen's wives, like Dr. Rouen's scientific community—we, the regular members of the audience, formed our own grouping, bound by familiarity with the wobbly chairs, the smell of floor polish, the narratives we followed together each week.

It was our custom to arrive early and save a seat for Cal. Ordinarily he and Hy took chairs while Tilly and I settled on cushions up front. But this night Tilly disdained a seat on the floor, electing instead to group with the adults. I followed her lead. She declined popcorn as well—this I could not bring myself to do, but I did try to eat it quietly, letting the pieces melt on my tongue one at a time, while we listened to Cal tell about the fire of '26.

Neither Tilly nor I had ever witnessed a real fire. We thought them rare and exotic, and found something bizarre, even mildly comic, about having a whole building, a whole profession, devoted to extinguishing them—the only services we had ever known the Lefferts Engine Company to provide, besides these Monday-night movies and popcorn, were its annual clangorous appearances in the Memorial Day parade, and its response, one time, to a false alarm at school (which instance had left deep, muddy waffle marks across one corner of our athletic field). Cal's reminiscences, on the other hand, offered proof of real danger.

But, "Do I really remember seeing that lady?" he mused now, and put two fingers to his lips and peered at the empty chair in front of him. "Or is it something I just remember being told?"

"If you remember the hat being feathered," Tilly reasoned, "you must have really seen her."

"Maybe," said Cal. "Maybe so."

The place was filling up. Hy, being so tall, had taken a seat on the outside aisle; then came Cal, with Tilly and me on his other side. Cal always smelled of pipe smoke; I liked to sit beside him. He spoke very soft and low and his breath made a sound as it passed through his nose hairs.

"Why did the lady give the firemen bananas?" I asked. It sounded like a sentence in a joke book.

Cal's eyes smiled, and he shook a cough drop from a cardboard box, then handed the box to me. I took one, returned the box, waited. Cal was generally slow to answer. He gazed around the room a full minute, then nodded and said, "She was thrilled by their bravery."

I liked the way he said this: decisively, after consideration, and I turned his words over in my mind, and with them a picture of a hatted lady, gaily extending bunches of bright yellow fruit, until I was confident I'd be able to transfer it all onto one of my recipe cards later that night.

On the wall of the meeting room behind the popcorn table, preserved under a glass in a cheap black frame, was an ochered newspaper clipping about the fire of '26 and an accompanying photograph, whose blurry subject was mostly smoke. It hung above my eye level; this summer, on tiptoe, I could make out approximately the bottom three-quarters of the story. It had been for a long time part of Tilly's and my ritual on movie nights to brush along the back wall, half scouting for school friends, and pause before the frame, always somewhat as if by chance.

We'd peer past the glare on the glass to note again the grainy image, the printed words that officially explained the otherwise mysterious remnants of structures we were always coming across in the woods around our house. The photo and words made a kind of scaffold on which we could mount and decipher such discoveries, and in this way encouraged our tendency to take the

fire personally, to treat it as a knowable part of our own past—
as we did all the found objects behind Pillow Lake.

Unexplained, however, excluded from any story or memory,
remained the dead house, intact and vacant all these years. We
somehow linked it neither to the time before the fire nor to the
present. It figured in none of Cal's stories. Hy didn't speak of it.
Tilly and I, although we treated the rest of the area behind the
lake with a near-filial proprietorship, avoided it. Until this summer, it had belonged to nothing so much as the murkily animate
woods into which it seemed to recede.

But now it had that car always parked out front, dusty and
squat, slung in rakishly over a corner of unmown weeds. It had
footsteps clattering across the porch, hands carrying groceries inside, cooking food, twisting knobs, opening windows. It had people sleeping in it, each night turning their heads on the pillows,
slow-breathing the air, filling it up with their dreams. And still
Tilly and I did not speak of it and still it was a mystery.

From the midst of all of these thoughts I was startled by Tilly,
who, having been deeply slouched and curled up in her seat, with
toes propped against the chair in front while she waited for the
movie to begin, now abruptly dropped her feet to the floor and
boosted herself erect. On the other side of Cal, Hy was half rising.
The Rouens had come in—not all of them: Bill Rouen and the
three oldest kids—and they were making their way toward us,
cutting across the middle aisle and sliding down our row with
their backs to the screen.

As soon as they reached us Tilly slouched again. She shook
her bangs forward, then finger-combed them back, quick and
automatic.

"Hello there," said Bill Rouen jovially, and, "There's some seats right there, kids," pointing to the ones in front of us, so that they had to back out and go around. He himself stayed in our row, wedged sideways, one leg hoisting a chair askew, while Hy introduced him. ("The Rouens are the ones staying in the cottage," was how she put it to Cal, and it took my brain several moments to distill "dead house" from "cottage.") Bill leaned forward and stretched his hand across Tilly and me; he and Cal shook. And then, "You mind?" Bill asked Tilly with exaggerated courtesy, his eyebrows somewhere up near his hairline, and he pointed to the empty chair beside her.

"No."

He sat. Isobel swiveled around and rested her chin on the back of her chair. She rubbed it there, back and forth across the wood, and looked at her father.

"Come here often?" asked Bill.

"It's just in summer," I said.

"You might find it boring," said Tilly.

Bill Rouen laughed. "Do *you* find it boring?"

"No." Tilly faced forward, and up into the cool moon of her face I saw a thin blush rise. She said curtly, "But you may have different tastes."

A smile wobbled in the corners of his pale eyes and his voice came out in a thickish way from back in his throat. "Well, yes. I have been known to have different tastes."

From the way he said this, I wondered whether it was a joke for Hy's benefit, something over our heads like when he had called Tilly a pragmatist, but when I glanced down the row, I saw she wasn't paying attention to us; it occurred to me his voice would be too low to reach her ears.

"I a little bit can't see, Daddy," Isobel said suddenly and in quite a high voice.

"I think you may be facing the wrong way, my love."

She took immediate offense, lifting her chin from the chair back and eyeing him with reproach. "No," she corrected, "there's a lady's *head* in my way." Her enunciation was pristine; accuracy of fact seemed of comparatively little concern, the seats in front of her clearly being occupied by a crew of young boys, all roughly my height.

"You can trade with me," said Tilly, and the lights went out.

In the new darkness Tilly rose and brushed past me and Cal and Hy, and then Isobel came in the same way, stepping on my feet as she did.

"Ah, much better," chirped Isobel, borderline-fresh, as she sat down. On the screen, the numbers started reeling backward from ten.

The Rouens had parked down the street, between the shuttered windows of the liquor store and The Sleeping Dog; after the movie we accompanied them to their car. We said good night to Cal (he lived right in town) on the concrete steps outside the Lefferts Engine Company, and for fifty paces proceeded like a party, like carolers, revelers, making our way down the warm, dark sidewalk, all of a group. Walter led, his white T-shirt softly aglow in ambient light from the gas station. He had asked for and gotten his father's keys; they jingled invisibly in his hand. Norah and Isobel, behind him, made a game of walking: they crossed their feet over each other, hips swishing out at every step, the jerking gait of arthritic dogs. When we reached their car they fell against it, laughing, with little metallic thuds.

"Mole, did you see us?" they asked. "Did you see what we were doing?"

Walter unlocked the door for them and they tumbled in. The others drew close, our little procession folding up like an accordion.

"And you parked . . . ?" Bill Rouen looked around.

"We walked," explained Hy.

"Ah. We'll give you a lift," he pronounced, and held out his hand to Walter for the keys.

"That'd be nice."

But Tilly appealed softly to Hy. "I'd rather walk."

"*I'd* like to walk," Walter said, so quick and solemn it might have been manners.

"There's room in the car for everyone." Bill patted the roof smartly twice and held the rear door open wide. No one made a move to get in.

"Do you kids want to walk back on your own?" asked Hy.

"That's silly," began Bill, but Hy had already turned to him.

"It's safe," she said. "Tilly knows the way."

"And me."

"Yes, Mole does, too."

So he had no choice but to close the rear door and let Hy into the front passenger seat. As I watched her gather up the hem of her skirt and shut the door, I had a queer sense of disappointment in Hy—not because she'd helped us get our way, but because her doing so had been inadvertent, or coincidental. There was a blindness I was noticing in Hy that summer, a genuine lack of knowing.

We waved and started down the sidewalk, three abreast and silent. In a moment the car passed us and Bill called out the window, "Race you back!" and then we watched the taillights grow little and snuff out around the bend.

It was clear: no moon, hundreds of stars. They reminded me of Walter's freckles. He walked in the middle. It was a mile home. I felt like a stowaway, brave and lucky.

"Your father didn't want us to walk," said Tilly.

"He's not my father," said Walter.

We passed the lot next to Steve Day's Auto Parts and I could smell the smell of warm tires and something else, like melon rinds left out in a heat wave. Tilly kicked a bottle, gently. It sang low over pavement and went mute in the grass.

"For real he's not?" I asked.

"He's my stepfather."

Just the fact of walking together seemed intimate, a kind of three-way privacy in the dark.

"The other ones," said Walter, "he's their biological father." I'd never heard it put that way: biological. It seemed to imply all sorts of alternatives.

"What happened to your real father?" asked Tilly.

"He lives in Montana."

"Oh."

A car drove by and got us all in its headlights, sharp as a flashbulb, snapping a brief, brilliant image of us on the road's soft shoulder. I felt swelled with the power of being seen.

Then Tilly said, "Our parents died when we were babies," and my bones became like water.

I never heard her tell it to anyone but me.

"They drowned in the Kittiwake when we were two and three."

She might have been reciting an old ballad; the words spun from her throat in the darkness with a certain inevitability.

"A storm came." She drew in a next breath as though to deliver further details, but no more came.

"Wow. And they drowned?" said Walter, prompting her, and I found myself, surprisingly, craning to hear what else she might say, as if there were anything new she could tell me, a portion of the story she'd kept to herself all this time.

"They were trying to rescue some other people." Her s's and l's slipped like pearls from a velvet tongue. Walter turned to her as we walked, watching the quiet majesty of her, his gaze like car headlights. "A boat full of people out on the water . . ." Again her voice trailed into ellipses; it sounded as though she would continue, but then she didn't. I wondered what she was doing, whether she meant for me to pick up the thread of the story.

She soloed on. "The boat tipped over in the storm, so our mother and father had to try to save them."

The boat tipped over.

It was a little enough slip. Not slip. But a slight enough way to introduce a fissure.

The story and every element of it, as I have said, had been fixed long ago, the shell of it passed down by Hy, the trappings furnished by Tilly and me, sometimes only after heated battle— but that was the point; we had literally fought to establish a single, ritualized version, constant enough to double for fact. Until Tilly changed a phrase.

The boat tipped over, she said, and the words smacked me in the face like a wet sponge. Should I say it wasn't true? Did she mean for me to? And, after all, what evidence could I offer? The only person I could ask to confirm the story I knew was the same one offering up this altered version for Walter. I wavered in the medium of my own liquid bones, governed by inaction. Tilly, beside me, fell intriguingly silent.

After a bit, Walter said, "Wow," but this time quietly, thoughtfully.

My head swam. What made her do it, without warning, without permission? What made me not correct her? I ought to have been indignant, ought to have piped up righteously in a high, clear voice like Isobel's. But I couldn't say it, and so made myself complicit. Tilly was the one who broke the rule; I was the one who let her.

We walked without talking then, in a manner that struck me as very grown up. The silence stretched among us like a bottle we might all pass around, all drink from. Soon we came to the beach path and the sign that said, "Public Swimming and Picnic Area," and then to the old wooden shingle, nailed to a fat oak, that still read, "Short Clove Lodge—12 Air Conditioned Rooms," and showed an arrow pointing down Short Clove Lane (now only a dirt path to a stunted-looking clearing, the lodge having been long since torn down). Walter, reading the sign, said, "What's that?" and Tilly said, "Just nothing now. We'll show you sometime," and I was encircled by that promise, by her saying "we," and began to enjoy the watery feeling in my bones; it became pleasant to go along, swept on the tide of Tilly's decisions; it was pleasant to have Walter know nothing about us or Pillow Lake, to have him to teach, to show ourselves to.

We started up the steep part of Ice Cart Road and it immediately got darker and our feet seemed to make less noise on the asphalt. In winter, I thought, on the same road, our steps would sound brittle, cracking.

"How come the hotter the night, the quieter your footsteps sound?"

"I didn't know that was true," said Walter.

We listened to ourselves walk.

After a bit, Tilly said, "At night there's no such thing as color."

"Of course there is," I said. "What do you mean?"

"Without light, your eyes don't see color, only shades of darkness."

We looked around.

"Then how come I can still tell those trees are green?"

"You can't," said Tilly. "You only think you see that because you remember what color they are in the day."

"I can too. Look. You can see green. Very dark green."

"You can't. It's just your brain."

And we walked on, looking at the sky and at our feet, checking our perceptions.

"All right," said Walter. "Here's something cool; we learned it in math. Okay, say you're walking home, well, like we're walking home, from the fire station: first we have to get halfway there, right?"

We murmured agreement.

"Okay, and then we have to walk half of what's left. And then half of that. If you keep dividing the remaining distance in half, it's like you keep passing these invisible halfway marks, see?"

Again we murmured, with foggy anticipation. Ice Cart Road began to climb.

"Well, actually, we learned it with a frog," he said.

"A frog? As in ribbit?" Tilly asked.

"Yeah. Pretend there's this frog trying to jump home to its lily pad in the center of the pond. Only each time it leaps, it can only go half the distance of the leap it just took. We had to use calculators and try to figure out how many leaps it would take."

We walked and thought. The lake was invisible, the tree shapes filling in like smoke.

"It would never get there," declared Tilly.

"That's the thing!" he crowed, and they each seemed pleased. I told them I didn't get it.

"It would just keep getting closer," Tilly explained.

"But it would always be farther away from getting there," said Walter.

"What do you mean, farther away?"

Tilly said she would explain it to me later, but Walter said no: we'll show her. He sent Tilly up ahead till we could barely make her out—only the zipper on her sweatshirt when she turned—and he said she was the lily pad and he was the pond edge and I was the frog, and he had us act it out. He coached me halfway to Tilly, and then half of that, and half of that, cutting the distance I traveled each time until I was taking teeny baby steps and then barely moving at all, only in my mind.

I stood suspended somewhere between the two, on a curve of road so dark it rendered us all faceless, and the distance between us kept shifting phantasmically, depending on whether I looked directly at one of them or a bit to the side. Their commands seemed hushed and close to my ears, but their figures grew furrier, progressively less substantial, as though the shadows were thickening, taking on matter. And falling into a cruel game with myself, holding my body rigid, I found it possible to believe that I had become trapped like the frog, had fallen under a spell that locked me into infinite half steps that would keep me from home forever.

Tilly. I tried to speak, but no sound came out. I had not spoken up earlier, had kept silent and even enjoyed letting my bones become watery, pliant; now, as the price, I had lost control over my limbs, my tongue, forever: they had been turned to stone. Walter's voice had discontinued far behind me. Tilly was invisible. Maybe I had grown invisible to them. Maybe hours had passed; they'd given up searching, left me for a stone in the road. Deep in the woods a tree creaked.

"Tilly!" Sound clambered up from my gullet; I hit two notes at once. "I can't see you!"

"I'm right here." In speech, her teeth glimmered, apple-clean and even, much closer than I'd expected. Her voice came swiftly, soothingly, big-sisterly. She stepped toward me, sweeping behind her ear a handful of hair, which was somehow the color and texture of the night air, and as she neared, crossed back over the line between shade and flesh, it occurred to me for the first time that my sister was going to be what people in the world thought of as beautiful. I shivered.

She put an arm around me and said, "Mole, don't be scared,"

which made me fake another shiver. She gave my arm a pat. Then she called, "Come on, Walter."

He loped up to us, speaking again, his voice charged with light, easy enthusiasm. "It's called somebody's paradox. I forget who." We resumed walking. "And the cool thing is, the really neat thing—anytime we go anywhere, we're passing those halfway marks. I mean if you break it down, in theory, we have to go through infinite numbers of halfways, so in a way, we should never get anywhere. Isn't that pretty neat?"

Suddenly Tilly dropped behind us, and I knew she was testing it out. I stopped and Walter stopped and we watched her watch herself put her foot slowly through space, thinking about the halfways. Her foot touched down and she looked up and smiled, half foolish, half triumphant, and announced, most un-Tilly-like, "I just did infinity," and then she said, "Let's run."

We took off as if chased. We ran the whole rest of the way, thrusting ourselves forward into the dark silky air, mouths open, eyes tearing, hearts slamming in exuberant terror—a kind of nameless game we all knew how to play. We slowed only when the dead house came into view: its husk lit from within.

"Okay: bye," said Walter. I thought he sounded different, subdued. He started up the path.

"See you," called Tilly.

We looked after him, curiously intent on seeing him enter the house. Only as he reached the steps did I notice the man, sitting very still in a chair on the porch; I could see just his outline, and dangling from the fingers of one hand the shape of a glass, which he raised, almost imperceptibly, as if toasting Tilly's words.

*   *   *

In the morning I watched them go by as usual, the mother and the father, on their morning walk to the river. I liked to pretend that one morning I would follow them, although inevitably I remained where I was and let them dip out of sight. This morning I did the same, but after a yawn and a good scratch, I did then hop off my bed and put on some clothes. I had not been to my mussels in more than a week.

The doors to Tilly's and Hy's rooms both stood shut. I went softly down the dim staircase, one hand trailing across the flowered wallpaper: snow roses, said Hy. I stole fig newtons from the pantry, two for each hand and one for my mouth, and stepped outside.

It was cool yet in back of the house. A breeze made me notice my knees. I took the zigzag path to the lake.

I could not find the mussels where I had left them, pushed back under a twisty gazebo of tree roots, and thought at first that I had the wrong place. But on closer inspection I recognized them after all—the rooms scattered apart, toppled, knocked free of their furnishings, some choked with sand, some half-sunken in it. They looked almost incidental, natural; someone coming upon them might not even recognize the traces of a little house, might register only an odd number of shells washed up in one spot.

I was still holding three cookies; I laid these on a rock and set about tending to the ruins, extracting them piece by piece from under their latticed root-roof. One shell had been cracked down the middle. I examined the two halves, then chucked them aside. The others had lost their luster, their insides clotted with sand and soil. The moss carpets, those scraps I could find, were dried up and tattered; these, too, I threw aside. The twig and bark furniture was gone, also the scoop-pebble easy chair; I ferreted around for it with both hands, uselessly.

I was not upset. I had known this would happen. There had been the storm on the Fourth (perhaps it had hailed here, too) as well as other afternoons of rain. Now it was up to me with my giant's hands to come set them right.

I knelt at the edge of the water and rinsed the shells back to iridescence, then crept up the bank and harvested new moss, which I separated, with surgical care, into precise ovals. These carpets I laid into four clean shells. In the fifth, a chip of mica and a flat white pebble became mirror and toilet. Then I began to rummage for a tiny cupped-up bathtub shell, but soon stopped: my neck felt stiff and creaked, faintly, if I moved my head just a fraction, and behind my eyes a tweezerlike ache had started.

I sat with my neck very straight and ate the rest of the fig newtons. The lake was perfectly empty, perfectly quiet, except for the old rowboat and the melancholy slap, slap of water against its side.

I pretended I could see ghosts of ice cutters and horses shimmering out there on the lake's surface, our grandfather guiding a plow across the water's thick winter rind, dividing it up, length and width, this way and that, carving great squares across the whole expanse. I could see them, all men, in black coats and mittens, with visible breath. I put Cal out there, too, as a young boy in a red woolen cap, following the men around the placid grid of ice. That had all really happened; that was something we could teach Walter about. Of course, we could say it even if it hadn't really happened.

I put my hand into the sand, ran it back and forth through

the still-chilly grains—and scraped against something. I drew out another mussel shell, this one whole, but splayed open on its hinge like a locket or a pair of wings. I blew it off and turned it over between my fingers.

Bill Rouen had said mussels attach for life. With—what had he called it? Bushel thread? I turned the thing over, looking for signs of this strong thread, maybe a ragged end where it had been severed. How thick would it have to be? Like embroidery thread? I drew my finger across the silken inside and over the coarse blue-black outer shell. Nothing. Perhaps it was still attached to the animal. The thread must be a kind of muscle, I thought. That must be where it gets its name.

And who would ever guess such a little creature would be so strong? For life, he had said. I looked into my palm at the thing that had been washed loose from the lake; this was a skeleton, then. Where did dead mussels go? Did they float? Did their bodies sink to the bottom of the lake? What were their bodies like? Pinkish? White? Did they bleed? I turned the shell facedown, scraped at the flaky black part. I bent it along its hinge, pressed it back wider and wider until it snapped apart. My heart lurched when it snapped like that, and a guilty, racing heat broke out along my forehead. I told myself, out loud, not to be a ninny. They were my shells to break. And I went on with the pieces in my hands: I tested the strength of each half. They were quite easily cracked. I threw the bits; they scattered in the shallows.

My stomach clutched with morbid thrill. I looked down at the shells I had just refurbished: they were lined up prissily at my feet, four with their silly soft beds of moss improbably thick, and the bathroom (bathroom!) with its flimsy wafer of mirror. Foolish little house of my own creation. I raised my foot above them, and with more curiosity than anything else, watched myself bring it down in slow motion like Tilly doing infinity.

CHAPTER ✦ FIVE

WE GAVE THINGS up to be with them. Lunches with Hy, of course, but that's not what I mean, what I think of now as the important change. Tilly relinquished (and unbegrudgingly: this was what surprised me) a great portion of the privacy and aloofness she'd worked to establish. She maintained it more with Hy than with anyone else, which made me sorry, but not so sorry as to jeopardize my own good fortune by calling attention to her unfairness—Tilly was behaving in a more sisterly manner than she had for months; at times I felt even indispensable. With Walter in particular and the Rouens in general, she manifested a new openness—truly new; it was not any echo of her old sturdy ingenuousness, but something altogether unrelated, a determined loosening of spirit that felt as tenuous as it did tantalizing.

What I gave up was the story of our parents' death. When I did not correct Tilly on the walk back from the fire station, when I chose not to dissociate myself from her words, I surrendered certain rights. We neither of us would have put a name to it, but by the codes of childhood a definite shift had occurred. Anyway, I didn't mind. What I gained was well worth it: it was brilliant spending time at the dead house with the Rouens, going around with Tilly and Walter. The summer seemed promising again; it might yet yield whatever it was I'd been hoping for so deeply and shapelessly. I looked to Tilly with fascination for signs of it, of what it might be.

For my sister—well, more than just her consonants were in flux that summer. She was by turns irritable and serene, radiant and remote. Within minutes she could alter, even her features, which behaved somehow out of synch with her moods; one moment she'd look stern and lovely, the next cheerful and angular, almost homely. She seemed to shimmer, slightly, as if two selves lay superimposed one over the other: a familiar thin shadow over a paler, emergent form. Now I have access to words I didn't then: "menarche," "hormones," "pubescence." That summer I thought it was all the Rouens, that their presence was bringing about a change in Tilly, in us, in our lives; that collectively they made a kind of key, unlocking us.

"Mole, you're blocking me." Tilly opened her eyes, shaded them, and frowned at my shadow, blanketing her torso.

We had come down to the public beach for a change, Tilly having decided she ought to "work on her tan."

We had been sunbathing since eleven; it was now nearly twelve. Working on our tans turned out to be an endeavor that precluded conversation, and I was bored silly. We'd flipped once, on the half hour, and bickered sporadically since then. Tilly complained that every time I sat up I blocked her sun, and furthermore that my fidgeting wrinkled up the sheet and got it full of sand. I insisted that the sand was coming up of its own accord through tiny moth holes.

"Moths don't eat sheets."

"Look. There are holes. I'll show you if you would open your eyes for one second."

"That's unnecessary. Moths eat wool."

"Well, then, what are these little tiny holes?"

Her face was utter peace and silence.

"I think it might be time to flip."

"Not yet."

"I think it might be."

She sighed, reached out a hand, felt languidly for her shoes, extracted her wristwatch from inside one, and held it out to me, all without opening her eyes.

"Eleven fifty-two," I read. "No, three. Two. In there."

Tilly, silently correct, replaced her watch. Her eyelids looked shiny. And above her lip.

"You're blocking me again," she said.

But it was not me this time. I looked up and there was Walter, standing behind Tilly's head, wearing only his eyeglasses and a pair of red trunks.

"Hola, Chiquita bananas," he said.

Tilly opened her eyes and propped herself up on one elbow. "Hey," she replied, as though accustomed to being addressed this way.

"I brought the littles down. They make me batty, cooped up inside." He nodded down the beach to where Norah, Isobel, and Gus were arranging towels, pails, bright plastic things, I could tell he wasn't saying it in order to sound old; in spite (or because) of this, he came across as captivatingly experienced. He also seemed blandly unself-conscious about his appearance: for me, the mix-

ture of wire-rimmed glasses and nakedness produced a queer effect, the stateliness of the former making the latter more
pronounced. The spread of his ribs showed clearly across his chest
and reminded me of a fir tree. His freckles, I could now see, went
all over.

Tilly sat up and Walter sat down. She let him have a corner
of sheet. "You're in charge?"

"Whenever our parents go out."

"Aren't you a little young for that responsibility?" Only Tilly
could ask that and not sound rude.

But he shot her a look of merry mock offense, his eyebrows
going up and together in the center like a circus tent. "You dare
call me young, miss?" His voice didn't quite crack but teetered as
it came out, a warbly bass.

And Tilly did the unexpected thing of laughing, and turning
a little bit prettily red, and backpedaling from her slight imperti-
nence. "I just meant—"

"Me?" he went on, still in sort of a rough Shakespeare-voice,
his brows knit haughtily. "A ripe old gent of fourteen? And how
old might you be, prithee tell?"

When she told him she'd be thirteen in the middle of August,
he asked her the date and then said, in his normal voice, "No
kidding. That's the same as my father's birthday."

"Your real father?"

"My step."

"The one we met."

"Right. Bill."

"Oh."

The mention of him was like a curtain dropping on their

comic little sketch. I tried to reproduce the cadence of their quick-woven banter. "We should have a party then, shouldn't we?" I said. "A joint party. We could have it at the dead house."

"Mole!" Tilly's voice was as sharp and shrill as the teakettle.

I blinked and shut up. Tilly went stony, rigid, her eyes watering from the terrible affront of my suggestion. On those rare occasions when Tilly lost her composure, she generally lost it all at once. The smooth, pale expanse of her face would become mottled with rough patches of emotion, and her lower jaw would pull forward slightly, and her eyes grow glassy, opaque. (I did not react this way ever, since, Tilly was fond of saying, I had so little composure to lose in the first place.) I wasn't even sure what exactly I'd said wrong: whether it was the idea of sharing her birthday with Bill Rouen, or my calling it the dead house, or even my speaking at all, when the conversation had been between her and Walter.

Then Walter said, lamely, I thought, "That's a pretty odd name: Mole. Where'd you get a name like that?"

But Tilly seemed grateful for the rescue. She swooped in and answered for me, very flat and offhand. "Oh, that's my doing. I couldn't pronounce Martha when I was little."

It was the tiniest scrap of misinformation, insignificant really. But my heart skidded sharply, caught on a ledge. That was not the story at all, not what I'd been told by Hy, who'd said it was me, my littleness, the furry brown hair I'd had even as a newborn; who'd said I was such a small, warm, brown thing they couldn't have called me anything else. As if it were my proper name, inscribed on my body for them to see. This was the story I'd always known about my name, and I opened my mouth to contradict my sister.

But I did not contradict her. I realized with a lurch like an aftershock that her explanation sounded truer, more likely, than Hy's.

"And it stuck," said Walter.

"And it stuck," Tilly agreed.

Then Norah and Isobel and Gus came over, swinging their bright shovels, greedy for whatever it was we were doing, so we broke off our conversation and buried Gus to the knees in sand, and then various ones of us went swimming and the awkward moment was left behind. But later, while Tilly was still in the water and I was toweling off, Walter approached me quietly and asked, "What is that, the, what did you call it?—dead house?"

My ears went hot. I scanned the lake for signs of Tilly, her lime-green suit, and saw that she was well out in the middle of the swimming area, hoisting herself onto the float. "Oh, well, that's, it's what we call the house where you're living, actually." Trying to sound casual, dismissive.

"Where *we're* living! How come?"

"We just do."

"Well, did somebody die there?"

"No." I couldn't make the stupid grin go away. "I never really—Tilly just made it up, I think. We've always called it that. I don't know." I felt queerly ashamed, yet I repeated it twice more—"I don't know, I don't know"—before bending my wet head forward into the towel and scrubbing it hard under that dark hood.

*   *   *

Dr. Rouen, the mother, we rarely saw. I had thought that after that hang-gliding day she and Hy might become friends, but this did not happen. She was always working, down at the river or in the house, but mostly at the river, all the time. I thought of her down there, gathering information. I still saw her in the mornings, wearing her same white cardigan, disappearing over the drop in Ice Cart Road; sometimes, too, in the afternoons. Or getting into their black car and driving somewhere in it—I thought maybe bringing samples to the lab. Samples of what, I did not know, but that phrase, "samples to the lab," had unfurled in my mind and would not go away. I even wrote it on a recipe card and drew an illustration: a laboratory in a white brick building, with gleaming metal tables and bubbling beakers and long-nosed scientists waiting around for samples to test. It came out not very well, the drawing (the scientists resembled mice without whiskers), but I knew what I meant, and put the card in my underwear drawer.

I was sorry we didn't see more of her, and sometimes tried to engineer our schedules so as to be sort of loitering around the dead house at times when I guessed she might be there. But I liked it, too, that she was so serious in her work; I ascribed to her a tenderness toward her work, a purity of intention that seemed noble, almost heroic; that seemed like a quality for a mother to have. I envisioned her eventually discovering that I shared such qualities; it would happen gradually, this recognition; it was happening already, imperceptibly, under the surface of the days. When we played around the dead house on certain afternoons, one piece of my self I tried to hold continually in check for her. I imagined her glancing out the window, up from her notebook, and taking note of my certain quietness, my special worth. Eventually, I imagined, she would learn about my mussel houses, and then we would have much to talk about.

Bill Rouen was different. Bill Rouen we saw often. He'd turn up at our house in the late afternoons, to borrow some vinegar, or return Hy's socket wrench, or offer us a lift into town.

"We have our bikes," Tilly would say, holding the screen door open a few inches with her toes.

"It's mighty hot, though," Bill would return, not looking at her but squinting off one end of the porch. He'd slide his tongue consideringly over his front teeth that overlapped. The way he said "mighty," it was the same as if he were wearing a costume.

"We can take it," she would tell him, always plain and serious.

He'd laugh then—as if she'd said exactly the thing that would delight him most—and pretend to tip his hat, except he didn't wear any. "I'm sure you can," he'd say, and the sound of his boots retreating off the porch, carrying the full weight of his body, would crack dully. "I have little doubt."

It had grown like a game between them now. Somewhere Tilly had entered into it; she was playing, too.

Walter asked us once did Hy ever have a husband.

At midday, when his parents came back from the river and he got off minding the little kids, Walter had taken to coming over to our house, which he called "an oasis of respite." He said this in his Shakespeare-voice. We looked forward to his coming. Sometimes he ate with us; Tilly would make tomato and mustard sandwiches, and I would pour little hills of potato chips on three plates. We kept the curtains drawn against the heat, and after lunch the downstairs was all bathed in a kind of filtered, water-hued light. On the hottest days we three would do nothing but go lie on the pantry tiles with just the backs of our heads propped against the baseboard and pass around a two-liter bottle of seltzer. That was what we were doing when he asked.

We told him no, Hy never had a husband.

Walter drank and swallowed with a loud glug, because of how his neck was scrunched. He always did things like that without any self-consciousness: made noise when he swallowed or chewed, left crumbs on his lips, burped—and it wasn't gross when he did it; Tilly didn't mind it as she would have if it were me or Hy. Walter said, "I would like to be a hermit," and I could think only of Hy's little brown, baked molasses bars.

"What's that?"

"It's somebody who lives in the woods," said Tilly, "and doesn't cut their hair and doesn't talk to anybody, except about once a year, when they buy groceries."

"How come?"

"How come they live in the woods?"

"How come Walter wants to be one?"

He was silent long enough that Tilly raised herself on one elbow and looked at him.

"I just think it would be cool," he said. "Not to have to . . . to do any of that, talk to people, be nice to people."

I felt personally insulted, but Tilly said, "Yes. I think that, too," and then I felt jealous.

Another time, Walter told us his mother was not in love with his stepfather.

We couldn't understand it, because it seemed like if you were going to be in love with anybody, Bill Rouen was cut out for it. He seemed designed to be in love with. With that slow way he spoke, like a person scraping his lower teeth along an artichoke leaf, and that cowboy manner of squinting his pale, pale eyes against the sun, you had the feeling: when I grow up and am supposed to fall in love with somebody, that's what he's supposed to be like.

Dr. Rouen had a romantic name: Delia—but she herself was not our idea of romantic. It was interesting to consider her being in love and not being in love, and it was especially interesting to consider her having the power to not be in love with Bill Rouen.

Walter told us this without any clue to how we were supposed to react. He just said it, out of the blue, in his deep, thin voice. We were in our usual positions on the pantry floor. Walter said that time was adhering and that was why his parents were together. He made it into science then; he told us that in science "time is adhering" meant this: you could put two pieces of gold in a vacuum and they'd adhere, they'd become one piece, because the atoms wouldn't know, as they buzzed around the edges, where one piece of gold stopped and the other began, and so they'd move around and bump into each other and overlap, until it'd all be one piece of gold.

Or, he went on, the other way you could make things adhere was in real life, not in a vacuum; it was simply a matter of a long enough time. For example, he said, if you wanted to store a car, you'd have to put it up on blocks in the garage and then put some oil in and turn the engine over once; if you didn't get that protective coat of oil in there, the different parts of the engine would eventually fuse together. It's the atoms not being able to tell where one object stops and the other begins that makes everything join. The natural tendency, over time, he said, is for everything touching to adhere.

He had lost me early on—I didn't see what a car and a vacuum cleaner could possibly have to do with his parents' staying married—but what did strike me was this last part, the word "adhere." I remembered that word from the picnic blanket, from Bill and Dr. Rouen teaching me about mussel shells and the way they held on so tightly. A fly buzzed and collided repeatedly against the window screen. I thought guiltily of my mussel houses, neglected now for—one week? two?

"I wonder if that's really true," said Tilly. She pressed the fingertips of either hand neatly together and looked curiously at them.

"It is. It's proven," said Walter. "Scientifically."

"I don't mean in science, I mean in people."

A series of images, like slides, slid unbidden into my mind. Hy and Cal: them in the boxy little garden behind Coffey's, drinking iced tea, each with their old callused feet stuck up on chairs. Then bluer, dimmer, an image of my parents: gliding, melting, one after the other, over the hill's dark ridge and into the river. And then I thought of Walter's father, the one he'd called biological: not really an image at all, just the word "MONTANA."

The three of us were lying so that no parts of our bodies were touching any other's. On Tilly's shins, lined up perpendicular to me, was stubble, the tiniest dark specks, like pepper, pricking up through the skin. "Check it out," she said, sitting up and holding one palm out toward Walter. He hesitated for a moment before obliging her, propping himself up and extending a palm to mirror hers, which she pressed against it. She lined up the heels of their hands exactly and their fingers rose like two fences, one tall and one short. "Like that?"

"Basically," he mumbled, and leaned back swiftly against the wall, drawing up his knees and wiping his hand on one of them. I wondered what had happened to make him embarrassed.

"Pass me the seltzer?" said Tilly, as if she didn't notice.

Walter sloshed what contents were left in the bottle. "I think it's pretty much just backwash." He removed the cap for her.

She leaned forward again and received it from him, tilted it toward her mouth. "I don't care," she said.

That surprised me, too.

We brought them to Coffey's one afternoon when Walter had charge of the little ones. The younger ones. Isobel hated to be called little. "I'm not at all little," she would correct anyone severely, and she was right. She was short but solid. She had wide wrists and a broad back and round calves, ballast.

Norah, on the other hand, objected to "younger." She had done the subtraction. "There's three years between Walter and Mole and only three years between Mole and me, but there's almost five years between me and Gus, so I don't see why I get called younger and Mole doesn't."

We were all standing around Walter's crouched figure, waiting for him to finish chaining the bikes to the parking meter in front of the shop. The Rouens had rented bikes for the summer: kid bikes for Norah and Isobel, and a five-speed with a child seat for Walter to ride Gus. Tilly knelt to help him thread the chain through all the spokes.

Feeling precarious, I kept quiet and tried to look both humble and mature.

Walter gave a little grunt as he tried to hook up the lock. He wiped some sweat from below his eye and told Norah, "It's just relative."

Norah's lower lip jutted.

"Mole doesn't play with dolls," Tilly tried to explain, making me dizzy with gratitude.

"Neither do I play with dolls!"

Walter said softly, "What about Miss Lollypodge?"

"I don't *play* with her!" Norah sounded aghast.

"Then can I have her?" Isobel asked with sudden interest.

"Be quiet," her sister hissed.

"Anyway," said Walter, snapping the lock shut and rising, "there's *six* years between you and me," and in the end she had to give in to the simple math of it.

I was relieved that Norah did not win her point, but in a way I liked her for her willingness to argue, to take them on, and I had to admit I thought Walter had not been altogether fair with her. Mentioning her doll's name in front of Tilly and me. And then using the numbers against her, turning the math around on her with such empty, grown-up logic.

Inside the shop, I watched them case the aisles, Norah and Isobel with Gus in tow, prowling through racks of chamois cloths and putty knives, ladders and light bulbs, coming upon the great peacock display of paint chips with chirps of delight. Norah, apparently grudgeless, approached me with several strips from the magenta family, saying, "Do you have a pocket? Hold these for me until we get back—don't let me forget!" and bustled along to the back garden, where Hy was pouring cold drinks and Isobel was teaching Gus Miss Mary Mack, their palms slapping sweatily over the sound of the rhyme. They were so bodily, the Rouen children, so messy and ripe and unapologetic. They smelled to me like hot dogs and ketchup. Smudges of dirt or lunch on their fingers and cheeks, their hair catching fire in the sun. It never occurred to me that anything could be missing from their family, that anything in it could be sad or not just right.

In every instance they were unshy about expressing intent. On our way back out, passing through the cool body of the shop, we heard Cal cutting a key on the noisy machine. Norah and Isobel went instantly on tiptoe and peered over the counter at the operation. Gus regarded them. Then he turned to Walter and in a fine, lucid treble said, "Pick me up. Don't hold me, please, just pick me up so I can see."

Bill Rouen said things to Tilly like she cleaned up pretty. He came over once in the evening and knocked (he was coming to tell Hy that water was coming out brown from their kitchen tap), and Tilly answered. She had just washed her hair and combed it, close against her scalp and glistening with tooth marks from the comb still in it; she looked like an Indian with it so black and tight, or like the lady in the cameo brooch Hy kept on her dresser. She was wearing a yellow T-shirt that came to her knees and nothing else. Bill Rouen looked at her face and her hair and her face and her T-shirt and her face and her bare legs, back and forth his eyes flitting like a candle flame, and she waited to see what his comment would be.

He told her then that she "sure cleaned up pretty." Whenever he said anything like this, it was always in quotes, as if he were half fooling, or meant something ever so slightly different from what the words implied.

Tilly did not reply, but kept her eyes on him while she angled her face toward the stairs and called "Hy!"

I was standing in the doorway to the living room.

Tilly said, "Hang on," and ran up the stairs.

Bill Rouen followed her with his face. As soon as she was out of sight, his face changed; something focused and bemused dropped out of it; he looked tired, and scratched inside his ear with his pinkie. He ventured a few steps inside the hall, and then saw me. "Good evening," he said with the ghost of a bow. He never used our names.

"Hi," I said. Even as he spoke, an ironical stiffness crept back into his posture and his lips, and he stood regarding me now with his hands in his pockets, the scorpion buckle winking softly between them. I wished I had washed my hair, too, wished it were black with being wet and combed against my scalp in a way that looked sleek and interesting. "How is your work coming along?" I asked.

He arched his eyebrows.

"With the mussels."

His brows went higher; creases appeared at the sides of his mouth. "Have they been sending you to cocktail parties?"

I didn't understand.

"Versed as you are in the social graces?" He made a sweeping gesture with his hand. "No, no, after *you*, Alphonse."

I didn't understand that either.

He took his other hand from his pocket, hooked both thumbs behind the brass buckle. He didn't answer my question.

"I'll see what's keeping Hy," I said after a moment, as coldly and politely as I thought Tilly would have done, and cut my eyes from him and started up the stairs.

On the fifth step I felt his hand close around my ankle. It was warm and firm, thrust through the banister. "My work, since you inquire, is coming along adequately," he said, his voice honeyed and polite. I tried to pull my ankle away and he tried not to let it go, which I wasn't expecting; I yanked again and the circle of his fingers tore open and he laughed. In spite of myself, I laughed, too, as I stumbled, reddening and furious, up the rest of the stairs.

They had in their house a book about shells.

They had, as well, a round kitchen table whose surface was glass, so you could peer down around your lunch and see the base, the white-painted iron bands twisting gracefully around each other and curving into legs, and in the center there, below the surface of the table, a round place where a bunch of cloth flowers might go, although the Rouens themselves did not actually keep a bunch of flowers there and I did not know where I got the idea that someone might.

And they had, by the entrance, built into the wall next to the front door, some shelves and pegs and a boot area and even a compartment for umbrellas, all ingeniously fitted into a little, unstained pine recess by the door. And they had downstairs bathroom curtains decorated with pale orange airplanes, and a large dark rectangle on the living room wall where a mirror might have hung. These things and others I saw, but did not register, when I went into the dead house.

I went to see the book on shells. Walter took me. First we had lunch on the glass table, baloney sandwiches he made for everyone: Gus, Isobel, Norah, Tilly, and me. It was a day when the parents stayed late at the river, and Tilly helped Walter with the baloney sandwiches and black olives and powdered milk that got measured with a plastic scoop and mixed with tap water. And then, after we ate, he turned especially to me and said, "Come on, I'll show you that book."

Tilly had told him about my mussel houses. She had confessed without apologizing. "I told Walter about your shells," she said.

"You what?" I pretended to be stricken; I don't know why; maybe I thought she would be impressed.

She was unfazed. "You know you don't care about privacy, Mole. Just the opposite."

This was entirely true. Her act, then, was one of generosity; I dropped my counterfeit indignation, and real gratitude replaced it.

"He knows a lot about shells, because of his parents. He said he has a cool book he'll show you."

So we went over for lunch and afterward Walter took me upstairs. The book, he said, was in his parents' bedroom, which was on the north side of the house, cool and shaded and dim. I stood in the doorway while he walked around their bed to the books piled on the floor below the dresser. I had not been up-stairs before. On the dresser top I could make out lumpy shapes: small garments, socks or underwear, and the glint of loose change, and a large oval hairbrush, bristles up. Walter knelt over a toppled stack of books and I saw the backs of his elbows and the soles of his feet and the pale of his lower back where his shirt rode up. Then he went forward on his hands and knees and reached for a book that had gotten pushed under the dresser. His khakis were loose on him, and beltless, and I could see the shadowy indentation at the base of his spine that marked the beginning of his bottom. I felt shy to look at him, at his hindquarters, and shy also for some reason to let my eyes rest on anything within the private space of the bedroom—the money on the dresser, or the bed, unmade but covered with a dark red spread, or the still-damp towel hanging over the back of the closet door—and maybe it was shyness, really, at the way my eyes ached to travel thoroughly over the room, to dwell and luxuriate in every shadowy corner. Behind the bed was an alcove with a window; I fixed my gaze through that. The view was purely branches, nothing remarkable: the top of a stooped apple tree and then farther away a reach of lean, dark pines, which cut a W into the sky at the top of the pane. But it gave me a funny sensation, looking out that window, as though I'd overstepped, intruded into something I had no business seeing.

I became so self-conscious I needed to distract myself, and so said, in a high, abrupt voice, "What *are* shells? You know? I mean, are they like bones?"

I could tell right away, from an eager sound he made, that Walter knew the answer. He didn't turn around, though, and the view of him was still rump and pale, narrow flashes of lower back and legs. "Shells are made of lime," he said.

"Limes?"

"Lime. Lime. As in a mineral, they, the animal gets from the water, and then their body somehow secretes tiny particles of it back out into this"—he rummaged the air with his hands for a word—"uh . . . *paste*. And it builds up, layer upon layer, into this hard shell. And they live in it." He rose and turned toward me. His glasses flashed a white reflection. "It's more like a house than bones. Here."

He crossed the dim room extending a fat maroon book, which he'd flipped open to a section of color photographs, and said, "The phylum you want is mollusks," tossing this off so casually that I thought he must be kind of proud of knowing it, and then he left me to sit in a rhomboid of sunlight on the landing outside his parents' room while he went down the stairs.

I sat there, on the second floor of the dead house, watching the back of Walter as he left me to thumb through the pages, whisper the names out loud.

False Angel Wing, Dwarf Tellin, Atlantic Strawberry Cockle, Three-lined Pandora, Unequal Spoon Clam, Blood Ark, Rough-mantled Doris, Comb Bittersweet, Warty Sea Cat, White Paper Bubble, Mouse Cone, Ida's Miter, True Tulip Snail, Lightning Whelk, Emerginate Dogwinkle, Crescent Cressinella, Gum Boot Chiton, Bleeding Tooth, Common Baby's Ear.

I wanted my recipe cards. The pages were smooth and heavy, the photographs darkly, richly colored. An ink-and-dust fragrance lived deep in the paper; the binding dug into my thigh and left a red impression. From time to time I looked up from my lap and over my shoulder, into their room, sipped glimpses: the hastily thrown spread, a pair of flip-flops on the rug, the curtains tied back from the alcove window. From downstairs came the sounds of the little girls' make-believe voices, animated and breathy, and of chairs scraped back and the fridge door shutting and water running in the sink.

More like a house than bones. Each shell a home, a chamber of lime, custom-secreted from the inside out. I found the ones I wanted.

The sea mussels: Dusky, Rubbed, Lemon, Scorched, Hooked, Cinnamon Chestnut. And the freshwaters, called naiads: Wavy, Nose, Bruised, Shaggy, Ocher Lamp. The Confused River Mussel. The Plaited Horse Mussel. The Fragile Freshwater Mussel, *anodonta cataracta*. This one I recognized. I moved my tongue around the Latin. Left my oily olive-thumbstreaks across the corner of the page.

On top of the hill on a clear, windy afternoon, we leaned against field rock markers for shelter. I against "Harriette Flemming Cates, Wife and Mother"; Tilly against "Barnabas Bradley Cates, Ice Cutter." Walter, who was spooked by the grave site but wouldn't admit it, sprawled several feet away from us on his stomach, regarding an anthill. ("Come sit here, Walter," Tilly had invited, patting "Jeremiah August Cates" beside her; "No, sir," is how Walter had answered, and Tilly received the appellation like she did "banana": with a wise, serene hint of a smile.)

Tilly and I had used to invent stories for the people named on the stones up here. We'd take what scant information had been carved into the markers, and note the connections to other names on other markers, and then craft whole histories from the broadest details to the most intricate anecdotes, taking turns laying out the facts. Some of the names we'd ask Cal if he recognized; some of them he did. The blending of fact and invention ran through all our childhood games, and the sense that one was transmutable into the other stayed with us to the very borders of childhood.

Here at the old cemetery the wind made a racket in the trees, which grew in stubby fashion along the high ridge. It made a racket like water, and far below us we could see whitecaps on the Kittiwake, and brief pearly nosegays where foam tipped up along the rocky shore. Straight below, tucked close against the rock wall, lay the marsh where the Rouen parents spent their mornings, but we could not see this from where we sat, lazily curled back from the wind.

"Our mother loved weather. Loved storms," Tilly was saying, telling Walter the story that only she and I really knew. She had been telling it to him in fragments: a sentence or two along Ice Cart Road, another day a detail offered up on the beach, a few words spoken across the floor of the pantry, some more dished out across the glass table in the dead house. Some of what she told him was familiar to me and some of it was not. "She was a little bit dense about storms," Tilly said now. "A little bit, you know, irresponsible."

This was unfamiliar to me; my listening grew sharper. I wondered if Walter knew that parts were true and parts improvised. He had his chin on one fist. With his other hand he brushed a dirt moat around the anthill.

"Her name was Violet. His was David."

Old hat.

"Our father had to watch out for her. Sometimes when a storm came, there she'd be, slipping out the door."

Unfamiliar.

Tilly didn't look to me for permission or agreement. In the weeks since we'd walked back from the firehouse, her telling had gained momentum and assurance. There was no question of my being a part of it now. It was Tilly's game. Walter and I made up the audience.

"He'd have to go get her, bring her back inside," said Tilly. "It was like—" She broke off, searching for the phrase she wanted, and I focused all my attention to hear what it would be. That was the funny part; even though I knew she was making it up, I attended to the story as if there were something I would really find out from it. A white butterfly, the common kind, stitched a wavy line across the crests of gravestones, then, overwhelmed by breeze as it gained altitude, fluttered over the drop.

Tilly tilted her head, as though listening herself, as though the phrases were coming to her from some sure external source. "It was like she was oblivious to the danger. Like she thought it couldn't harm her."

I sampled the image: our mother, Violet, her braid soaked and coming out in wisps, her ankles bare and mud-splattered, picking lightly around the side of the house, slipping through trees, eyelashes beating against the drops as she raised her face toward the top of the hill. In my mind, she was draped in white, filmy clothes, tattered by branches and fluttering in strips behind her as she ran, half mother, half water nymph, like an etching in an old book of fairy tales, with her arms (very pale, very articulated) cocked balletically away from her body, one leading, one trailing. I did not like the picture. It did not seem like a picture of a mother that a daughter should have. But once conjured, it persisted, like Tilly's words, sinister and compelling.

Walter raised his chin from his fist so he could move his jaw to speak. "Are they buried up here, your parents?"

I felt a queer, startled rush of shame, just as I had when he asked about the dead house and why we called it that. Tilly was caught off guard, too, but she tried to recover quickly. "I don't— well, they couldn't be, could they?" she said, and twisted around and scanned the gray tablets leaning through the tangled foliage. "I mean, obviously not: these are all from the twenties, and teens, and, like, the eighteen hundreds." Wind kept whipping the ends of her hair into her mouth; she spat out a strand and hooked it behind an ear.

"But?" Walter had not missed her flusteredness, and asked with gentle surprise, "Do you not know?"

And that was when she took it to the next level—not of distortion; that wasn't what it was. Because it was *our* story after all, had been ours and solely ours since Hy had handed it down with such a paucity of detail. It had been strictly up to us to make it work, to adorn it, cover its bones with flesh, line its stark shell, make it suffice. And we had done that, molded it and clothed it to the best of our abilities and left it, then, undisturbed for so many years.

But the Rouens' arrival, their coming to the river and into our lives, had acted as a disturbance. Their moving into the dead house, and passing daily along Ice Cart Road, and noticing Tilly and me—somewhere in all of this, the story of our parents' deaths had gotten jostled. And once Tilly had removed it from its wrapping, once she had started to tell it over, refashioning it more or less minutely as she had over the past few weeks, its bones had grown pliant, its shell gone soft. So that, really, it was only a matter of time before some larger change was introduced. And I was not as surprised as I might have been then to hear Tilly say, "Actually, no. Actually, there's a lot of unexplained things about how they died."

The sky was terribly clear, a kind of fervent blue, arcing across the Kittiwake to the opposite shore, and I strained my eyes against it, braced my ears against the wind's racket, scuttling around the cemetery behind our backs.

"We haven't ever told this to anybody," said Tilly. "Not even Hy."

I closed my eyes and leaned my head back against the stone marker. She was not so much distorting the tale, perhaps, as restoring it to an earlier state of ambiguity.

"But Mole and I have thought for a long time that there was something fishy about their death."

I am not sure whether Walter accepted this as the truth or as part of a game.

Violet and David.

The Violet pebble: roundish, butterscotch, with a tiny face of mica. The David: long, maroon, and a fine belt of white quartz across the diameter.

I found the David wet and it looked better wet, but it was all right dry.

One shell, butterflied open, the two cavities joined by a fragile hinge. Their bedroom. I found the softest moss, then scraped muter-toned lichen with the back of my fingernail gently, gently, off a rock and transported it—coverlets—to dark green beds. Laid them each on a bed. The butterscotch and the maroon. The mother and the father.

I plucked, from a wild-blueberry bush back among the trees, two hard July berries, tiny pale kernels, the waxen white-green of ghost-skin. Apples. And set them in a tiny, glossy leaf-bowl. The bowl on a flat gray rock. The rock in another shell, the one rinsed and unlined. Kitchen.

Half a scrap of white birch bark (with whispered sorry and thanks as I tore it from the living tree, something Cal said never do); mattress ticking. Brittle brown pine needles, crushed to bits between my fingers: fragrant crumbs of stuffing. The other half a scrap on top. This laid into the smallest shell with the curvingest bottom, nestled between the valves of the butterfly shell. Cradle.

CHAPTER ✦ SIX

THEIR BIRTHDAYS FELL not on the same day but side by side—
Walter had been off by one. First, his, then hers. I thought Bill
Rouen would make a joke about it, but he only said, "I graciously
offer to postpone mine a day so that we may have, as Mole puts
it, a 'joint party.' "

Tilly said nothing.

Hy said, "That's fine," and set her drink, not quite empty, on
the porch floor.

"Another?" asked Bill.

"Oh, no, thanks." She rose from the rocking chair and gathered her things from the porch railing—a crescent wrench and
pliers and a handful of washers, which she dropped into the deep
side pocket of her skirt. She'd come to repair their kitchen faucet
again and stayed, afterward, for a drink with Bill. He'd fixed something colorless for Hy, with ice and lime, and a gold one for
himself, with nothing, and brought them in thick, stubby glasses
out onto the porch.

Tilly and I had been playing an after-supper game of running
bases with the Rouen kids on the road in front of the dead

house—Tilly and Walter, with mitts, throwing, while the rest of us ran—but as the sky grew dusky with evening and it got harder to see the softball, we had drifted back across the lawn and onto the porch steps. Walter tossed the ball repeatedly straight up, high, so it looked like a baby tooth against the velvet sky. Now the fireflies were coming out. Isobel and Gus stalked around the bushes at the edge of the porch, chasing the glowing arcs with their hands held cupped before them.

"Let's ask Daddy for a jar," I heard Isobel say, but Walter, one step below me, said, "No, that's mean," the softball socking into his mitt and his voice carrying straight and low across the grass, and they left it at that. The lawn and the road and the trees across the road all seemed to have slipped together in a charcoal smudge, and I remembered what Tilly had said about night. Only the sky held its color; acres and acres of ultramarine, spotted now with stars, as if in answer to the insect light on earth.

"All right, then," announced Hy, mobilizing herself, crossing to the steps. The washers in her pocket sounded just behind my head. "You two going to stay a while?"

Tilly gave a little grunt that few might have recognized as assent. I said, "Mm-m," going along with that. Hy touched the top of my head for a second and I was irritated by the lightness of the pressure. Then she said over her shoulder, "Good night, and thanks for the drink." Norah and Tilly and Walter and I all leaned to either side of the steps, making room as she walked down the middle of us.

Bill Rouen spoke up from his chair. "Thank *you*. For the sink."

She held up the back of her hand in acknowledgment and receded down the path, swinging her tools at her side. As she

turned into Ice Cart Road she began to whistle "Pine Apple Rag."
I tried to think whether I thought it odd that she was leaving and
letting us stay. We could hear the song even after her tall figure
dimmed from sight, swallowed by the evening's shadowy husk.

Then we were just the six of us kids and Bill Rouen. Over to
the left of the house lay an empty tract of flattened crabgrass
where their car was normally parked. When we stopped being
able to hear Hy, we listened to that silence, and then Bill began
to whistle, her rag at first, but quickly lapsed into nothing with
any tune, and then into nothing at all.

"It's too dark," pronounced Norah, very sensible. She stood
and walked across to the door.

"Are you turning on the porch light?" asked Walter.

"Yes."

"Don't. Bugs."

"Get the citronella," said their father.

Norah went to the far end of the porch and came back with
a small metal pail, which she clunked at Bill's feet. He took a
lighter from the pocket of his khaki trousers and bent forward.
The pail was filled with wax. The lighter snapped open and flared;
Bill touched it to a wick at the center of the wax. A lemony glow
burned out from the pail. The lighter clicked shut. Bill slipped it
into his pocket, leaned over sideways, retrieved Hy's glass from
where she had rested it, half-full, and settled back again with it
cupped in his lap, the cane chair creaking softly under his weight.

A song came into my head: *What can you do, Citronella, Citronella? What can you do, Citronella little girl?* I wasn't sure whether
I'd just made it up.

Gus and Isobel climbed up on the porch, fireflyless, and sat by their father. Norah took the rocker.

"What do you normally do for your birthday?" asked Bill Rouen.

Tilly was quiet for a moment. She was sitting on the bottom step, just below Walter. "Have cake."

"Angel?"

"Chocolate."

"I would have thought angel."

"Chocolate."

"Ah." The dull mutter of ice cubes as he drank. The low rhythmic heaving of the rocker as Norah worked it, pointedly. "And is this the birthday where you become a young woman?"

Isobel was sticking her fingers in the melted wax, dipping them one at time. She whispered, "Ow. Ow. Ow. Ow."

"I don't know," said Tilly. Her tone of voice said, *I don't know, stupid,* but she had turned her body sideways on the step, offering him her profile, very sharp-jawed.

Walter said nothing. He continued to toss and toss the ball, letting it drop with that steady socking sound back into his open mitt, and Norah rocked in the chair, and Isobel let wax cool into horny little caps on each of her fingers.

"How come mussels are called mussels?" I asked. "Is it because they're so strong?"

"Pardon?" said Bill.

"Like you said those threads they have, that grip, that are so strong."

"Oh." He shifted; the cane back creaked. "Well, you know it's spelled differently from, from muscle *tissue,* you know."

"I know."

"It's from the Latin," he said, and then, "What's the largest muscle in the human body?"

"The leg muscle," guessed Isobel.

"There's about a hundred different muscles in the leg," Norah informed her.

"Your knee?" asked Gus.

"Trapezius, maybe?" mused Walter. "Or, no."

Bill Rouen let us wonder a minute longer, considering our bodies.

"What?" Tilly finally asked.

"The cardiac muscle," he said. He appeared to toast her, faintly, with Hy's drink. "The heart." He held up his other hand, made a fist, and pumped it open and shut. Norah ceased rocking, and Walter let the ball lie in the mitt, slipped the mitt off his hand. "It works like this," said Bill Rouen. He showed her.

We heard the sound of a car approaching slowly along Ice Cart Road. Headlights fluttered through the trees.

"Mommy!" said Isobel. Norah jumped down from the rocker.

The car swung into view, turned, and coasted, very gently, onto the grass. With the motor off we could hear, through the window, Dr. Rouen singing.

Walter brought something to us, a story. It was in a small book with a red plaid cover.

He brought it to us on a day when it was going to rain. A single cloud had spread its woolly tarpaulin across the sky. We sat on the stone step outside our pantry door, facing the stable and the rise of the hill. The step was worn in the middle by years of feet and, in spite of the overcast day, was warm against our bottoms. The trees had flipped their leaves, so that the silvery-green undersides were facing up.

Walter opened the book and handed it to Tilly, who, starting from where he showed her with his finger, read out loud, "When a young woman—"

"It's about this place in Scotland," Walter interrupted. "Sorry, go ahead."

And she began again:

"When a young woman combed her hair at night, she put every loose strand in the fire. If the hair did not burn, it meant she would one day drown.

"If a girl did drown, she might become a seal. Then once a year she could, if she liked, step out of her phocine skin and walk the earth as a human being. The shores of the Hebrides have always been populated with seal maidens, sunning themselves on boulders above the waves, their sealskins draped nearby. Once, a mainland girl betrothed to a young man of Colonsay was drowned on the voyage she was making to the island to marry him. In his melancholy, he hunted the shores for years, and finally he found her. He stole her sealskin and hid it, and then he took her home with him. He married her. Seal maidens could live among mortals and could marry and have children, and frequently enough they did, but they always felt a powerful draw to the sea, which they sometimes found irresistible. This one bore the children of the man of Colonsay and had good years with him, but her longing finally overcame her. She found the sealskin where her husband had hidden it, and she disappeared."

Marking the page with her thumb, Tilly closed the book, smoothed its plaid jacket. "Phocine is seal, I guess?" she murmured to herself. The drizzle began; it wetted the fine dust of the yard, and our legs and feet. Walter and I waited. Tilly sighed. She tapped the book on her knee. She said, "Only it wasn't the sea with our mother, it was storms."

And, in saying so, granted the likeness.

I felt a throat-ache as round and full as if I'd swallowed a whole metal flashlight.

At bottom lay the terrible carelessness of the mother, her lack of attachment, her lack of attention: her failure to avoid drowning in the first place. At bottom lay fault.

Tilly slid the book under her thighs to keep it dry. Walter had brought it to her as a contribution, and she had seen that and seen what she was supposed to do: feed it, like a log, into the fire. I was equally awed by the boldness of his offering and Tilly's acceptance of it. We sat and let the rain fall on us, we three in a row, savoring the heaviness we felt.

The Pillow Lake Public Library was built all of stone. The building dated back to 1929, only three years after the old hamlet had burned down, and like several of the older edifices in town—the Dutch Reform Church, the post office, a few large houses—it had been constructed to withstand another blaze. The facade was squat and gray and half covered in ivy. Above the main entrance, chiseled into a wide block of stone, it read "PLPL *1929," almost perfectly symmetrical. I often thought what a shame it was that it hadn't been built one decade earlier. I thought if I had been in charge of inscribing the stone, I would've just cheated on that detail.

Inside, centered along the back wall, was a huge fireplace in which I could have stood had it not been filled with books. Every niche, every alcove, was similarly crammed. The stacks themselves were gorged; overflow books had been more or less tidily arranged at the foot of every stack, spines facing up. Dusty wandering Jews and philodendrons dangled over window seats appointed with red velvet cushions (faded watermelon-light), where a person could sit and read if she didn't mind stepping over double rows of books to get there.

We brought the Rouen kids there on a hot day, a heat-wave day. The little ones were grouchy; they wanted to be at the lake. They complained the whole while Walter was chaining the bikes to the rack out front. Eventually Gus started to cry, not the sad kind but pouty, and Isobel said, somewhat obscurely, "See!" and Norah said, "Fine. Fine. Unlock my bike. I'll ride back alone," just as Walter got the padlock shut and stood, pocketing the key.

"No, sir," he answered. "Look, the three of you: how about a little cooperation? I told you, the lake after lunch."

I marveled at his authority, the sealed logic of his appeal, at the same time as I felt cut off from him because of it. He had his hands on his hips, little and ring fingers loose in the air. His shoulder blades protruded and his T-shirt hung off them, swung in folds at the small of his back. The base of his neck looked broad and pink, and gleamed sweatily. From the back he looked practically like a man.

"Why do we even have to come here?" demanded Norah.

Walter glanced at Tilly. "For a school project. I'm helping Tilly with something she has to do for school."

"There is no school in summer."

"When you get older," said Walter, beginning to walk toward the entrance now as he replied, "sometimes they assign you projects for over the summer." He did it so easily.

Norah did not budge. "How come I've never heard of such a thing?" She was fierce and brave and skeptical: her instincts told her something was fishy, and she trusted herself.

But, of course, now he had maneuvered into the false part of the lie—he'd got her questioning the one detail that was true, and with breezy confidence he tossed back, "Oh, well, I'm sure you will in a few years."

So Norah, stymied, trailed up the steps to where Walter was patiently holding the door.

We had come because Walter was going to help us look up our parents' death. Tilly had asked me the night before, while we were sharing the bathroom, what I thought of this. She was rinsing off cold cream with a washcloth and I was sitting on the hamper.

"He said there's this thing in the library called microfish."

"Microfish?" I had to repeat it, feel it coming off my own tongue: it was lovely. "Microfish." And I could see them zipping through water: minute aquatic oracles with silky, prismatic fins.

"It's all the old newspaper articles on slides, and you look at them under a projector," Tilly continued.

"Newspaper?"

"Yeah, the actual articles from decades back. Walter said we could look up the date of when they drowned and read if it says anything about what happened."

I was struck, unpleasantly, by the apparent seriousness with which she proposed to undertake the search, by her leap from seal lore to historical data. I didn't understand how much of this was real and how much play. Did she really mean to find something out? "Tilly . . ."

"We could just see what it says." She spoke while rinsing her washcloth in the sink, paused in the intervals while she bent and drew it across her face. "I mean, if it says anything." She wrung the cloth a final time, draped it over the metal rod. Her face looked flushed, tender. "So what do you think? Do you want to?"

"Do you?"

She straightened the cloth on the rod. "We could go tomorrow, he said. Bike out in the morning."

The next day it was hot by eight. We ate toast and nectarines and wandered throughout the house, upstairs and down, picking up books and abandoning them, switching the television on and off, until nine-thirty, when Tilly announced it was time. We pedaled to the dead house and didn't dismount, just rang our safety bells until the Rouen kids came wheeling their own bikes around the side of the porch.

I had a sickening, kindling sensation in my stomach the whole way to town. I was afraid Tilly had lost track of what she was doing, that she'd misstepped badly by permitting our story to intersect with real library records, and I wondered if Walter knew, wondered even whether he had suggested the library as a test, to try to unmask us, to unfrock her fictions. This idea lasted only a few seconds before I corrected myself: why should he risk offending Tilly? Tilly herself seemed peculiarly calm, which I took to mean either that she didn't think we'd find anything or that this was not a game at all, that she really meant to learn some facts, that she thought there were facts important enough to have been hidden from us, and her hope or trepidation was so dangerously great she felt the need to monitor it.

Tilly rode out front, alternately pumping very hard and coasting, and didn't look back at all. I rode behind with Norah and Isobel. My palms were sweaty on the handlebars and I kept having to adjust my grip. I wondered what Hy would say if she happened to be standing in the doorway of Coffey's and saw us pedal by, single file and solemn in our pursuit. But though I slowed as I passed the hardware store, the doorway stood empty. No grown-up watched us, noticed what was going on.

Immediately upon arriving at the library, Tilly put down her kickstand and strode off a few paces into the shade. She scooped up her hair with one hand and began to fan her neck, vigorously, with the other.

"You're just making more sweat," I told her when I had dismounted as well. In school, after recess, we always ripped sheets of paper from our notebooks, pleated them, and then fanned ourselves with them at our desks, until one day we had a sub who made us stop because, he said, we were creating more friction, and in turn more heat, with the motion of our elbows. "It's scientific," I advised Tilly, but she ignored me, continuing to fan herself until Walter succeeded in persuading his siblings inside. Then she went, too, ducking neatly under his arm as he held the door. She looked fairly white around the mouth, and her eyes, adjusting to the relative darkness, took on their distant, reclining look: the centers growing huge and black. But she took command and led with brisk grace to the children's room.

This was not really a separate room, but a very large alcove at the rear. Its entrance was hung with a green-and-blue-daisied curtain, which, since it was always tied back on both sides, did not provide a separation between children and adults so much as a frame, a sort of proscenium beyond which lay a stage of infinite and sublime fantasy worlds. Posters of illustrations hung on the walls; games and puppets adorned lower shelves; a fish tank burbled behind the librarian's desk. Every time I stepped past the drawn curtain into the children's room, I seemed to enter a charmed space immune to the intrusions of adult knowledge: here flowers and tugboats had yearnings, and pigs wore bonnets, and little trains conversed with their passengers. Isobel took herself instantly, dreamily, off toward picture books, and the impulse to follow her was powerful.

I became aware of a slight fuss a little ways from me. Walter was squatting before Norah. He had taken one of her hands in his, and he spoke to her very quietly, looking up into her face. Finally he rose and clapped his hand on her shoulder in the manner of a gym teacher. Then, "C'mon, Gussie," she said, and held out her hand, and led her little brother over to the low shelves.

"Okay," said Walter, with a nod at Tilly and me, and I was split between admiration for the sureness with which he'd placated Norah and a small, indefinite ache as I looked at her handing Gus a book and saying, "See if you want me to read this one."

Then Walter said, with a meaningful glance at his siblings, "I don't know how much time we'll have here," and I was reminded that I was grouped with him and Tilly. The three of us pushed past the daisied curtain and moved toward Reference.

They did have microfiche. The very thin librarian whose name I always forgot, but who always said hello and asked how Hy was, rose from her desk and led us to it. She said we were lucky because they'd only recently gotten the *Kittiwake County Gazette* on microfiche, and only the past ten years' worth (quick math: we ought to be covered, barely). The librarian's breath smelled of licorice. She was sucking something, and I could see that her tongue was dyed black. She showed us the indexes where we could look up any subject we wanted. Then she showed us the slides. These were bigger than I expected, floppy indigo squares that fit into white paper sleeves the size of folded napkins. She said when we found what we wanted, she'd show us how to view it on the machine. Then, without asking any questions, she left us to it and returned to her desk, her flat shoes noiseless on the carpet, the licorice candy rattling against her teeth.

Tilly went to the earliest indexes. The dates, handwritten in felt tip on sticky tabs, curled around the narrow bindings. We halted before them. We did not know what date we wanted. We knew the ages we had been when it occurred, and we both felt certain it had occurred in warm weather. But we did not know the day or month. This was strange; clearly Walter thought it was strange that we did not know the date. Stranger still, I realized I was reluctant to learn it. To learn a number for it.

The library had ceiling fans, slow-turning wooden paddles to churn the air, and their light, motorized current pulsed over us.

We all just stood there for a moment. Then Tilly slid out a volume. April/May/June.

She laid it on the counter in front of me (I stood in the middle) and returned her hand to her side. The cover of the booklet read: "*Partial Index to The Kittiwake County Gazette. Selected, Compiled, and Produced by Pillow Lake Public Library.*" It had a homey feel, being typed and staple-bound.

"Go ahead," she whispered to me.

I flushed with surprise. "Look under what?"

Tilly whispered, "Grummer," which was our last name. I opened it flat on the counter, found the G's. I could feel the heat from each of their bodies as the other two tilted in to read over my shoulders, could feel each of their breaths angled from different heights—Tilly's, slightly rapider than Walter's, against my cheek; Walter's stirring the hair above my temple. We scanned down the page.

Groundhogs

Grouse shooting

Growth stocks

Gubernatorial race

"Not there," Walter whispered. I closed the book, shoved it back on the shelf.

Tilly reached for the next volume: July/August/September. She opened it herself this time, found the page, and generously pressed it flat for all of us to read. She was the first to conclude; still holding the page for us, she looked up and shook her bangs. "Nothing." Each time one of them whispered, I felt as though someone were stroking a finger along the rim of my ear. It was a funny thing, the combination of discomfort and comfort I felt standing there, squashed between them in the stuffy, whispery air of the reference section, the queer kindling feeling still hot and shaky in my abdomen, but also the novelty of being included in their serious business (or serious game).

"Is it worth checking October? Or March?" asked Walter.

"Check them all," said Tilly. They each looked through another volume apiece, but replaced them without reporting any findings.

"Hang on a sec." Walter retrieved the first index again and was flipping through it. I craned my neck to see which part of the alphabet. The D's.

"You don't think first names?" queried Tilly.

"No. Wait." He kept turning pages. "Look." He held it up for us to see the headings: *Drownings.*

Drownings. More than a column of annotated entries.

"Let Mole hold it," whispered Tilly, for convenience's sake, and he set it before me. I laid my palm sideways across the bottom of the page. We bowed our heads and read silently.

Drownings—
—A nine-year-old girl who was pulled from a frozen pond while trying to rescue her German shepherd, died soon after . . .
—Divers recovered the bodies of two men, who apparently drowned in a fishing accident, along the western banks of the Kittiwake River . . .
—The second of five boys who were swept into the rain-swollen Quashpeake Creek, apparently while they waded alongshore, was found drowned . . .
—The body of a woman was pulled from Slaughter's Falls,

where she drowned while swimming, in an apparently inebri-
ated state, with friends . . .

I started out skimming for our parents' names, prepared only
to filter in the most familiar details, but I found I was incapable
of doing so. Each entry, each blunt capsule of news, as it touched
my vision, impelled an act of imagination that was really a form
of respect. I saw each entry as I read it; not to do so would have
been impossibly crude. And with each it was like having the wind
knocked from my lungs; the tidiness of the newspaper language
got shaved off by the images, by the weight of ruined flesh and
grief, as I, involuntarily, imagined them. And there was no pleasure in this shaving off, no mystery, no thrill, nothing I would
save from this to copy down later on recipe cards. What remained
was a kind of violence: the sheer ugliness of the facts. And the
thought that I might come across our parents' names here, in that
same heedless type, *David and Violet Grummer*, followed by a short
string of recorded, impassive details, sickened me. Tilly couldn't
want that.

I stood in the sweet middle spot between her breath and
Walter's and found myself unable to read on: the page had
blurred. I made myself skinny and slipped out from between
them, rubbing my nose and eyes on the shoulder of my T-shirt.
If this was a game, I had forgotten why we started it, and if it
was in earnest, I had never been told.

"It's okay, Mole." There she was at my side, having turned
away from the book. She rubbed my arm. A few long-fingered
boy-pats landed on my other shoulder. "It's okay if we don't
find it." She thought I was crying from disappointment; they

must have gotten to the end of *Drownings* and not found our parents' story. "There's still the other months," she whispered encouragingly.

The licorice librarian lifted her head and gazed pensively in our direction. I wiped my lashes with my knuckles. The librarian looked as if she knew we were doing something not quite right. I thought she must be contemplating suggesting that we belonged on the other side of the daisied curtain. But then a grown-up approached her desk and she was diverted.

I wouldn't look through the index anymore, though. I sat myself at one of the long, heavy wooden tables, facing the children's room with its posters of winged blue dogs and ghosts drinking milk and kids riding the backs of clouds, and I listened to Tilly and Walter check the other volumes behind me. Tilly *had* misstepped, she had, badly, by bringing our parents' story out here into the adult room, by bringing us into the adult room of our parents' death. I was angry with them for taking so long, for bringing us here at all to do this thing whose purpose I found I did not understand.

Then I heard volumes being replaced and Walter whispered, "Nada," and Tilly said, "I know. It's weird," and made that *tsk* sound with her tongue, but she did not sound upset; and when I turned, I saw that they were almost grinning at each other.

She was going through trees in the night in the rain. The rain fell hard as cherry stones, broke like beads of mercury on bushes and pine needles and on her skull and arms. Behind her, someone was calling and she ran from him. She was smiling. She was going up the hill where the trees grew thick and dark, wending her way through the muscley stalks of their trunks. Pale, tattery tendrils of her dress fluttered out behind her. She ran smiling with her mouth open. The water was coming into her mouth. Someone was calling her. At the top was the ridge and she ran toward it. She saw the great mercury light, the poisonous silver flash along the top. She found it irresistible. She moved through the trees and her wet dress unraveled and she was naked and the rain fell on her like the tips of fingers, begging her, crying, scraping at her hair. Her hair unraveled, came away from her skull like corn silk. She reached the ridge. Someone was still calling her. She tipped, smiling, over the drop, and her mouth was filling up with water.

I woke to a cry, my own tiny cry, a mean sound dragged pitiably from sleep. I looked out the window, waited for the lightning, for the thunderclap, but none came. I heard crickets singing, saw stars. After a moment, I realized that although I felt damp, it was not raining.

The covers were twisted around my legs, my nightgown bunched around my middle. I kicked the covers off and tried to straighten my gown, but I couldn't get it perfectly smooth under me; every time I lay back down, something would ride up and make a lump, a mocking, spiteful wrinkle. My heart was still beating from the dream. I rose.

The air in the hallway was as dark and grainy as chocolate cake. The stairway was even darker than the hall. I navigated it by feel and memory, one hand brushing along the kindly wallpaper. In the front hall the heavy oak door stood closed, locked up for the night. In the kitchen the light over the stove had been left on. Passing it, I felt heat. But not until I reached the entrance to the pantry and, looking through, saw the familiar figure sitting out on the step, her back silhouetted against the moonlit stable, did I make the connection between what I had observed and what was obvious. A cup of something steamed at her side.

Hy turned. "Mole! You are a mouse: I didn't hear you."

"I had a nightmare."

"Are you okay?" She moved the cup. "Come sit."

She sat with her big hands on her knees. She was wearing a faded brown shirtwaist with white eyelet along the hem and pocket. Her hair wasn't in a kerchief; it fell in a crinkly cloud midway down her back. It had much gray in it, and the gray in the moonlight looked like silver.

"It's a gibbous moon," said Hy.

"What's gibbous?"

"Between half full and full. Would you like a cup of milk?"

"Yes, please."

"You know, when I was a child I used to believe the moon rose each night out of the stable. There was a huge old wasps' nest, like a big, huge, gray bulb, up under the eaves around back, that you could see from the ground. I used to think that was where the moon went during the day." It was a nice story, but she wasn't telling it for me. This was Hy gone off. Lighthearted instead of cross, but still remote, elsewhere. She had forgotten my nightmare. "That was when we still had a horse living in the stable," she added. "Frieda. She was gray and she loved green beans. I was afraid of her teeth, though."

"I thought you'd gone to bed."

"Oh, no; no, I hadn't." An owl hooted. "Listen, Mole, did you hear that?" She stood. "I think it lives close by, in one of those trees right over there. Sometimes you can see its eyes. Like two . . . two yellow eyes." She took a few steps toward it, white eyelet waving along her hem.

"Hy . . ."

"It's all right, I'm just looking if I can see it. Hey, old hooter, where are you hiding?" Her voice came back to me as she wandered out to the hill edge of the yard, where the thick trees began. I could see her, and then not, as she passed in and out of their shadows. She had left her cup behind on the step.

"Hy."

I heard twigs snap over there, and wind pass through branches, and the burred prattle of bugs. I realized I had no idea what time it was. The step was cool under me; I wrapped my nightgown like swaddling around my legs. I could see no light in the east, over the stable. I did not smell dew.

"Oh, well." Hy's voice came drifting back before her body reemerged, moving slowly toward the house. "He doesn't want company, I guess." She sat beside me again and took up her cup in two hands between her knees, as though it were something purely to hold.

"Like a hermit."

"Mm."

"Hy?"

"Mm?"

"How did I get my name?"

"Which—Mole?"

"Mm-hm."

"Ohhh," said Hy, "I don't know. It suited you, I guess." She was looking at the stars, and rocking her knees in and out a little. She seemed to be humming a tune inside her head.

"Tilly said she made it up."

"Did she?" It was unclear whether she was saying, *Did she make it up?* or, *Did she say that?*

"But that's not really how I got it, right?"

"Oh, goodness, Mole. It might have been partly that."

I laid my cheek sideways on my knees. She should have been more careful, Hy should, to be certain, to keep the story straight. Because I counted on the things she said. I remembered them, wrote them down, preserved them beneath my underwear. The owl hooted again. "Hy?"

"Mm?"

"Where does Dr. Rouen the mother go all the time in the car?"

"I don't know, Mole."

I sighed. She had forgotten also about my milk. I traced her mug rim with one finger. "We went to the library today."

"What books did you find?"

"No books."

"Mole, smell! Do you smell those roses? I can't believe how strong. I always thought it was funny how they smell so strong even when it's too dark to see them."

"That's what Tilly said."

"Did she?"

But she hadn't; Tilly's thing had been about colors. The homesick feeling swelled intolerably.

"Hy?"

"Mm?"

"Nothing."

After a while, absently, she put her arm around me.

CHAPTER ✦ SEVEN

TILLY, AFTER ALL her talk of privacy, became the one who led them through the woods and showed them our secret places. Sometimes all the kids; sometimes, when he didn't have to mind them, just Walter. I'd come, too. I'd help show them our things. But it was Tilly guiding.

We took them to the fort. This was a dank square pit on the lake edge of the woods, three sides partially walled in stone, one side caved in and thick with bramble and ivy. Tilly and I, when we were younger, used to climb down in it and gather sticks and pretend we were stockpiling arrows for an enemy attack. In winter, when it filled partway with snow, we would leap into this cold mattress and make angels there. We had an idea that any snow that fell in the fort was purer, somehow—we used to lie there, looking at the white sky between dark branches, biting snow from our mittens, and tell each other back and forth what we thought it tasted like. ("Vanilla." "Milk." "Watermelon.")

Calling it the fort was our invention; it was, in fact, the remains of one of the old icehouses from the early part of the century. We had learned this, years back, after finding a long iron rod with a rectangular dip at one end and a spiral at the other, and taking it down to Coffey's to show Hy and Cal. "It's an ice auger," Cal had said, hefting it with one hand. He held it where it jutted out and cranked it clockwise in the air, translating the strange shape into its function. "They used it for drilling holes in the ice, to measure the thickness."

"An ice auger," I'd repeated, and made Cal spell it so I could copy it down on a recipe card.

Cal seemed unaware of the value of such facts, and in this regard was as maddening as any adult—but Tilly and I believed instinctively in their worth. Therefore her sharing of these facts with the Rouen children was an act of almost ceremonial significance, which they in turn received with due solemnity. She passed along not only Cal's various bits of historical information, but other things, too, our old private customs.

She took the Rouen children back in the woods and showed them our special haunts. Isobel and Gus rode the dragon trees; Norah tasted the cursed spring; Walter got in the front seat of the rusted-out truck and talked at length about the mechanics of hot-wiring a car. Through it all, Tilly was the knowing, generous, and beautiful host. The broad planes of her face shone. She had cultivated a habit of standing with her weight all on one leg, the neat plane of her stomach pushed forward, arms loose at her sides, neck tilted so hair spilled across one shoulder. It was as if she had just realized the pleasure of exposing herself in a measured fashion.

I do not think that I was jealous, but it is true that I was gratified the day Tilly suggested showing Walter my mussel houses. We took him alone down the zigzag path to Tilly's and my rocky cove. He had said he would help me match my type of mussels to the proper picture in his parents' book, so that I could know the proper name. I led the way, picking quickly and proudly down the irregular slope, instructing Walter which roots to use as steps, which branches to hold.

They were there, I could see when we reached bottom, in their spot under the root-roof, but when I reached to draw them out I jerked back, pressed my hands into my stomach with a violent shudder. The opening had been encased, thickly, by web. I possessed a morbid fear of spiders. This web was so thick it looked like fiberglass, looked smug and malevolent, like the filmy third eyelid of a snake. I knew it might make a queer, dry tearing sound when broken. My throat clutched and I backed up some more.

Tilly knew; she went and rummaged among the leaves and bushes for a stick to dismantle the web for me. But Walter did the odd thing of getting right down on his hands and knees. "Coool," he said, with something like reverence. He inched closer, leaning his face toward the web as if looking through a porthole. "Any critters in there?" He moved his face around, inspecting. "Nope. Uninhabited." He answered his own question with a mild disappointment I could not fathom. Sometimes he was such a foreigner, it was disconcerting. I didn't like it that we could have two such different understandings of the web.

"Isn't it a beauty?"

"Mm." I stood several steps behind him, twisting my hands in my shirt, trying to swallow without gagging.

"It looks like a caul," he mused. "Doesn't it?"

"Yeah." I had never heard that word. Tilly said I always did that—not lie, exactly, but be too eager to agree.

"She doesn't know what a caul is," said Tilly now, coming back with a stubby piece of blueberry bush in her hand.

"I'm not sure what one is," I amended.

"What's that for?" asked Walter, looking at the branch.

"To get it away with." She nodded at the web.

"Oh, you don't need that." And he scooped it away with his hand, wiped his fingers carelessly on the sand.

I regarded him with a mixture of fascination and repulsion and suppressed another shudder. I said, "What is a caul?"

"It's a thing some babies are born with, on their heads. Like a, what do you call it, a membrane. It's supposed to be mystical if you're born with a caul. Like a good omen. I *think* good."

I studied him, and could feel myself frowning. Often I was unsure whether the things Walter told us were true. It wasn't that I thought he was lying; I just couldn't sort the science from the pretend. The frog jumping home, the gold in the vacuum, the seal maiden, his biological father—all of these he spoke about in just the same tone of voice. And with us for him—did he under-stand the differences between the ice auger and our parents' drowning? What was real and what was made up all seemed to have jumped track this summer. Tilly and Walter appeared not only unbothered by the confusion, but to be tempting it further, egging it along, with their blending of story and science.

"Show him your shells," prompted Tilly.

"Never mind," I said quietly.

"What do you mean?"

"She doesn't like spiders," explained Tilly, misinterpreting my resistance, and she, like a kind big sister, knelt beside Walter and slid the shells out for me one by one.

Their knees did not touch, but her arm made a shadow across his lap as she reached. He teetered on the balls of his feet for a moment, then relaxed into a kneel. "Spiders are good, though," he said. "They eat other insects."

"So?" I said. "I know. I've heard that a million times."

"Well." Walter shrugged as if that clinched it.

"Well, so that doesn't mean they're good. Maybe I prefer the other insects."

Tilly snorted. "Since when do you prefer *any* insects?"

I looked at her a bit wildly, feeling ganged-up-on, and a little foolish. "Cicadas," I exclaimed, grasping the quickest thing to come to mind.

"What's that?" Walter asked, and I was amazed to know something scientific that he didn't.

"A kind of bug. They were on TV. They only come out every seventeen years." I looked to Tilly for affirmation, but she offered none. "Remember?"

"No."

"Yes, you do! We saw that special—yes—that night when it rained? Hy bought ice cream? It was really hot?"

She only shrugged.

"At the beginning of *summer*." I stamped my foot and sand flew up.

Tilly just brushed it off her bare thighs and said, "I don't *not* believe you," with terrible, gentle helplessness, as if she were being truthful.

My face tightened. I didn't want to know something alone. I wanted to know it with her.

"Let's not make a federal case of it," said Walter. "Aren't you going to show me your shells?"

"I guess Tilly already did that," I said, and walked away.

What we could not tell them about was the dead house. We were spending more and more time in it, sometimes having lunch at that glass kitchen table, sometimes sitting around the candle pail on the porch after dinner. Each night darkness settling in a touch earlier.

In the evenings, often Bill Rouen would be there with us. Dr. Rouen might be there, but inside the house, in some lit, curtained room. Sometimes she would not be there at all, but out on a late errand. Bill, though, would sit right out on the porch with us, in the cane chair, a small glass in his hand and a newspaper spread across his knees. Even when he didn't become part of our conversation, we behaved with the understanding that he listened, and with the belief that he listened interestedly.

And so when Walter sat on the steps one evening eating a scooter pie, and Tilly, beside him, said, "You know there's horse tendons in the marshmallow part," with a certain contained archness, it might have been that the remark was as much for the father's benefit as for the son's. Because it was just the sort of utterance that seemed to arouse such amused delight in Bill.

Walter might have had a similar idea, because he only said, in a heavy kind of way, "On postage stamps, too," and continued to eat.

Bill said nothing, but he cleared his throat behind us.

"What do you mean, on postage stamps?" asked Norah.

"The part you lick," said Walter, and he licked the web of skin between his thumb and index finger, where a crumb of chocolate had fallen.

"Gross," said Norah.

"What's gross?" asked Isobel.

"There's horse tendons in the stuff you lick on stamps."

"Oh," said Isobel. And after a moment, "But is that true?"

I loved it that she said that; it seemed a novelty to ask.

In the absence of any of us answering, I could feel us all sort of leaning toward Bill Rouen. We called upon him in language that should have been obvious, but somehow he failed to respond.

"Dr. Rouen?" said Tilly, with a little ironical ring she'd developed. It sounded funny to hear her address him; it made me realize she never did. He was silent.

I looked over my shoulder.

He was very much in shadows, outside the circumscribed glow of the citronella. He appeared curiously engrossed in the glass in his hand, and in a moment I saw why: a yellow jacket clung to the rim, its wings just grazing his knuckle, and it moved with dizzying, slow imprecision. It wasn't clear whether it wanted to get in or out of the glass. Bill Rouen had lost himself in the yellow jacket; his posture was slack, and his lips had fallen slightly open, and his empty hand lay upturned on his knee. He looked a little goofy, but I liked him this way, plain and interested in a bug.

Then Isobel said, "*Daddy*. Is what Walter said true?"

And he straightened with a jerk, which must have rattled the yellow jacket, because then, with a bewildered wince, he sucked air between his teeth and said, "Ow," and looked back down at the hand that held the glass.

"What!" cried Norah, and "What's the matter, Daddy?" exclaimed Isobel.

Bill removed an ice cube from his drink, sucked it off, and placed it on his knuckle. His lips were tight and pruney-pale against his teeth.

I had thought that I was the only one who'd noticed the yellow jacket and therefore realized what had happened, but Tilly suddenly pivoted around and got to her knees in one swirl, positioning herself over the hand that held the glass. With smart efficiency, almost rudeness, she lifted away his hand that held the ice, said, "Did the stinger come out?" and, as quickly, bent low over the knuckle, holding it steady with her left hand, and used her fingernails as tweezers. It took her one try. In the almost darkness, I saw her inspect something between her nails, then make a flicking motion away from the light. Bill Rouen, allowed his hand back, inspected his injury and stuck it in his mouth.

"What—what, Daddy!" Isobel and Norah, still excited and confused, scrambled up the steps and pressed close to him.

"I got shtung," he said around his knuckle.

"What?"

He removed the injury from between his lips and nursed it again with the ice cube. "I got stung by a wasp."

"It was a yellow jacket," said Tilly. She was still on her knees, but sitting back on her heels now, so there was distance between her and the arm of his chair. She had that look of impossible flatness, even in the play of dusk and citronella, as if some injustice had been done to her.

Bill Rouen looked at Tilly with a scowl, most likely from the sting, but it made him seem annoyed. He said, "What a stickler for detail you are."

I wondered why he didn't praise Tilly for acting so cleverly, didn't thank her for taking the stinger out. But when I thought about it later—I mean long after that summer—I figured that that wasn't what he wanted from her.

Tilly shrugged, and rose, and walked to the top of the steps. Walter remained there, working on his scooter pie with his back to the porch, as if he were no part of us.

We spent days at the dead house, too, keeping Walter company while his parents worked at the river and he minded his sisters and brother. We played spud and blindman's bluff and red light, green light, one two three. The lawn was mined with thistles, which added an element of danger, and with slippery wild strawberries, which stained our clothes. When it rained we sat in the kitchen and played cards: go fish, slapjack, spoons. Spoons was our favorite. It was the most exciting game still easy enough for Gus to play.

In a way I preferred these times, with Bill and Dr. Rouen out being scientists, and Walter and Tilly and me not free to go off on our own. In the absence of the Rouen parents, and under the self-imposed ban on discussing the mystery of *our* parents in the presence of the littler ones, a certain dramatic tension lifted. Walter was more fun. Sometimes Tilly forgot to lisp. It was less complicated, easier, somehow, even with all the fighting that went on, and we did fight (*quarrel*, Tilly would say), especially during one rainy spell that lasted the better part of a week. During this week our drive grew so muddy that Hy had trouble pulling the car out one morning and Tilly and I had to push. The doors, swollen with moisture, would open and shut only with full-body maneuvers. My bedroom ceiling got a new leak; I fell asleep each night listening to a saucepan catch it.

The weather did not keep the Rouen parents from the river. I watched from my window: in army-green rain ponchos, they walked without hurrying. The ponchos had hoods, which gave them a faceless, creaturelike look. They dropped out of sight in the rain over the ridge.

Nor did the weather keep Tilly and me from the dead house. We'd fallen into a pattern now, and every morning it was the same. Hy would drive off to Coffey's, and Tilly and I would eat something and then tarry about the house, and after an hour or two, one of us would say, as though the thought had just occurred, "I think I'll go over to the Rouens'," and the other would say, "I guess I'll go with you," and we'd put on flip-flops and go down the road. At the dead house we were greeted like long-lost kin. Norah would bring us a dishrag for our muddy ankles. We'd eat grilled cheese and popcorn and count the seconds between lightning and thunder.

By the fourth or fifth day of this, however, we had grown sick of the rain, each other, even spoons, a peevish game of which we were playing around the kitchen table. Norah kept snapping at Gus, who was on her left, to pass faster, until Tilly finally suggested she calm down, and then Walter told everybody to shut up and play cards, at which Tilly said didn't he get sick of always telling everyone what to do—when there came a solid white-blue flash and the lights went off and the refrigerator shushed. Tilly and Norah simultaneously began to whisper-chant, "One one-thousand, two one-thousand," and were interrupted right at "three" by a great rip-crack-into-rumble. The pettiness crumbled; we all grinned at each other across the gloom.

"Sar*dines*," said Norah, dragging out the syllable as if stroking it; for just a moment, she reminded me of her father. "This is perfect for sardines."

Immediately, the lights returned. She blinked and looked insulted.

"We could turn them back off," offered Tilly.

She brightened. "Okay."

"Boundaries?" asked Walter.

"The house."

"Too big."

"It is not."

"Anywhere in the whole house?" He looked at Gus.

"Yeah. Gus doesn't mind, do you, Gussie?"

"Sardines is the opposite of hide-and-seek?" he asked.

"Yeah," Isobel told him, and announced, "Me and Gus can go around together."

"Who'll hide?" asked Walter.

"One of us has to, because Tilly and Mole don't know the good places."

"You, then," said Walter.

"Okay." Norah got down from the table. "You have to cover your ears while you count. Count to a hundred."

"No way. To fifty," said Walter.

"Fifty-five," she said, and as she left the kitchen, flicked off the lights.

The dead house was perfect for sardines. It was smaller and more crooked than our house, with narrow, angled hallways, and storage spaces built cleverly into walls under sloping ceilings, and rooms that connected, opened surprisingly into each other. After reaching fifty-five, we departed the kitchen separately. Soon creeping sounds were reverberating from all parts of the house, like a scritter of squirrels in the walls. The downstairs hall smelled of apples and oil soap. Through a high window streamed shadows of rain, phantom rivulets coursing down the wall and across floorboards. It was day, but so dark the colors had partly drained. Lightning cracked open like a bed sheet and vanished. I took myself upstairs.

The window at the landing rattled as I passed; my body took on, then shed, the rippling lace of water-shadow. At the top of the stairs the door to the parents' room stood shut. I turned the glass knob slowly, went in.

The room looked different than it had the other time. I stood just inside the doorway, wondering why. It was much darker this time—the rain, of course—but then I noticed the alcove window: its curtains were closed. Without thinking, I crossed around the bed and spread them apart. Light the color of ashes fell into the room. I leaned my elbows against the sill, forehead against the pane, and stared at the pines, transfixed by the W-shape that the treetops cut into the bottom of the sky.

Some shifting of weight within the house, the sound of heavy shoes moving without stealth, reached me in the alcove, where I had grown lost. Was the game over? Could everyone have found Norah? Were they now looking for me? I lifted my brow from the glass and listened.

"Hello!" The mother.

"Hi, kids!" The father.

The house was little enough that I knew all of us could hear—Norah, wherever she was hiding (I pictured her on her back, beneath a piece of furniture, wide-eyed with suspense), and the others, either roving furtively through rooms or, already having discovered Norah, smashed in with her there in her hiding place—and I listened for one of them to answer.

"Hel-lo-ohh!" Dr. Rouen sang it louder this time, with a note of amused insistence. I imagined she had her head cocked, listening. I listened with her. The only next sound was stillness and the rain, and then the parents' voices resuming conversation, and then their footsteps on the stairs.

They must have been halfway up before it occurred to me that I was in their bedroom. I looked around. There was only the bed. I got under it.

"Get the kind packed in water," Dr. Rouen was saying, her voice reaching the top of the stairs.

"I know," said Bill. I heard a click and, from beneath the drooping red bedspread, saw electric light warm the room, and two pairs of sock-feet. The feet crossed in and out of my field of vision as the parents continued their conversation and moved around the room.

"'Because last time you got it in oil."

"I did?"

"Uh-huh."

"Will I need to get gas?"

"I don't know. I think yes. Oh, and a quart of skim."

The feet passed around the room. Another lamp was switched on. A dresser drawer opened.

"Do you remember seeing lights on in their house when we went by?" Dr. Rouen again. She sat on the bed and springs dipped close to my head. Beside my face were her feet, and then her fingers, coming down to peel off a wet sock.

"Can't say. Do you want me to call over there?"

"You know, I really wish Walter would have left a note."

A kind of quivering, silent laugh seized my chest. They were talking about our house; they thought their kids were with us at our house.

"When I go out, I'll swing by."

"I'm sure you will," muttered Dr. Rouen. The bed sighed and lifted and she walked over by the dresser, and I couldn't tell where Bill Rouen was; it remained so quiet I wondered if he could have left without my noticing. Then I became aware of a sound, utterly familiar, although it was a moment before I could identify it: cloth against cloth and cloth against skin and hair against skin.

"Delia." He spoke her name as if it were an entire thought, a lengthy explanation, a stream of facts.

She said, so softly I had to strain, "This is not going to happen."

"Delia."

More of the soft friction, then someone knocking lightly into the dresser.

"Go," said Dr. Rouen. "Get the groceries."

After a moment, the sound of coins scooped, cascading into

a loose pocket. Then just silence, stillness, no one moving or talking. Rain blew against the window glass.

"What?" said Dr. Rouen.

I closed my eyes again. I was breathing too fast, too loudly.

"You are very full of shit," said Bill Rouen, very softly. He didn't sound angry and he didn't sound like he was joking. Then he left the room, his footsteps receding heavily down the treads.

No sound at all came from Dr. Rouen. I had the idea that we were both listening to his footsteps together.

From downstairs came the sudden scrape of furniture, followed by voices and giggling. "We're here!" Isobel cried. I heard Norah's boisterous laugh, Gus's triumphant peal. "We were hiding! Mommy—oh, I mean, hi, Daddy—you didn't know we were here!" The sounds of easy laughter and voices released and overlapped enticingly.

In the bedroom, Dr. Rouen blew her nose extensively, sniffed, and walked brusquely to the door. I listened to her go down, and counted to twenty before following. In the living room, Bill and Dr. Rouen stood more or less ringed by their festive children, who seemed frighteningly oblivious to anything amiss.

I thought Tilly and Walter had dropped the game of the story of our parents' drowning. I thought, after the dead end of the indexes at the library, that they had decided to leave it alone, to cultivate other, more fertile plots. I thought Tilly had moved on to revealing different sorts of things: the fort, the springhouse, the truck. My mussels. I thought Walter didn't care what game they played, so long as it contained plenty of room for facts and theories, an appearance of grave importance, and plenty of exploring missions from which the little kids were barred.

But the evening of the day that the rain finally stopped, Tilly resurrected the subject. She had come up with the idea that we ought to search for our parents' graves.

We were washing up before bed; I was in my usual spot, atop the hamper, and Tilly in hers, at the sink. Tilly had a bra this summer; she was hand-washing it. She did this very frequently, every few nights, with great care and special liquid soap that she kept in her room.

"But you said yourself they couldn't be buried on the hill," I said when she told me the plan. "All those people died in the eighteen hundreds, I thought."

"Not there, dope. In soup field."

Soup field was Tilly's and my name for a wide sunken meadow that stretched beside the main thoroughfare on the north end of town. Mist that burned off grasses elsewhere at sunrise lingered here till midmorning. Our bus went this route on the way to school, and all year long, every day, it reminded us of driving past a giant's bowl of steaming-hot soup. Part of this area was a horse farm, and then came a fence, and the part on the other side of that was Pillow Lake Cemetery.

"So they're buried there?"

"We can look."

I listened to the *plap, plap* of the material being dunked in the water, and looked at Tilly, her neck bent over the sink, shortie pajamas hanging lightly off her body. I counted seven scabs on the backs of her two legs: mosquito bites she could not leave alone. "With Walter, too?"

"Yes. He thinks it's a good idea."

She'd asked him first. Rage came upon me so abruptly it caused my temples to throb. "Oh—oh, of *course*. I'm sure he has a very important opinion about it!" I spat the words right out with no dignity or coolness, and then they continued, sputtering and unstanchable, and my mouth felt ugly. "I'm sure it matters *so much* to him . . . he's just so . . . he cares really a lot about finding out . . . out . . . the exact location of your parents' dead bodies!"

Tilly turned from the sink. Suds dripped from her hands onto the floor. "Lower your voice, Mole," she said.

"Why should I?" I slid off the hamper so I could be standing, too. "I don't get what's so private about it. Since you've made the decision to tell it all to a boy who doesn't even know us. Who's it supposed to be a secret from now?"

She didn't answer. Soapy water continued to drip from her fingertips. Below us, a man's deep voice droned unintelligibly. It was the radio in the kitchen, broadcasting the great glaring fact that Hy was in the house below us; Hy who ought, of anyone, to know where her sister was buried; Hy who was clearly the answer to my question.

Tilly said, quietly, "For your information, he does care. He's interested in helping us find out about them." She said, "I would think you'd want to, too."

I leaned back against the hamper, picked at its wicker side.

"But don't come if you don't want to," she said, and her eyelashes came down, soft black shutters, as she turned and resumed washing her bra, going *plap, plap, plap* in the sink.

The next day I biked single file along the thoroughfare with them, and with them pulled over in front of Pillow Lake Cemetery. We didn't bother with Walter's lock, but toed our kickstands in the sand. It was late in the day, and the sun steered through the iron gate and laid slatted shadows at our feet.

"G-R-U-M-M-E-R," said Tilly.

"I know how to spell it," I said.

"I was doing it for Walter."

"Oh."

Since the rain let up the previous afternoon, the weather had turned dry, weightless, just the thinnest layer of summer. A breeze spun across soup field, scattering dandelion clocks and causing the grass to quiver. Tilly stepped forward, laid one hand on the iron gate and the other on her hip. She was wearing an old denim work shirt of Hy's with the sleeves cut off, the ends knotted at her navel. Her arms angled long and slim out of the frayed blue holes, and I noticed for the first time a supple roundness to her shoulders, slender eggs of muscle gliding into the flat length that ran to her elbows. It was lovely and utterly strange how she looked, standing there backlit at the cemetery gate; I wondered if she knew she was making a picture.

Walter stepped up beside her and placed his hand on the dark metal next to hers. His hair was red and hers black. Some plant nearby was smelling of sugar. One or both of them put pressure on the gate; it opened, and we all crossed through it to search, stone by stone, for my and Tilly's family name.

I don't know why she invited me at all. It was the last day I would be invited to go exploring with them, although I didn't know that yet. I only knew that for the past several weeks, whenever I'd felt a little lonely or cross, I'd found myself yearning after my invented scientists' daughter, that pensive ash-blond fabrication, and that now, this afternoon, as I followed them through the iron gate, I found myself yearning instead after my own real sister, who, though she tramped flesh and blood two yards ahead of me with the low light streaking over her muscled arms and scabby legs, seemed as inaccessible and remote as someone who'd never existed.

We split up inside the cemetery, which, except for a single cross that cut two major aisles through its center, wasn't particularly mown. As I pushed out toward the margins, I had to step high, like a marcher, and the tramping had its own rhythm and crushing sound every time my sandaled feet came down. Forget-me-nots grew in such dense patches that from a distance it looked as though someone had dropped blue handkerchiefs all along the graves. I saw black-eyed Susans, and chicory, and purple clover and white, and every now and then a small American flag, poking out of the earth near a marker.

"Too bad it's not alphabetical," Tilly's voice came thinly over a distance. I stopped and looked over my shoulder. She was wading slowly through growth on the far side of the cross, perusing epitaphs. Walter was in the front far quadrant. I saw him under a fruit tree, hands on hips, walking sideways, bent at the middle, in order to read.

It came to me how hollow her words were, how meaningless his actions. We were none of us here to find our parents' graves. If we happened to locate them, Tilly would find a way to extend the game from there, and if we didn't, she would think up another avenue for us to explore. She had vandalized our parents' story not for the sake of learning anything true about it, or about them; they were in fact immaterial to her game.

I sat. A screen of grass all but eclipsed me. I had no idea what to do. My indignation was imperfect: I had done nothing to defend our parents' story all these weeks. On some foggy, languageless level, it occurred to me that that silence might have constituted my usefulness, and an aching fury clotted my heart.

Peering over the top of grass, I saw Walter move from the fruit tree to where Tilly stood, near the center of the mown cross. Sunlight smacked from his glasses like a skipped stone. She drifted to meet him, speaking, I could tell, by the way she moved her hands, although as their proximity to each other increased, their voices were lost to me.

My knee tickled. I looked down and flicked off a Japanese beetle. It landed in a patch of clover. Hy said in every patch of clover grew at least one stem that bore four leaves. With faith in Hy, I parted this patch and, very methodical and determined, searched inch by inch with my fingers, but finally gave up, and when I looked up again, Tilly and Walter were gone.

I scanned the cemetery, front and back, and looked up toward the gate, where our bicycles still glinted, but saw no sign of them. They could have disappeared only by doing what I had: lowering themselves into the high grass. I moved my head back and forth, seeking a glimpse of Tilly's denim shirt through needles of grass. Twice I was fooled by slivers of sky. What I finally made out was the pale flame of Walter's hair, burnished by the low-slanting sun, and from this point of reference located Tilly beside him, sitting with her arms clasped round her knees.

They were chatting. Not even pretending to look. Our bikes

like calling cards parked by the iron gate, and them in here hidden, in over their heads among grass and graves, not even pretending to do the thing we'd said.

I went to them, pushing through the brownish-green, untended growth. They looked up when they heard me come rustling. The sun was at my back; they had to squint.

"Did you find it?" I stood over Tilly. In the harsh angle of light, a fine down, faint as pollen, was illuminated along her wide, flat cheek.

She visored her eyes. "What?"

"Their grave."

She chewed the inside of her bottom lip. "We're just sitting for a while."

"Why?"

"Well, gee, Mole, I guess because we feel like it."

"What are you doing?"

"I just said. Sitting."

I looked at Walter. He smiled at me. He had removed his sneakers and socks, and was leaning back on his hands. The tops of his ankles looked as if they were getting burned. I looked back at Tilly. The story of our parents by now was riddled with fissures. Mentally I picked it up, weighed it like an egg in my hand. I said, "I think this is a waste of time."

The muscles of her face shifted and hardened, almost as if her ears had picked up the sound of shell cracking. We met each other's eyes with cold surprise. "No one's making you be here," she declared.

"I just think this is stupid."

"You can think that if you like."

"I know." My throat needed clearing and I cleared it. I tossed the egg high into the air. "Obviously," I said, "we could just ask Hy."

Tilly's face looked like a peach ripening in time-lapse photography. Above our heads, the egg somersaulted in slow motion. Tilly opened and closed her mouth. She dropped her gaze to somewhere past my ribs.

"We should ask her tonight," I said. "When she gets home from Coffey's. What do you think?"

"You can ask her anything you want."

"I know I can."

"All right."

"All right." The egg fell slowly back toward earth, still holding together. I caught it. It was in my hand now, and I held it, and stood there, and rolled it between my fingers, and refrained from crushing it. Tilly didn't look at me.

It seemed I had to walk away then.

I went without hurrying, choosing a not-quite-straight route toward the gate. I took in the stones that bordered my path, their colors, damask and gray and bone; their shapes, curved and corniced and tiered; their ornaments, a sheaf of wheat, a lamb. And the words themselves—names, dates, the quietest of prayers, the briefest of explanations.

As today our bikes had not been threaded together on Walter's chain, there was nothing to keep me.

Alone through town I rode, past the gas station, past Coffey's. Hy's car was parked out front and the door to the shop propped open with a brick, but I did not stop. The weight of this egg was a terrible surprise; I pedaled very fast, streaming down the streets, passing all the familiar buildings.

I veered diagonally across the intersection before Steve Day's Auto Parts. A car beeped at me, one long, complaining note. I cut out of town, angling around the rubbish-smelling vacant lot, and slanted up Ice Cart Road, around the great curve of Pillow Lake, past the public beach and Short Clove Lane, and finally gave in to the incline and my trembling muscles. Here where the cool began, I braked. This was the part of Pillow Lake where the pines grew thick as army blankets—and where, at intervals, the woods was pocked by stubbly clearings and occasional human arrangements of stone: the part of Pillow Lake where the old hamlet had been. I touched my sandal to the pavement, dismounted.

And we were the only ones left here now, we and those scant others scattered through the woods, in those few houses that had not burned or been abandoned and torn down when the rest of town moved across the lake. A handful of houses, large and old like ours, with pointy attics and gingerbread along the eaves.

I was pushing my bike up the hill now. Below me, on my right, lay the public beach. High above, where I walked, only wan apricots of light fell, between the stiff pine shadows at my feet. It had always been something special about us, that we lived up here, at a remove, in one of the few houses harking back to that other time. One of the few old houses, old houses, old houses . . . I was just wheeling up around the bend now, panting, the words revolving senselessly in my brain, as though they'd worn a tired groove there, losing their meaning and becoming only sound, and I saw what I had looked upon a hundred, a thousand, maybe a million times before.

The dead house sat back from the road. Squat, plain. A cement foundation. No chunkily irregular stone cellar. No attic lifting into a high pointy brow. No gingerbread: no curvy brackets or carpenter's lace. No stable in the rear. It was an altogether different species from the other houses that remained in the woods. I stood holding onto the handlebars and dried out my lips, breathing with my mouth open. The house, with its lucid glass panes and neat window fittings, stood gilded by the hour, opaque, speechless.

Then from inside came an ordinary sound, the hard chink of dishes: a drying rack being emptied, or a table being set for supper. I wondered if I was being seen, and had to picture for a moment how I would look: a girl in yellow shorts, small for her age, standing perfectly straight beside a red bike, holding it with two hands. I wished I were being seen. Dr. Rouen would come to the door and say, "Hiya. What're you doing?" in her creaky city voice, and I would have to lie. I would say, "Looking for Tilly. Is she there?" and Dr. Rouen would maybe know I was lying; she would say, "Nope. Haven't seen her or Walter all afternoon. Come in, though, if you like. We'll be having supper soon." I would say, "Okay," and I would wheel my bike across the yard.

And I could get rid of my egg, set it discreetly perhaps on the glass kitchen table and leave it there—because I hadn't meant to take it, didn't really mean to smash it, only wanted Tilly to leave it alone and come back. But the dead house would not be a safe place to leave it; I knew this as I stood there looking at it now.

I did not hear the car until it idled up beside me, and then I whipped around and there was Hy, resting her elbow out the open window.

"I'd really like it if you didn't stand right in the road, Mole. Cars can't see you, coming around the bend."

"I know. Sorry."

"Okay, well. Don't be sorry, just don't do it." She looked tired, but in a pleasant, relaxed way. "Where's your sister?"

"I don't know."

She looked at me. She laid her big hand gently against the outside of the car. "Hungry?"

"I guess."

"Come home. Help me get supper." She said this kindly.

"All right."

It was only a short way down the road, and I knew I had my bike, but when she drove on ahead I felt bad.

CHAPTER ✦ EIGHT

AND THEN I was by myself. It wasn't as if we had really fought. Just, everything had changed. The Rouen parents still went over the ridge the next morning, and Hy still went to Coffey's, and Tilly and I even still had our breakfast together; she was even pleasant to me, sliced half a banana into my cereal. But then, after we had placed our bowls in the sink and run a little water over them, Tilly said, "Well, see you," and I said, "Okay," and she headed off, alone, to the dead house.

From the kitchen I listened to the screen door smack and her footsteps clatter down the porch steps and die in the grass. The silence of the house became gigantic, the way a tiny cut can feel huge inside your mouth. Even though I had just finished breakfast, I went to the pantry and found some cookies and ate five. Then I drank some water, and then I looked at the bookshelves in the living room, and then I went out on the back step and looked at the yard for a while, and then I had some more cookies. Then I went to Tilly's room.

The heat upstairs was moist, palpable. I stood in the doorway of her room, listening to the house; it came back hushed. I felt

I was swimming as I drifted through the densely humid air to the bed, and there I knelt and reached one hand beneath the dust ruffle. My fingers struck first the smooth, dense block of a magazine, and then a single sock, and then a kitchen garbage bag stuffed with winter woolens and mothballs. My confidence was already waning by the time I came into contact with what I sought. I pulled it toward me; the tin rasped against the floor.

Sweat slid straight down the middle of my chest. I brought the tin around to the far side of the bed, by the open window, and sat with it between my legs. The cover—*Danish Butter Cookies*, scripted white on navy, the shapes of the words so familiar they hardly registered as language—came off with a concerted but brief effort, one hand bracing the tin against my thighs, the fingernails of the other inserted under the rim, so that, as it came free, my nails bent back and caused me a shuddery little ache. Also familiar.

There followed the smell: the dry, sepia-colored smell, intricate, aged, strangely pristine. I laid the lid aside and—two hands, eyes shut—raised the tin to my nostrils. And then, with the particles of scent deep in my nose and throat, I laid the tin back on the floor and bent over its unchanged contents.

Even sitting directly in front of Tilly's window, the curtains of which stirred with some gusto, clearly identifying a breeze, I continued to sweat. Beads meandered down my ribs and spine, clung to the wisps that grew in front of my ears. (The elastic of my underpants was wet, and also behind my knees.) I wiped my palms on Tilly's braided rug and picked up the snapshots.

It had been a long while since I'd visited the tin, but there was nothing new here for me to notice: one dozen photographs, gazed at so often as to have been practically used up, like beaters licked down to the metal. The faces, the poses, the maddeningly poor focus, all appeared just the same as a hundred times before. I flipped through the stack with growing impatience: the mother the father the mother the mother the father the mother and father both. Violet David Violet Violet David Violet David. Each picture slightly blurred, flat, confined to a single angle. Eternally unaccountable.

They seemed even less revealing than I had remembered. I flipped through them again, a little violently, as if each shadowy face, and hand, and bit of shelf or door were intentionally stingy, tauntingly vague. And the third time—I could not stop—I was even rougher, twisting edges as I shuffled each picture to the bottom of the stack, gouging corners with my thumbnail, studding the images with little crescent dents. And I was overcome with the impression that the pictures themselves were amused at me, that behind their perfectly concealing facades they tittered mockingly; the very *shhp, shhp* I made riffling through them seemed like smug, whispering laughter, and I threw them suddenly, flung them all against the wall.

One ricocheted back, faceup but tilted sideways, between my legs. It was the picture of Violet, the mother, wearing a black dress and a half smile, sitting on the edge of a bed. But it was not the mother herself who caught my attention, it was that shape behind the mother, out through the window over her right shoulder, a shape I hadn't quite ever noticed with the picture right side up, a shape layered dark onto pale so tiny at the upper left edge of the frame that it was impossible to be certain whether it was actually the tops of pine trees biting a W into the rim of the sky.

I looked at the picture for some time, and I looked at the wall for a little while after that, and then I gathered up the other pictures I'd thrown and I smoothed the edges I'd crimped and I piled all twelve pictures together and put them in the tin and put the tin's lid back on tight and pushed the tin back deep under the bed until it rammed up against the sack of winter clothes. We had been looking for something like concrete evidence about our parents, some piece of information that had been kept from us, for weeks, and only now did I fully realize how much that search had not been in earnest.

I missed Tilly, but discovered I also had that same bitter sensation of power I'd had the day I walked away from her and Walter at the rocky cove. I felt superior to her. Loneliness swept through, flooded me. I fell upon her bed and sobbed.

When I opened my eyes I thought I had slept, but the light outside looked unchanged and the house was quiet and the air had the same quality it had earlier: languid and moist and rather sweet-smelling. A chickadee sang outside the window. I felt hollowed out, bereft of anger. I got up and smoothed Tilly's bedspread and, on my way out, drifted over to Tilly's dresser and lifted the back off her little pewter pig. I did this more or less mechanically, by force of habit.

The fact is I often sifted through her room when she was out, as well as Hy's, as well as, for that matter, most of the rest of the house—closets and cupboards, bookshelves and milk crates and trunks. I conducted these investigations with an almost embarrassing lack of guilt. I did not consider myself to be prying, or snooping, or disturbing what I did not have a right to disturb. I felt it almost as a duty, a responsibility, a kind of obligatory paying of attention.

Inside the pewter pig this morning I counted four fire-station movie ticket stubs, eleven thumbtacks, and a tiny gold safety pin. I replaced the lid; it nestled back in its groove with a fine, heavy click. I opened a Sucrets tin (empty), and a pencil box (three ballpoint pens, an eraser shaped and colored like a cheeseburger, a stick of gum), and moved on then to her top dresser drawer.

I didn't kid myself that Tilly or Hy would be quick to understand why my inventories didn't constitute trespassing—especially not Tilly, with her great, moody privacy—but even with this, the full knowledge that she would be appalled to find me here, I did not feel remorse. Their secrets, Tilly's and Hy's, even their—not secrets, but *things*, trappings, personal effects—I felt were in some way details of my own life, to which I was entitled. As if locked inside their private artifacts lay information about me.

Sweeping against the back panel of her underwear drawer, my hand brushed into contact with a small wad of tissue paper. I took it out and unwrapped it. Inside were eight tiny glass beads, garnet red. The hang-gliding day came back to me in vivid spurts: the severed bracelet, Tilly's hand cupping her wrist as though it were injured, the beads trickling into the grass.

I had not realized she'd salvaged any of it. The weight of that information sat with me for a moment, as light and consequential as the tissue in my hand. I was inexplicably glad.

I shut the drawer, folded the tissue back over the beads, and stuck it in my pocket. Her birthday would be soon.

*   *   *

The car was gone from in front of the dead house. The two girls' bikes were there, leaning against the wall at one end of the porch. The curtains in the front window were drawn. I mounted the steps and rang the bell and heard it *dong* inside the house. Both doors were shut, screen and regular.

I waited longer than seemed natural, and then I put my hand on the knob and gripped but did not turn it. I went on tiptoe, trying to see through the glass at the top of the door. I cupped my hand against the pane to try to see in past my own image, and this was how Bill Rouen found me when he came to the door, loomed up suddenly on the other side, his chest breaking through the murky reflection.

He opened the door and stood there, one hand against the frame. I backed up a little and he pushed open the screen for me, too, held it in place with his bare foot. He had, in the hollow part of his cheeks, a gingery stubble that flickered when he moved his jaw. He looked strangely devoid of intention.

"Hi."

He dipped his head curtly. "Afternoon." I wondered if he had been sleeping.

"I didn't think anyone was home."

"The bell doesn't always work." He delivered this lie blandly, impatiently, and hooked a thumb behind his scorpion belt buckle.

"Who's here?" I asked, my gaze traveling beyond his body into the dark hall.

He shot me a look of mild surprise, as if at my effrontery, and made a show of turning sideways so that I might inspect past him. The bland sleepiness dissolving fast.

I flushed. "I mean, I'm sorry, I just meant, if Tilly or anyone was here?"

" 'Anyone' is here, yes: *this* one." He pointed at his own chest with his chin.

"I meant—"

"Delia has taken them all. Out. Somewhere. Miniature golfing. No." He was kidding now, but there was a blunt edge to it. "I do not know where the kids've gone. Out somewhere with my wife. Your sister," he added sibilantly, "very likely among them."

I didn't think so; it seemed more likely that Dr. Rouen was with just the little ones, and Tilly and Walter off elsewhere on their own—but I noticed that Bill Rouen had withdrawn his foot from propping open the screen door, which he let swing forward on its hinge a few inches before catching it with his hand. He was waiting for me to leave.

"I didn't come for Tilly."

"No?" he said with little curiosity.

"No. Do you have any fishing line?"

A pause settled like a vacuum between us.

"Fishing line," he repeated.

"Yeah."

He pursed his lips.

"You know, like for fishing."

"Oh, for *fishing*."

"Well, not actually *for* fishing."

"I see, not for fishing." Behind closed lips, he ran his tongue across his upper teeth. "And what," he asked, "are you hoping to catch?"

"No, *not* for fishing. It's for a project. Like an art project."

"Well," he said. His feet were very large and white; they reminded me of something. Flounder. "Let's have a look." Abruptly he pulled back into the dimness of the house. I stepped after him.

The light in the hall was the slow honey of late July, strained through curtains; it fell in slender shafts and loose washes across the floor, lit the wooden boards so that they shone deep sorrel, like the backs of violins. Disinterested constellations of dust revolved through the honeyed stillness. The screen door moaned shut and caught on its latch.

For a moment in the hall, Bill Rouen just stood there, thinking.

"It's okay if you don't have any," I said.

He turned to me slowly, as though I had not quite distracted him from an idea he was weighing.

"What's the matter?" I asked with a small laugh. A kind of pressure seemed to grow.

He still didn't speak, but frowned more deeply at me, and then he removed one thumb from where it was hitched behind the buckle and rubbed it across his lower lip.

In the closeness of the house, I felt sweat break out like a wet rash. I passed a hand over my brow, and, automatically, reached out and touched the wall beside me to wipe it off. But a thing happened when I did this: my hand bumped into the built-in shelves there, and I turned and looked at them, all but forgetting Bill Rouen, his silent, frowning carriage. I experienced a rush of light-headedness that made me brace myself against the middle shelf for balance. They were, these blond pine shelves, recessed beside the door with their row of fattish pegs for scarves and mittens, and that special hole built as an umbrella stand, the sister shelves that matched those others, the very ones built in beside our own front door, the ones Hy had said our father had made. I ran my hands over them, picked up a coat of dark gray dust.

"Nothing's the matter," said Bill Rouen behind me. "I was just thinking. Come, we'll look upstairs for your line." He closed his fingers around my upper arm. "Come," he repeated, turning me back toward him.

The middle shelf had a small gouge along the edge where a crooked strip of wood had been torn away. As Bill Rouen pulled me around, my hand dragged across the rough spot, and a piece of the wood entered my palm.

"Please to come up to my bedroom," he said with a small bow and a Russian-type accent. I looked at his face in some confusion, tried to assimilate the different things going on in my mind. The flatness with which he'd answered the door had all cleared out now. His eyes were like glass disks and his stubble looked darker here inside the hall. He still held my arm. It occurred to me that I had presented myself here, had rung his bell and asked for his help.

"Do you want it or not?" he asked, a little hardness creeping into his voice.

"I got a splinter." I held my palm between us. I could feel my face going worried, and my voice came out small and plaintive. I reminded myself of Isobel.

"What do you mean? Just now?" He sounded annoyed.

I nodded, and looked over my shoulder at the ragged-edged shelf.

He released my arm and straightened. "Let's see."

I let him bring my hand up near his eyes. It felt sweaty, ridiculous, in his.

He said, tersely, "I can't see anything in this—move over to the light," and led me by my outstretched wrist across the hall, over the violin-back floor, and through the honey spokes of light, until we stood beneath the square hall window. He pushed the little curtain back further on its rod and bent, frowning, over my palm.

"First of all, I still can't see anything," he said, and blew on it, two quick, sharp puffs from his lips, scurrying dust. Then he rubbed his thumb over it, none too gently, and I flinched. "Sorry," he murmured. He had forgotten I was there, the person attached to this hand. "Eh yup," he said neutrally. "It's going to take a needle."

"Are you sure?"

He shrugged. "You could try soaking it first." He was still looking it over, tilting my palm either way. It might have been a specimen, something on a slide or in a jar, unattached to my body. "You want me to get it out for you?"

"How?"

He looked at me.

"With a needle?"

"It's up to you. It'll take two seconds."

"Okay."

I followed him to the upstairs bathroom and sat on the toilet lid while he sterilized the needle with the same lighter he always used for the citronella, clicking it smoothly open and shut. Then he began to pierce my skin. I made red half-moons in my knee with the fingernails of my other hand, but it didn't really hurt very much; he had an expert touch, not gentle, but precise, and what is strange is that I savored those moments of finite pain, those needle-pricking seconds when I was the recipient of all his concentrated attention—not an oddly accented, please-to-come-up-to-my-bedroom sort of attention, which in some ways only bounced off me and circled back to himself, but a clean, detached attention that was almost tenderly impersonal. Then he said, "Done," and handed me back my hand. "Rinse it in a little warm water," he directed. "I'll get a Band-Aid."

As completely as his demeanor had changed when I asked him for the fishing line—had gone from flat to sinuous, dull to mannered, spiritless to alert—it had been altered again by the splinter, by my second need for help. Only this request had summoned in him seriousness and practicality. Fatherliness. When else had I seen this? The other night, when he'd been stung. The yellow jacket and the splinter, both. Two little emergencies. No, three—that day at Bluefields, when we all thought the hang glider had crashed.

He continued now to be all the father, all distracted and kind: poking through the medicine cabinet, knocking an emery board out by mistake, finding the Band-Aids and being clumsy fishing one from the box, patting my hand dry and jamming the hand towel crookedly back over the rack, applying the adhesive to my palm with a final pat and a "Not too tight?"

I nodded. A second time he removed the warm nest of his fingers from my hand. I wondered at the two Bill Rouens, felt curious about my own power to summon either of them. He was putting the Band-Aid box away, cleaning the needle. I looked at my hand, at the Band-Aid he'd pressed on with his thumbs.

"You said one time you could read palms."

"No. Me?" As smoothly as when he'd said the bell didn't always work.

"Yes. Once, I remember."

"You must have misunderstood."

"No, it was at Bluefields, on the Fourth of July, we'd just met you, practically, and Tilly—"

"I must have been kidding." He shut the water off in the sink. The bathroom fell quiet. "Now," he said briskly. "Fishing line, right?"

I followed him to the bedroom, and stood in the doorway while he knelt over a plastic tackle box by the dresser, right where Walter had knelt to get me the shell book. I watched him sort through things. The soles of his feet were white and wrinkled. The bed was unmade. The alcove window was open. I looked out it, at the shape that was now not only familiar but locked in, identified.

"This is the parents' room," I whispered, my cheek against the doorframe.

Bill Rouen breathed with the heaviness of a grown man bent over and rummaging in humid midsummer. He gave a grunt as he stood. His knees cracked. "Sorry. I know we have some. I don't know where she's put it."

"Oh. Well, that's okay."

"Right." He came toward the door, waited for me to move. He was finished with my visit.

"This is a nice house," I told him.

He gave a funny kind of smile, with a cocked head and a soft weariness around the eyes. "Is it?" He looked around the bedroom in its dim sloppiness. "Well," he said, and opened one hand, and I saw it was a gesture to conduct me out of the doorway and down the stairs. His manner had changed again, shed its playfulness and then its fatherliness. He was hurrying me out.

On the porch, with the front door shut behind me, I peeled off the Band-Aid and examined the spot where the splinter from my father's shelves had gone in. There was a tiny dot of blood, from Bill Rouen's pricking me, on the gauze pad. I smoothed the adhesive back in place. He had disappeared quietly back into the cool shade of the house. Across the yard, the black car was still missing, the mother and the children still gone. Again a chickadee sang, and all the hollow, dead space behind Pillow Lake seemed to swell in the wake of its thin song. I reached into my pocket and, squeezing the thin folds of tissue paper, counted there with my fingers Tilly's eight red beads.

Cal turned out to have the fishing line, and the clasp I needed, too. He was sitting behind the register when I walked into Coffey's, reading a book and holding a cold pipe in his mouth; it clicked some across his teeth when he drew it out. "Hiya." He inserted his bookmark (a shred of newspaper), laid the book on the counter and the pipe on the book.

"Hey. How come you're not really smoking?"

"Ask your aunt."

"Why?"

"She's after me to quit."

"Oh. But then why're you still pretending to?"

He eyed me from under brows like steel wool, and sighed

through his nose. "Call it habit," he said. "Call it you can't teach an old dog."

"You can't teach an old dog new tricks."

"Right."

I came over and hung on the counter. It was an old wooden counter with a yellowed Formica top, which was moderately cool and anyway smooth; I leaned my forearms on it and then my chin. The point of my chin was not a point but a flat bone; I pushed it against the firm countertop.

"Hot out," said Cal.

"Boiling." I laid my cheek on my arms.

"You're out of sorts today."

"I know." I lifted my head again and looked at him. "Cal, you know everything."

"Hardly."

"But you do." I picked a miniature carpenter's level from a display rack next to the register, tried to get the air bubble centered in the tube. "You've known us since before we were born, right?"

"Inasmuch as you can say so."

"And our parents, too, right?"

He nodded his head once and rubbed his chin with two fingers (why was the same motion entirely different on him than on Bill Rouen?), and if he did not volunteer more, neither did he shift his weight nor pick up his book again preemptively.

"Very well, did you know them?"

"Pardon?"

"Did you know our parents very well?"

"Your father not so well. He hadn't lived in this area long, I think. Your mother, of course, from growing up here."

My heart seemed to be tipping, sliding, like the pocket of air in the yellow fluid before me, because here was Cal with all his stores of knowledge and I did not know the questions I meant to ask. "Did you know her as well as you know me?"

He smiled now; I was still bent over the level, but I could tell from the way his vowels stretched out. "Noo . . . I wouldn't say so. I had much less contact with her. She certainly never frequented my store the way you and your sister do." He made it a compliment.

"Tilly doesn't really come in here very often anymore." I hung the level back up. "Do you know how I got my nickname?"

"How?"

"No, I'm asking, do you?"

"I do not."

I took a handful of pencil grips and began lining them up on the counter in rainbow order. "Tilly said she invented it. But she always says things that you don't know if they're true or not." I scooped out another handful and continued arranging them: red orange yellow green blue purple. "Like she said at night there's no such thing as color." The line stretched nearly the length of the counter. "And another thing she said is our mother was irresponsible." I fished back in the plastic tub for another yellow.

"I did not think of your mother as irresponsible."

I checked his face. He looked serious and solid, just like Cal.

I started to try to ask him more. "But . . ." Then I upset the tub and it tipped over and spilled all the rest of the pencil grips on the floor. I got on my hands and knees and picked them up, and then I stood and swept all the others I'd laid out back into the tub, and replaced it next to Cal. "Sorry."

He nodded.

Then I stood looking at him, waiting for him to dispense more information, the memories and facts it must have been apparent I hungered for, the answers to the questions I was having trouble framing. But he only smiled at me, very quietly, mostly just a wrinkling at the eyes, as though he understood a little but not enough. He just stood there smiling, his arms secured across his chest, and all around him hung tools and furnishings in their great candor and utility: hardwares and housewares, putty knives and spackle and light bulbs and carrot peelers, oilcloth and cheesecloth, canvas gloves and rawhide dog bones, all dangling from hooks; and for a moment I thought he *did* understand, was being deliberately, intricately mean, and—just for that moment— I thought I hated him. Then I was ashamed, because it was my fault; I was too weak or chicken to know what to ask, and I looked down and cupped my elbows and traced a line with my sandal in the thin film of sawdust.

Cal reached inside his pocket; I could hear him shift his girth, and then the sound of him fishing a cough drop from its box. He slid it wordlessly across the counter. Wordlessly I picked it up. It was a funny kind of comfort to have Cal witness me in such a foul mood. I was almost glad for him to see me so ugly. "Shall I give you a job?" he offered.

"What?"

"I have some inventory that could use putting out."

"No, thanks," I said. "I guess I'll take off."

"Not going to say hi to your aunt?"

I shrugged. "I'll see her at home."

"Mole-Mole."

I smiled at him as best I could, and sighed and put the cough drop in my mouth. Halfway to the door, I remembered the fishing line and little metal clasp I'd come for, and I went back and Cal fixed me up with that.

At night I stood in the bathroom doorway and watched Tilly put lotion on her shoulders. She had gotten burned that day; her shoulders were a fantastic color, like roasted meat, and she was rubbing the lotion on with extreme care, trying not to actually touch her fingers to the skin.

"Does it hurt?" I asked.

"Not yet." But she winced a little. She had pulled one strap of her pajama top down; it cut a pale blue smile across her arm. She had behaved pleasantly toward me since our not-fight at the cemetery the previous afternoon. I found this more alienating than had she been outright snippy or cold.

"Did you have fun today?"

"Mm."

"Where did you go? The cemetery?"

"Nn-nn."

"Bill Rouen said something about miniature golf. He said maybe you went to do that."

Tilly snorted. "He's berserk." That was a word I had not ever heard her use. "When did he say that?"

"This afternoon."

"What were you talking to him for?"

"I was over there. I got a splinter."

"Were the other kids there?"

"Just him."

She turned, looked at me over her burned shoulder. "Don't go there when he's alone."

"Why not?"

She turned back to the mirror. "I don't think he appreciates being disturbed. He was probably working."

"He wasn't."

"Just don't, Mole."

"You're not my mother," I said, and then, "What's wrong?" because she'd suddenly leaned her face close to the mirror and was peering fixedly into the dark reflection of her open mouth.

"Nothing," she said, still intent, and reached a finger into the back recesses of her mouth. "I think I have a wisdom tooth coming in." She felt it for a moment, then rinsed her finger under the faucet, slid down the other strap and started lotioning that shoulder. She watched herself do it in the mirror, looking serious and abstracted, wholly absorbed in the task. Her face had been richly colored that day; it contrasted almost violently with the white tiles and her pale blue pajamas, made her appear both fierce and exhausted.

"Tilly."

"Mm."

"Can I go with you tomorrow?"

"Where?"

"With you and Walter."

She squeezed more lotion onto her fingers, circled it into the skin, following all her motions in the mirror. "Mole, no."

My heart suddenly matched her face. I had been leaning against the doorframe, but now I stood up straight.

She spoke before I could, saying almost gently, "You were the one who decided not to stay."

"But—"

"Just: no, Mole."

"But there's something I wanted to show you!"

"What?"

"I have to *show* you."

"Just tell me."

I stared at her red, red reflection, the mesmerizing calm with which she attended her burned skin, encased it in cool lotion, and I wanted to scratch it, pierce it, tear at her with my fingernails. I stepped over the threshold, crossed to her, grasped the bowl of the sink. My heart and throat and brain pounded in concert as I leaned between my sister and her reflection, breaking her communion with herself. She settled her eyes on me: two cool black olive pits. I said: "We used to live in the dead house."

Nothing in her face changed. "I know," she said. After a moment she dropped her gaze back to her shoulder, continued to massage lotion in deliberate circles onto the burn. She said, lightly, coolly, "You knew that."

I stepped back from the sink, swallowed, and shivered, just a little, as though it were chilly. She didn't notice.

She said, "You knew it, Mole."

AUGUST

CHAPTER ◆ NINE

I WENT BACK to the library by myself. It seemed impossible now that I shouldn't go back, and after a few days I got up one morning and set off boldly; anyway, I felt bold, and the daylight through which I biked seemed very broad.

I went to obtain information, not for myself but for Tilly. I wanted to find the story that would finally prove there was no mystery around our parents' death. A piece of evidence that would bring her game with Walter to an end, make her sigh and admit what we both already knew. Whether I meant to defy or impress her with such evidence, I didn't know. Possibly both. I went heedless of outcome, as if on a dare.

I pumped through town—over yielding asphalt, its delicately putrid smell; shop awnings making blue blocks of shade on the yellow sidewalks; cars baking, their windshields slinging headache-bright flashes of sunlight—operating on a stripped and heady determination that I mistook for courage. In front of the library, I chained my bike to a meter, and as I pushed the parts of the padlock together (always Tilly's or Walter's job), I pinched my finger.

The street was very quiet and bare, as if everyone in town were at the lake or fast asleep, and it gave me a feeling of trespassing and also of time being distorted or halted. The library stood still enough to be frozen, or painted on. I thought of Walter's frog stuck halfway home for eternity, and the predicament seemed nearly enviable. With resignation I moved toward the steps. The door blinded me for a moment as it swung open and a mother and two girls came out. I stopped and watched them go down the sidewalk, books tucked like colored parcels under each of their arms. I mounted the steps and heaved the door open; it was very heavy, and I did feel again how much it was the case that I was here alone, and my mind brimmed and roiled with thoughts of Tilly.

Tilly had gone off. She would be mortified to hear that expression applied to herself, but it was true. Ever since the night of her burned shoulders, she had gone off—both in the Hy sense and in the ordinary sense, for she and Walter had gone on cycling trips every afternoon. A whole succession of days had passed with both of their bikes absent from their respective porches, both of their selves gone away from behind Pillow Lake. I know because I had looked, some, on my own. I had searched the fort and the old weathered graveyard at the top of the ridge, looked inside the abandoned truck, gone down to the scrubby clearing at the end of Short Clove Lane where the lodge no longer stood. I'd looked for them, too, at my own mussel cove below the zigzag path, checked all these places the past few days, stepping softly across pine needles, one foot in front of the other, searching for snips of clothing through fern and fir, but there was no pleasure in this spying, only disappointment.

She slept late. She kept the sash of her bathrobe tied. She began to peel and the lighter fringe of dead skin looked like the veins in marble, or the foam stains left inside a drained beer glass—a pale, papery circuitry diagrammed against her tan. I caught it only in glimpses. She stopped letting me sit on the hamper while she washed up at night. She waited for me to finish with the bathroom, and then she went in and shut the door behind her.

At first I thought it was all because of me, because of what I had said about the dead house, and I was stricken with remorse. But after a few days I realized it had nothing to do with me, and then I felt worse.

I would anchor her back in herself with the grappling iron of fact. I did not even know whether she and Walter were still engaged in the charade of unearthing the story of our parents' death, but it was the only subject I could think of, the only information that might startle her back.

Inside the old stone building my eyes adjusted to the dim. A woman with white hair and lots of blue and red veins, like a road map, covering her legs sat reading in a leather chair by the window, and a man in an olive-green bowtie browsed at the paperback rack, and other than that, I looked to be the only patron on this August weekday morning. I was sorry, because this made me more self-conscious, but neither of the older people glanced at me, and I was encouraged by the lovely, quiet seriousness with which they each seemed engrossed. I crossed back into Reference, to the messy wooden desk where the licorice librarian sat, erasing something from an index card.

She looked up. "Martha Grummer," she said without any effort, and the sound of my own full name went through me like heat. "What are you up to? How is your aunt?"

"Fine. Hi."

Her tongue was black. I saw a little white paper sack amid the books and things piled around her. She saw me trying to peep inside, and spread apart the opening. It was filled with small, chalky-looking gray tablets. "Want one? They're very strong."

They *were* very strong, more like medicine than candy.

"Something I can help you with?" I had always thought she was about Hy's age, but now I saw that although her hair was almost entirely silver, she was several years younger. Her eyes were navy blue, her hair close-cropped. I thought it was funny that I didn't know her name.

"I wanted to look up some information."

"Okay." She laid one hand on top of the other and spread her elbows across her desk, and she met my eyes quite directly and simply, without amusement or condescension or impatience or indifference, and I began to have the strange impression that she knew me very well. She had spoken my real name without hesitation, and given me one of her grown-up licorices, and now looked at me with such lack of mannerism; I felt disconcerted and drawn to her, both.

"If I wanted to look up something that happened in Pillow Lake, and I couldn't find it in those books"—pointing to the soap-blue indexes on their shelf—"then what would I do?"

"Hm." She wrinkled her nose. "Hm, hm, hm."

"Would there be another place I could look?"

She rattled her licorice over to one side of her mouth. "Well, if you know a specific date, you could look at the *Gazette* on microfiche for that particular day. The indexes are highly selective, unfortunately, so not everything in the paper is indexed. What is it you're interested in looking up?"

I was slow to think of a lie, and blushed instead.

"That's all right," said the librarian.

"No, that's all right," I said, angry with myself, and I mustered up boldness and told her, "Just . . . about a storm and some people who might have died in it."

She nodded.

I took the licorice out of my mouth because it was really too strong for me.

"Do you know that date?"

I shook my head. The tablet was slick between my fingers; I rubbed it back and forth.

She nodded again, and looked down at her hands, and index cards, and found a pencil, which she picked up and held between her two hands. Then she said, carefully, I thought, "Did you know I went to high school with your mother?"

I felt rash, exposed. I shook my head.

"Mm. She was younger, but we overlapped for a couple years. Actually, we had the same algebra." The pencil oscillated between her fingers. A smile. "She let me look over her shoulder on the final." Then, the smile ebbing, "You look like her."

I had no words to say. I was deeply startled and embarrassed by these unexpected, unasked-for bits of information. It wasn't that I didn't want them. It was just the idea that such information existed, lived in fragments in people all around Pillow Lake—people who'd known my mother, and some of them my father—and that for the most part it was irretrievable, if for no other reason than that I didn't know where it was located, in whom and in what form. The humiliating unfairness of it crashed over me: the idea that strangers, through no special industry and to no practical purpose, possessed facts, knowledge, that belonged to me.

The librarian paused. Then she looked down at my hand, where I held the wet licorice, and grinned. "I know; they are strong."

I looked down, too. The pads of my pointer and thumb were black. "I know."

She lifted a small, empty wastepaper basket from beside her and tilted it over the desk. I dropped the tablet and it went *tong* against the metal and she smiled again.

I sucked my two stained fingers. "Thanks," I said.

She waved a hand dismissively. "If you want to, come back when you get the date."

"Okay." Knowing I wouldn't.

I was unlocking my bike when it hit me about the algebra exam, that actually, I had procured a new fact about our mother, that I knew something about her now that Tilly didn't. Somehow this failed to cheer me, though; I doubted whether the news of this slim item would impress Tilly sufficiently to improve my standing with her. And I had failed to learn anything really substantial—if there even was any such thing to be learned. I might have asked the librarian a few good questions if I'd been serious, if I'd been brave. She had made herself uncommonly available. But then I hadn't come on the strength of anything so solid as real courage or conviction, only on that of such lesser fuels as spite and jealousy. As I rode home, a new, restive dourness settled over me.

I wanted to have an emergency. I wanted something to break. That day at Bluefields, I had thought something would happen and nothing did happen, only Tilly's bracelet had broken and then it had rained. A month had passed since then and still nothing had happened, only I knew about the dead house and Tilly and I were not friends. But nothing had *happened;* I kept expecting something to *occur.*

August is the dog's month, I thought, and wondered if I'd made that up or heard it somewhere. *August, dog dish* was a kind of rhyme. It had a nicely disparaging ring, and became a little thing I'd hum to myself as I hung restlessly around the house, waiting for something to happen. I didn't only hang around the house. I took myself off to Coffey's, where I spent two hours rearranging the wall of sponges and household cleaners for Cal and then got into a fight with Hy about whether I could buy a soft-serve before dinner. I took a magnifying glass up to the old graveyard at the top of the ridge and tried to set fire to a stack of picked grass, but the moment actual smoke began to curl from it, I got scared and doused it with a jam jar full of water I'd thought to bring with me from the house. I found a dead bee and stuck it under the sheet by Tilly's pillow, but she never said anything about it and I couldn't find it when I went back to look the next day.

Hy saw my mood.

"Why don't you come shopping with me, Mole?"

This was evening, late in the first week of August.

"What are you getting?"

"Food, groceries."

"I don't know." I pushed the newsprint away from me and rubbed my smudged fingers along the margins.

"Yes, come."

"All right."

On the steering wheel, Hy's hands looked raw and dry, a chappedness about the knuckles. I looked at her face. She was looking straight ahead, not happy, not sad. At the corner of her mouth it came down, as if in sorrow or disappointment, but this was only gravity. Grown-ups' faces in repose always told more than kids'. I looked at her for a little while without her feeling it and turning to me. Then I looked ahead, too.

At the supermarket I pushed the cart. Hy got noodles, lettuce, bread, ketchup, toilet paper, eggs, lemons, hot dogs, raisins. In a cart a baby was singing. In another cart another baby wore tiny gold earrings. I steered carefully around other people's carts and other people. Hy said, "Why don't you pick out some berries?"

"Oh. What kind?"

"You choose. What looks good to you. Straw, blue, black. You decide."

I left the cart and went to the cool produce case and hovered my hand over the green plastic baskets. I chose strawberries, and brought them back to the cart.

"Get more," said Hy. "Get a lot."

"How much?"

"Get five or six baskets."

Then I knew what she was doing, but I didn't say anything.

We went back down other aisles, and Hy got sugar and wax.

Then I said, "What's that for?" even though I knew.

"Jam," said Hy.

"But you never make jam till the end of August, till Coffey's closes."

"Usually not," she agreed. "I thought you and I might make some, though. I was thinking you're right about the age to learn how."

I thought about how Tilly was older than me and Hy hadn't taught her. "When?" I said.

"Let's do it tonight, when we get back."

On the checkout line I leaned against Hy while she opened her wallet and counted the money. I could feel the fine detail of muscles working in her arm. When it came our turn, I helped unload the cart, heavy things first, fragile things last. I stopped for a moment, stumped on eggs.

Beyond the huge plate-glass windows the sky was getting dusky, the hushed blue of a queen's bathrobe. The supermarket was lit and almost cozy, the way a spaceship would be cozy if you were in outer space. I would've liked to tell Tilly about those two things, the bathrobe idea and the spaceship.

"Are those yours, too, ma'am?" said the cashier.

"The eggs, Mole."

I was still holding them. I set them on the conveyor belt, last of all.

Outside, by all the shopping carts collapsed in on one another, were Norah and Isobel with one lollipop, grape. They were slowly promenading the length of the sidewalk, which connected super- market, drugstore, liquor store, pizza. I saw them and Hy didn't; I listened to what they were saying while she shifted around the shopping bags on her hips. Norah was holding forth, using the lollipop as a pointer. "I get it to that thing that sticks out there, and then you get it to the mailbox, and then me to the end, and then we switch." She put the lollipop inside her mouth and they began to walk.

Hy got her bags adjusted and saw the little girls. "Hello!" she said.

They saw us and said hi. Isobel was wearing a short white dress that looked like she had eaten mustard in it, and she had a wilted daisy just barely hanging in her hair. Norah was wearing normal clothes, shorts and a T-shirt, but she was barefoot, and seemed surprised to see us, and it was funny to see them alone at dusk at the supermarket that you had to drive to. They stood looking up at us with sunburned faces and tired, overbright eyes. A car behind them in the lot turned on its headlights, giving them halos.

"Do you need a lift?" Hy asked with that mild suspicion grown-ups have when they're trying to apprehend whether children require their intervention.

"Oh, we have our car here," said Norah, gesturing toward the parking lot with her and Isobel's lollipop. "I mean, we have our mother, too," she added, and aimed the candy now at the drugstore. But then she waved at someone behind Hy and me, and when we turned, it was her father. He was walking from the direction of the liquor store, holding Gus on his hip and with the other hand gripping a lean paper bag.

"Carry me, Daddy," said Isobel.

He gave her a woe-is-me look. "Would that I had three arms, my sweet."

"I'll carry you, Izzo," said Norah, jamming the pop in her mouth and bending her knees to hoist her little sister by the waist. Isobel tolerated it for a moment, and briefly we stood there, Bill Rouen and Hy and Norah and me, like sad, funny statues, all holding things up in the fading light. Then Isobel struggled to get down. Her underpants showed as her dress rode up as she slid through her sister's arms.

"Good evening," said Bill Rouen, nodding to us. As he did, the light from inside the supermarket struck him and showed quite plainly a dark purple mark framing his left eye.

"Evening," said Hy, nodding back as if she didn't see it. She hefted her two bags up with a little jerk; she had given me the light one.

"Mole." Bill Rouen nodded my own good-evening just to me.

It was plainly evident to me that Hy ought to intervene. I didn't know how, but something was not right, something required attention, tending. The laying of a cool washcloth over that bruise, the disentangling of that flower from Isobel's hair, the dressing of Norah's feet. But Hy did not act, did not speak.

Isobel said, "Now my turn," about the lollipop, and Norah handed it over. I noticed she had a dark grape tongue. It nearly matched her father's bruise. I had a quick, vivid fantasy of bruises, bruises on everyone. And in a kind of dream-logic, I wondered whether that was why Hy hadn't commented on Bill Rouen's face; perhaps she didn't see anything unusual there; perhaps I was just learning to see what was normal.

Isobel bent her head down around the dark candy. The flower fell out of her hair and down the loose collar of her dress. I looked to the grown-ups to see what was happening. Bill Rouen was looking at me already, and when our eyes met, for some reason he laughed, a low, complicit sound.

"Don't laugh, Daddy," admonished Gus in his rare, piping voice.

Bill Rouen turned to his son and stuck out his tongue.

"No, don't do that," said Gus calmly and with no humor.

Their faces were inches apart, one serious and troubled and clear, the other complicated with muscle and stubble and irony, and the unnatural purple rimming one eye.

Bill Rouen set him down. "Hey, Gus?"

The small faced looked up.

"Peace." He held up two fingers. Gus did not smile.

"Well," said Hy. "We're on our way home." And to me, "Ready?" We said good night and walked across the parking lot.

While Hy unlocked the trunk, I looked back at the large, glowing hulk of the supermarket and the smallness of the people on the concrete apron out in front. I saw Dr. Rouen, just then, with a white bag from the drugstore, join her family. Gus went and put his face against her skirt. She handed the white bag to Bill and then fished something limp and white out of the back of Isobel's dress: the flower; she let it fall to the ground. And I was rocked by a stunning wave of pity, directed either at them in particular or more probably at us all.

It was not quite fully dark when we got home, but the sky was so dark it made things on earth—the stable, the side of the house, my legs as I got out of the car—look luminous and pale, and it was cool the way it is always cool behind Pillow Lake on summer nights, even those nights that follow hot days. We brought the groceries through the pantry door and unloaded the bags and folded them and tucked them under the sink.

Hy set me up with the potato masher and a large saucepan. She stood next to me and clipped the tops from the strawberries and plunked them one at a time into the pot, and I mashed them. Beside me, Hy measured sugar into the eight-cup measuring glass. She looked down into the sweet white avalanche and whistled.

"Isn't it kind of late to start jam?" I asked. The berries would have to sit a while in the sugar before boiling.

She whistled to the end of a phrase before answering. "Oh, it's the best time. The coolest part of the day."

When I had mashed enough, Hy let me pour the sugar into the pot, and then she said, "Now you get the cards." Playing cards were kept bunched with rubber bands in the drawer beside the sink. I found a deck that had all fifty-two and shuffled while Hy set over a flame on the stove a huge pot filled with water and glass jars. She let me choose the game. I laid the cards out for concentration, which Tilly said was babyish and hadn't played with me since I'd had strep last winter. Hy wiped her hands on her skirt and came to the table, and for a long while there was just the sound of jars knocking into each other as the water boiled, and moths colliding against the screen door in the pantry, and the cards as we flipped them over and back again. I pictured Tilly coming home then and finding us so cozy and not missing her. The windowpanes got bluer, then blacker. I was the best person I'd ever met at this game; I had six pairs to Hy's two when the phone rang.

Tilly asked for Hy, and I put her on.

"Where are you? . . . They're just eating now? . . . You're sure it's okay with . . . Mm . . . Mm . . . when did you get there? . . . It's too dark to be on bikes at that . . . Yes, but a month ago at that hour it . . . Just the two of you? . . . Mm . . . It doesn't matter, cars can't . . . A car can't see you, though, Tilly . . . Okay. Enjoy the pizza . . . By ten o'clock . . . Okay." She smiled at me as she returned to the table. "How many more pairs did you get?"

"No, it was your turn."

We left the game unfinished when it was time to cook the jam. Now outside the windows there were stars. Hy set blocks of wax to melting in a double boiler; they would be poured later onto filled jars to harden into seals. She gave the strawberry-liquid a stir with a wooden spoon, then walked through the kitchen and the open pantry door. She stopped on the stone step, stood in the middle spot, worn low. I followed and took a piece of her skirt between my fingers, conscious as I did it of Gus's earlier gesture.

"My mother taught me to make jam when I was even younger than you." Even though she spoke to me, it had the singsong lilt of her gone-off voice. "She made far more than I ever do. Enough to sell some down in the city."

"Like the ice."

"Well, yes, sort of like the ice."

Jam and ice, I thought. *Jam and ice, on a boat—how nice!—in the city to get jam and ice.*

"Sometimes," Hy went on, "we would go to the top of the hill, with pails, and pick our own crabapples, and use them to make quince-crabapple marmalade. Doesn't that have an old-fashioned sound?"

"Can we still do that, too?" I guess it was a little bit like lying that I asked that, pretending I didn't know the answer.

"Make marmalade?"

"Pick our own crabapples." Maybe I just wanted to hear her tell one story the same way twice.

"Not with those trees," said Hy. "They were blighted years ago."

"Blighted?" As though we'd never had this conversation. Maybe I was testing her. Maybe I wanted her to realize, to be the one reminding *me* of something I should have known, to take responsibility for a memory.

But, "Diseased," she answered with the patience of never having told it to me before. It occurred to me that Hy's mind didn't differentiate between those stories she'd told us and those she hadn't yet. It was all indiscriminate, arbitrary, what got said. She didn't keep things from us so much as neglect to tell them.

Bugs sang in the dark grass. I could feel with my bare feet where the stone step dipped from years and years of other people's feet. Hy was quiet and away from me, deep inside her own head.

"Hy," I said.

There were so many things it would have been appropriate to begin to ask or tell her. On the inhale, the seconds while my lungs swelled with air, they swam at me, blind, mothlike: the dead house shelves; the index books; Bill Rouen's bruise; the parents' bedroom, with its rumpled bed and dirty glass on the floor and W-bit of sky. The cemetery, the splinter, the seal maiden story. But the breath remained a speechless fullness in my chest; the words froze halfway home, as they had with Cal, as they had with the librarian. And when the breath expired, I had said no more to Hy than I had managed to say to either of them, and she, as if she hadn't heard me say her name, gave no encouragement but only said, "I'd better stir the jam," and turned away from me on the stone step, her skirt tearing gently from my fingers.

I have said that it was faith that kept me immobile that summer. So that in the face of Tilly's altering the story of our parents' drowning, her insertion of mystery and concealment and guilt, I said nothing. So that when Bill Rouen behaved strangely with Tilly, and no one else acknowledged it, I said nothing. So that when I saw the scientist family was not quite happy, not even quite all right, I said nothing. I have said that my quietness was the result of a stubborn, innocent faith in the people around me and the stories, like poured cement, in which they had been cast. I have said that it was not a result of cowardice.

But as I felt Hy's tall, blithe form brush past me into the house, it was not faith that prevented me from calling her back. Standing alone, securing my gaze on stars over the now-charcoaled stable, I thought of her selective blindness, her concentrated involvement in things like jam and hardware and pursuing owls in the woods beyond the lawn, and her seeming oblivion to certain details of the past and the Rouens' unhappiness and where Tilly spent all her waking hours. And it was not faith that kept me from asking, say, what had been the matter with Bill Rouen's eye ("Was something the matter?" I could almost hear the reply: "I didn't notice"), or what Tilly had meant when she told me not to bother him when he was alone, or whether our mother had been irresponsible, had been to blame for her and our father's deaths. Standing there in darkness at the edge of the house, I was conscious, in fact, of a stinging, vertiginous liberty from faith.

I don't know what it was that kept me paralyzed. Maybe it was cowardice after all, the fear of Hy's inability to see, the threat of exposing my thoughts only to find myself alone. Maybe it was just science, like that paradox of Walter's frog. I choose to think it was beyond my control. I was eleven that summer. But it troubles me sometimes, when I look back, to think I might have let slide a responsibility.

I went over then to Norah and Isobel and Gus. Some sort of shift had occurred. I noticed that now one Rouen parent or the other would go over the hill in the morning, singly, and I had observed the three younger ones playing on the public beach unattended, which left Walter free to go off with Tilly, and the other Rouen parent to do I did not know what, alone. This scattering realignment of people and schedules, coinciding with, and amplified by, my own recent lonesome status, struck me as so worrisome it dissolved my pride, and a few days after the black eye and the jam, I gave up my solitary skulking about the house and hill and was drawn, or drew myself, down to the public beach, where I knew the younger ones would be.

Norah was clearly delighted by my presence. As if I were a visiting dignitary, she immediately deferred to me on everything: should there be a drip-turret on this sand castle here? Did I think we'd waited long enough after eating those sandwiches to go swimming? How many miles down would I say the lake went? Isobel was less verbally welcoming, but, once when I looked up, she shot me a private, sturdy-cheeked smile, and later insisted on counting each different-colored fish on my bathing suit with her shy finger. Even Gus seemed excited I was there, in his sun-bleached, skinny-boned way; he flung sand at me and demanded piggyback rides, during which he shrieked and grabbed often at my ears. I was flattered by this.

I spent the better part of the day with them there. I realized the deep, unexpected pleasure of being certified as the eldest; their obvious delight at my presence made me feel powerful and kind. No one got cut or stung or bumped or anything, but I was sure that if someone had, they would have brought the injury to me, and just the idea that I would've been the receiver of the problem, the one charged with providing a remedy, made me feel noble in a thrilling, sophisticated way, like white chocolate: kneeling over a sand castle with the three littler ones' heads bent lower than mine, and the sun warming my back, I actually felt a bit tall for once, and supple and even lithe next to their more squat and awkward chatty selves. Gus breathed like a little dog as he worked.

Once I looked up from burying Isobel to the shoulders in sand and saw Tilly and Walter biking along the road that cut above the beach. They were coasting toward town, Walter without any hands, the sun turning their hair into gleaming caps, one marmalade, one black. I thought, *They won't notice us.* But they did; they looked, first Walter, then Tilly, and they waved, two lean salutes, and, without slowing, then disappeared around the bend.

I didn't care for how nonchalant their waves looked. It reminded me of Tilly's lisp, and the expert way she had of flicking back her bangs, and it took some of the edge off the novelty of being the big one, the kind and prestigious authority, here with Norah and Isobel and Gus.

A few minutes later, Norah remarked, "Your sister's snobbish."

"No, she's not."

Norah didn't respond, and I couldn't help feeling she knew she had the stronger position. "How come you're not playing with them anymore? Did she say so?" She didn't ask it nastily; if anything, she sounded sympathetic, which only irritated me more.

"Of course not!"

We scooped and patted sand in around Isobel. She watched us, watched the grainy cocoon encase her. It was packed so high and tight now that she couldn't move her arms.

I said, "You know how our parents died?" I hadn't known I was going to say that until I heard myself speak. Norah and Isobel both looked immediately up; they looked like echoes of my own surprise. Gus was out of earshot, down the beach collecting stones. "Well," I said, and it was a long "well," while I thought of what would come next, but it was a pleasurable kind of suspense I felt under the gaze of their four bright eyes. "They were out in a boat drinking beer, and they got drunk, and a wave came, and it knocked their boat over, and they drowned." I was not sure that what I had come out with was very good; I thought it lacked Tilly's slow-reeling seductiveness.

"Were they by themselves?" asked Norah with husky drama. I felt my confidence mount.

"Yes," I answered, making my voice as clipped and plain as I imagined Tilly's would be. "Tilly and I were just babies. They left us all alone in the house, and they went out in the boat and drank beer and brandy and stuff, and—" I shook my head and pursed my lips, pressing sand tidily around Isobel's shoulders. "Then they just drowned."

Norah thought. "How do you know how it happened if no one was with them?"

"Some guy was walking by and saw," I said quickly. My own easy wickedness amazed me. "But it was too late to get them. They went under the water, and nobody ever saw them again."

"Get it off," cried Isobel abruptly, struggling under the sand. She was little and the sand a bit damp; it locked her in firmly, barely shifted in response to her wiggles.

"It's okay, Izzo," said Norah, quickly pawing back sand. Her eyes were off me now and entirely on her sister, gentle light brown circles, clear and soothing. "She's just pretending it."

"No, I'm not!" I protested. "You can even look it up in the library."

"It's okay, don't be creeped," Norah clucked to Isobel. She got her undug, and Isobel, caked with sand, ran to the lake and splashed straight in, emerging after a minute to shake herself like a dog.

"Don't say any more in front of Isobel," suggested Norah.

My face felt hard and mean, taut. "What a baby," I said. "Anyway, it's true. I wasn't pretending."

"I know," said Norah. "But pretend you were."

I was furious and ashamed. It was a dirty feeling I had for having tried my hand at Tilly's fabrication. At the same time, I could not keep from wondering how she wove it differently to make it work.

Dr. Rouen came down to the beach in the late afternoon to

collect the girls for a snack and Gus for his nap, and I got invited back to the dead house. She didn't chat as we walked, but sang to us, or anyway sang, in some language besides English. It made it so she wasn't quite ignoring us.

At the house, she went straight upstairs to put Gus in for his nap. She didn't fix us snacks, only told us what we could have. I listened for signs of anyone else in the house. It was quiet. We three ate plums and popcorn cakes at the kitchen table, but Norah and Isobel acted like little children, showing each other bites of chewed-up food and pretending their plum pits were a cat and a dog chasing each other around and under the glass tabletop. After we got down from the table, I tried to get them to play older games, cards and jacks, but they weren't any good at it; Isobel couldn't remember rules, and the Superball kept going under the porch when it was either of their turns.

"How did your father get a black eye?" I kept wanting to say the whole time, only I kept not saying it. I wondered where Bill Rouen was. Dr. Rouen still had not come down; she was having her own nap while Gus had his. That's what Norah said, telling us suddenly, "Shishhhh"—we must not wake their mother.

Having abandoned cards and jacks, we had come back inside the house and were sitting cross-legged on the living room rug, sipping air out of plastic teacups that Isobel had poured for us: a dismally childish echo of the afternoons I'd spent on the pantry floor with Tilly and Walter and a bottle of seltzer, listening to talk of parents and vacuums and pieces of gold. We all had bare legs; mine looked big next to the others', and as we shifted in our tea-circle, our legs kept touching one another's with tiny, sweaty smacks. "Look, my knee kissed yours," said Isobel. She bumped her knees into our thighs and yelped, "Knee kisses!" and laughed.

Norah hissed, "Shishhh," then, around one stubby index finger. "Mommy'll be mad if we wake her."

Isobel shut up instantly and picked up the plastic teapot.

"Really?" I asked. "Will she be very mad?"

"Have some more tea," suggested Isobel, her whisper damp on my shoulder, and poured more air into my cup.

"Yes," said Norah. "Maybe."

"How?" I asked.

"Drink," Isobel whispered to me.

"But what will she do?" I persisted, suddenly curious.

Norah shrugged. One hand came up and began to play with her bottom lip.

"Drink it," ordered Isobel in a pinched whisper, waiting, watching, to make sure I drank it up.

I tried to picture Dr. Rouen very mad, her eyes hard, solidified in their cloudy whites, her shoulders and arms squared and clenched. I thought of Bill Rouen's eye, the purple-red lumpy ring. "Would she spank you?" I asked.

Norah's eyes swung back and forth vaguely across the rug. She stroked her bottom lip. Isobel poured more air into everybody's cup.

"Would she?" I asked. "If she was very, very mad? What would she do?"

"She would get in the car," said Norah.

"And drive?"

"Yes."

"Where?"

"I don't know." Her thumb went again to her lower lip. Tilly would have said I was being nasty. But I was curious.

Isobel pressed plastic cups into each of our hands. "Drink your tea, *every*body."

"Hold on," I said, standing, "I have to pee."

Norah had a frown on.

I went up the stairs as softly as I could, wishing they were carpeted, glad I was barefoot. I stepped on the wall edge of each tread like Tilly had taught me spies do, and talked to the wood in my head, coaxing it not to creak. Maple-syrup light came in from the landing window, filled with revolving specks of dust. Stairs were a place I loved in any house. Rooms got taken over by people; they tended to give off the character and essence of their current inhabitants. But stairs were only passageways, never fully claimed by those who lived in the house; they simply connected everything neutrally, without bias or judgment. Going up them, I did not feel I was trespassing.

As soon as I passed from the stairs into the second-floor hallway, which was shadowed and cool, I set my foot down on the floor and heard a creak and froze. But the sound didn't issue from me, I realized with relief when it came again, then twice more. It wasn't coming from Gus's room either, I could tell, but from behind the door directly opposite the stairs: the parents' room. A band of light showed under the door, widening where the floor sloped down and the bottom of the door didn't. That sight stopped me for a moment, that wedge of yellow burrowing into my memory until it met with recognition, and I was confused for an instant about which mother lay behind the door. Then the creak sounded again and my muscles jerked back to the present.

I thought, *Dr. Rouen's not napping after all. What would she say if I knocked on the door?*

But something kept me from going forward with this plan, and as I stood there, from the far side of the door came another sound. It made me queerly anxious. It was a womanly, medium-crying sound, a sort of feathery sob-breath, and the creaking grew stronger and regular, like someone in a rocking chair, but less tranquil. Like a child in a rocking chair, whose express purpose is to rock.

The sounds continued. They were not of grief, or of pain; they sounded fretful in an odd, almost babyish way, and something about them made me feel, not sympathetic, but rather angry; there was a ridiculous flimsiness about them. They were, to my ear, self-serving.

Then a man's voice broke softly through the little cries like brackish waves piling on top of each other—"*Delia delia delia delia*"—broken and low and infinitely mournful.

The creaking became slower and at the same time more pronounced, accented now, still reminding me of a child in a rocker, single-minded, intent. The sound of breathing was plain. The woman's voice shifted momentarily into speech. "... the children ... foolish ..." I heard, but the rest was indistinguishable. Now the creaking sped.

I turned and flew as quietly as I could down the stairs, jelly-kneed and strangely cold. In the living room, Isobel promptly filled my cup, and I took an immediate and large gulp of air-tea.

"You didn't flush," said Norah.

"What?"

"You didn't flush the toilet."

I shrugged. The feeling of white chocolate, of being the strong, benevolent elder, had gone flat in a single afternoon. I'd trampled it; it was my own fault.

I was not doing anything with them, not furnishing them or building new ones, but had simply laid the mussel shells, the mussel rooms, out on the sand in what seemed an appropriate configuration. I was simply looking at them, without touching, my hands laced around my drawn-up knees. I sat on a rock and looked upon them and made up actions inside my head. The mother rock, the father rock, the baby—well, I hadn't yet found a good baby rock, but a baby slept anyway in its crib, in its mossy cradle under lichen blanket. If I kept my eyes partway closed and didn't breathe too much, the words made up themselves.

"You are very full of shit," the father rock said to the mother rock, and it started to rain, drizzle, right inside their house, since it had no roof.

The mother rock lowered her smooth mica face and kissed the baby, fast asleep. *"Good-bye,"* she said to the father rock. *"I'm getting in the car now."*

"Wait, I'll read your palm," said the father rock, a little fat where the belt of white quartz ringed his middle.

"No," said the mother rock. *"Just, good-bye."*

She hopped right over the rim of the mussel.

"You come back," said the father rock, and caught her by her pebble ankle.

She tore out of his fingers, went laughing through the rain.

He was grabbing her hair; it came away in his hands. *"Wait,"* he shouted. *"What about Baby?"*

She opened her mouth to answer; rain spattered in on her teeth, and spattered hard into the cradle shell, knocking loose the lichen—

The story froze. Someone was coming down the zigzag path. My first throught was, *Finally, Tilly.* Then I noticed the step was far too careless and crashing and I thought, *Walter looking for Tilly,* and was annoyed. The crashing halted. I moved my head but saw nothing through the trees except other trees' branches. I rose up on my knees, my spine an antenna.

Crashing resumed. I jumped. Bill Rouen came blinking into view. His scorpion belt came blinking, too, catching midmorning light as he emerged from trees into the rocky cove and, in rapid succession, stumbled over the ledge of roots, half caught himself, saw me, planted a foot heavily, crackingly, into the midst of the mussel house, cursed, then looked up at me and made a charmingly bashful grin.

A roiling hotness flashed upward through my face, a kind of guilty heat, as if he could deduce what I had been playing.

All he said was, "Nice day for a swim." I knew him well enough by now not to take this literally, but as code for some private joke he had with himself. And then, as if he really did feel foolish, he took a step backward, and I saw him observe the disturbed mussel configuration but say nothing, and squint out across the lake.

Illogically, I thought, *He can't be here, because we never showed him the way.*

"Mole," stated Bill Rouen. He looked at me. He looked like he needed sunglasses. There was something not right with him. "Mole Grummer," he said, a pronouncement, and smiled so his gums showed, but the smile stayed fixed; it was a grimace maybe from the brightness.

I felt a second charge of heat, in my stomach this time, caused by the sound of my two names coming from his throat. It made me think he knew something about me. Something was not right with him. There was the bruise, gone yellow and green by now. It shimmered iridescently around his eye, beautiful fish colors. But it was not quite the bruise; he was stubbly also and had pasty-white bits, almost webby, at the corners of his lips. He looked like he needed a wet washcloth.

He said, "You're not your sister."

"No," I admitted, obscurely defensive. I was still kneeling on the rock, and wondered whether I should stand.

"What are you, fishing?" he asked as if it were not obvious I wasn't.

"No."

He looked around, smiling. "What are you doing down here all by yourself?"

I shrugged.

"Want to go for a row?" he asked, eyeing the aluminum boat.

"We're not allowed to."

"Come on, I'll row you out on the lake."

He did a funny thing then; he stumbled, even though he'd only been standing in place. "Sorry," he murmured, catching himself and scraping a hand over his jaw, back and forth. I could hear the scritchiness, a sound like gray plaid wool, and right then was filled with a melting pity, all the stronger for being tinged with revulsion. Tilly, I thought, would be curt with him right now, say something cool and cutting, and whisk herself up the path.

I rose. But I wasn't Tilly; I was Mole and I lingered. "Walter says . . ."

His eyes flicked to me, pale as cellophane, fixed quietly on my face.

The words retreated and reshaped: "He says these shells would be called *anodonta cataracta*." I pointed, and he looked at the disturbance of mussels at his feet, swirled in the sand by his own stumbling shoes. I had practiced those words, written them in eleven different styles of handwriting over both sides of a recipe card, whispered them against my own lips in the bathroom mirror.

"*Anodonta cataracta*," he repeated, but it wasn't a confirmation. He said it echoingly, bemusedly, and I wondered if he was trying to guess what I'd really started to say. Then he added, as if it were a fact in science, "That sounds like running water."

I hadn't imagined him capable of saying anything that would please me so much, and was startled into friendliness. "It does!" I cried warmly, in spite of myself. He looked full at me, so the sun cut into his eyes and they glittered. He looked up and down me and then swiftly away, seeming to shelve a smile at the back of one cheek.

"*Cataracta*, calamari!" He recited these words tricklingly to the lake, spreading his hands wide, like an opera singer. "Sperma-celli!" His lips and tongue looped over and under the words. I didn't know if they were real words, things in science maybe, or if he was making them up.

"Cello. Jello," I contributed.

"Bordello! *Cara mio!* Fellatio!"

"That doesn't sound like water," I said about the last, after a moment. Something about his face made me suspect the words were real.

"It sounds like wind."

"Oh."

He turned and regarded me, silent, enjoying himself. Suddenly I was not sure that it was not somehow at my expense.

"Whisper," I offered. He slitted his eyes. "That sounds like wind," I explained.

Then he spoke abruptly, decisively. "Come." He held out one hand. "Let's go out in the boat."

I hesitated and he smiled, and his smile was laughing and warm and wise, the lines around his eyes and his red-gold stubble like sun catchers, the overlap of his front teeth sweetly imperfect. I thought of how he was asking me and not Tilly, and then I thought: *Tilly is with Walter, but I am with Bill Rouen,* and I pictured us sitting in the boat and discussing mussels and cicadas and frogs.

Still, I checked. "Did someone say you could?"

"Did someone say you could?" he simpered, switching so fast it was like being punched in the stomach. Or maybe he hadn't switched at all; maybe a moment ago had all been a different sort of sneering.

"Forget it," I said, and my voice came out like a small, hard pebble. I cut my eyes away and prepared to walk coolly toward the blueberry bushes and up the zigzag path, but he reached out and caught me by the wrist, easily. I yanked back but he held on, smiling, laughing a little in a kindly way, so that I was embarrassed; I thought, *It's what Tilly always says, I'm too sensitive.*

"My apologies," he said. "Pray don't take offense." Up close, he reeked of something strong and odd, a hot, eggy smell.

"Whatever." I gave a kind of snort in my awkwardness and a drop flew out of my nose; I saw it and blushed, horrified, wondered with mortification if he had noticed.

With two fingers locked around my wrist, he brought it now very close to his face, turning the palm up. "How's the splinter-wound?" he inquired, peering. Breath came from his nose in short puffs against my skin. He had the wrong hand.

I felt deeply stupid. It would be awful if I tried to yank it back and he didn't let go; I pretended, instead, to participate as if it were my game, too. "Just fine." I wiped my nose with my other wrist, trying to be less sensitive. I could feel his breath in two spots, one for each nostril.

"The doctor was deft with his needle?"

"Um." I was pulling back some with my arm, but not so much as to be rude.

He looked past my hand to my face, amused at something—I wondered if it could be something as thin as my discomfort—and said, "Look how brown you are," his vowels stretching like a cat after a nap. "You are nut-brown. I bet you taste like a nut."

I wondered whether that was good or bad. He just smiled at me, as if pleased by his statement. I twisted my wrist again, not to be rude or actually struggling, just to remind him he had it, so he could let go. He only smiled, in that small way, firm at the back of his jaw.

"A little nut," he repeated.

I tried to think of something Tilly would say, very blunt and factual. "I do not."

Still smiling, he tightened his hold around my wrist, brought it higher, and licked it.

"Hey!" I yanked back violently and this time he let go. I stumbled backward.

He gave a small shrug. "No, you're right," he admitted, "Not like nut. Just girl."

I caught my balance, scowling, my insides shaking with anger and disturbance. I thought I ought to go up the zigzag path, but it seemed humiliating to show him I was bothered, and to abandon my cove to him seemed an utter indignity. "What are you doing down here?" I asked. "Don't you normally go to the Kittiwake? With Dr. Rou—with your wife?"

"This is generally true." He stepped away from me, unbothered, and reached into one of the many pockets in his vest, from which he drew a small dented canteen. He uncapped this and drank.

"Where is your wife?"

"Kittiwake," he said on the heels of swallowing, and a different odor came from him, not the hot egginess, but a dank, sweetish smell.

"What's in there, water?"

"No." He screwed the cap back on and slipped the canteen into another pocket. "Let's go swimming," he said. "Come on. Swim away with me. Last one in's a chickenshit." He proceeded to kick off his shoes and remove the vest at the same time, losing his balance again and this time regaining it by using the top of my head as a newel-post. I ducked away. "Come on," he said, "what are you waiting for?" He grinned at me. "Are you going to say to your mother, 'Bill Rouen took off his shirt in front of me'?"

"Mother!"

"Aunt. Are you going to say, 'Bill Rouen took his shirt off'?"

I didn't know what to say. He hadn't taken his shirt off. "My mother's dead," I said.

"I meant aunt."

"Why did you say mother?"

"Because I made a mistake." Now he undid the scorpion belt buckle, the belt buckle that wasn't a belt buckle for a father to wear. I meant to go up the path then. I watched him undo the buckle, remove the brass tongue from the eye, and unthread the leather, then in one quick motion that made a sound like wind, pull the length of the belt free from the loops sewn onto his pants. He tossed the belt on top of his vest, then pulled his shirt off over his head. His chest was covered with silvery hairs; he touched them, rubbed them with one palm. "This is your last chance," he said. "This is it. Now or never." After a moment he shrugged, gave a serious, formal salute, and turned toward the lake.

"How did you get a black eye?" I shouted to his back.

"Brawling." The question didn't even slow him.

"Who with?"

He was heading, not straight for the water but left, toward the boat, and he waded several inches deep to reach it, as if he'd forgotten about his socks and pants. "You should've seen the other guy," he called back.

"That's not your boat," I said.

"Come on. You row for me." He threw a wet leg over the side. His weight made the aluminum bottom grind screechingly against pebbles and sand, and he was not steady or agile enough to hoist his body in without the boat listing almost onto its side.

"What other guy?" I called.

He tried again to climb into the boat, lifted one soaking pant leg over the side, then braced his hands to lurch the rest of his body clumsily, smackingly, after. "Ta-da." He stood and held out his arms, then whisked the canteen from his pocket and uncapped it. The boat rocked under him. I looked at the rope that still tethered it to shore. His gaze followed mine. "Oops." He made a mock-embarrassed moue, drank, and wiped his mouth. "Untie me," he said. "Please? Untie me, nut-girl."

I shook my head, the tiniest motion. I should already have gone up the path, but I needed to see how badly a grown-up could behave.

"Please? Don't be a little priss. Please please please?" Then he let out a harsh sigh and started to lever himself cumbersomely back out of the boat.

I turned, finally mobile, and sprang toward the path, leaping out of daylight and into the dimness of leaf and soil, tripping blindly over roots in panting, nauseating urgency. I nevertheless remained within earshot to hear the two sounds that followed: one, the crash of a grown man's body capsizing a rowboat in two inches of lake; the other, apparently, laughter.

CHAPTER ✦ TEN

THAT NIGHT AT dinner, Hy told us about the social. We didn't know the word; she had to explain. "A dance." At the firehouse, it would be. Flyers had gone up that afternoon; a boy, she said, had come into Coffey's wanting to tape one in the window. "We used to have socials all the time," she said. "It was a very summer thing. The whole town." She drank thirstily, and when she set down her cup, water glistened in the invisible hairs on either side of her mouth.

This was our dinner: cantaloupe, carrot sticks, cheddar cheese, and crackers. All *c*'s, I had noted aloud when we first sat down, upon which Tilly had sighed and said could she please heat up some soup.

"*Can* of soup, get it?"

But she didn't answer, only made a soft guttural sound that made me think of curdled cream, and jerked back her bangs and went to the pantry.

Hy looked at me. She called out, "Does it get better or worse when you turn thirteen?" There was no answer to that either, only cans being slid around and thunked down with some force.

Tilly had indeed gone off, so completely I was embarrassed for her. Because we despised it so much in Hy. Tilly would be mortified if she could see herself, I was certain. She would be sorry and ashamed. Hy was, of course, different when she went off, less blatantly scowly, more muted and vague, but the quality of unbreachable distance was the same. I looked across at her now, saw a fondness lighting and crinkling her eyes. Not fondness for me; she was smiling at the light fixture. Smiling at something inside her own head.

I thought of Dr. Rouen getting into the black car and driving. I thought of Bill Rouen, behind his belt buckle and his accents, behind the ironical shifting mask of his face, and I wondered whether he was ever *not* gone off. And then I thought of Cal, his seeming gladness to volunteer answers that were never quite enough, never contained the information I sought; and even the licorice librarian fell into the mold, now when I thought about it, rattling that dark candy around on her black tongue, acting as though she meant to help. I had the terrible thought that all grown-ups were gone off, partly or wholly, but all of the time. You might think you were having a conversation with them; you might think they understood the things you said, and that you understood them in turn, but in fact it was an illusion. You could remember their exact words, even write them down on recipe cards, but later when you checked, they would say you had misunderstood. They would say they had forgotten. And now Tilly, too.

Tilly brought her can from the pantry and lit a burner. The gas caught fire with a sound like punching a sheet of metal.

I could not conceive of myself ever going off like them. It

frightened me to think of it. To retreat into a space that allowed no one else access, to allow for the possibility of the inexpressible—these were nightmarish thoughts. I could no more imagine exiling myself to this kind of mental solitude than I could imagine having secrets about myself that I would not want learned. What was the point of having secrets if not in the hope that someone would come along and find them out?

I thought of my mussels, of the lonely work of tending them down at the rocky cove, and the way that that work was made delicious by the prospect of their being happened upon. I pictured them right now, at this moment, with Tilly stirring soup at the stove and Hy spooning melon and the sky fading to powdery lavender; pictured them alone on the beach with the sand growing cold and losing its color and the frogs singing in the moss and water lapping at the sides of the aluminum boat and the first stars appearing so faintly and far away it made my throat clench.

I did have a secret. The mussels lay in disarray on the beach, stirred up by Bill Rouen's heavy shoes. I hadn't told about him coming to our private cove that day, how there'd been something wrong with him, how he'd held my wrist and licked it and used strange words and said "No" when I'd asked if it was water in the canteen. How he'd fallen from the boat. Taken off his shirt. I hadn't told about the parents arguing, either, and then making sounds of skin and cloth, and then arguing some more, on that day we played sardines. I hadn't told about the rocking-chair noise from behind their bedroom door, or what their voices had murmured beneath it. I hadn't told about him getting my splinter out, or about the way it had made him switch to acting like a father. I hoarded these items, gathered them uncomfortably into myself and did not pass them on. And it was not faith that kept me from telling. An involuntary shudder racked up my spine, tailbone to neck.

Hy noticed me. "Mouse run over your grave?"

"No."

"Anyway," she said, continuing aloud with whatever silent conversation she'd been having with the light fixture, "it'll be fun. You girls'll get to see what it's like." She had finished her melon and played with the spoon now while she talked. She said Pillow Lake socials used to happen every week, all summer long. Sometimes they would have live music, guitar and fiddle and drums, and sometimes they'd wheel in an upright piano, and Hy said Cal played the trumpet a few times. She said someone would make barbecue, or there would be tables of cold fried chicken wings and coolers full of soda, and that the kids used to snitch pieces of ice from them and slip them down the backs of each other's shirts.

She recounted all of this almost as though she were telling us for the second time, as though it were part of a history we ought already to know.

"You would dance?" I asked. I could not picture it.

"Well, yes. Everybody would." Hy's long fingers slid up and down her water glass. This irritated me greatly. She was gazing now at the black and silver pots that hung above the stove, and smiling. Tilly's back was to us; she stirred regularly and gave no sign of hearing, but the smell of her soup—tomato rice—reached us plainly.

"Our mother would dance?" I was a little startled by how harsh and impatient this sounded, but Hy didn't seem to notice.

"Yes, Violet of course . . ." she answered mildly, then cocked her head. "Not so much, maybe, Violet, by the time they stopped having them. She was twelve years younger—"

"I know."

"—and used to play more, I think. With the other children. There'd always be children running around. Under the refreshment table. Eating all the brownies. Families would . . . whole families, you know. But the single people, too. Oh, and dressed!" She had fallen into almost code now, speaking to herself more than to me.

"You would dance, what—like with men?" Each question I asked now had the effect of sending her farther away inside herself.

"Well, yes." She did not go on aloud, but her face grew more lively, and then her eyelids lowered a bit, like a gentle screen. She tilted her head and pressed the bowl of her spoon against her cheek. To watch her do this made me inexplicably incensed.

"What kind of dancing?"

"Oh . . ." She shook her head, then laughed a little.

"What?"

"Oh. Nothing, I . . ."

"What?"

"I was a good dancer." She blushed, and lidded her eyes more heavily.

"Don't do that," I said sharply. I felt like Gus.

Her gaze came down from the pots; she looked bewildered, but she also looked faintly uncomfortable, as thought I had in fact caught her at something. "Do what?"

"You're acting silly," I snapped. "I can't even picture you dancing." I didn't mean it to come out quite so scornfully.

And I saw in a definite moment what I'd done, the exact pricking of her tender reminiscence, when her eyes seemed to flinch and drain of light, and then she closed her mouth and set her hand down by her plate and looked down at the gouged-out melon rind. I was sorry for Hy. I felt a little like the wrecker I'd been at Norah and Isobel's tea, asking all those questions, making Norah worry her lip.

But I was not very sorry. I wouldn't have everyone going off.

With a pair of scissors pressed cold against me underneath my shirt, I mounted the stairs, dark with evening and creaky, the snow roses faceless, the water stains there only in my mind. I went to my room and shut the door, extracted the scissors, and laid them on my bed. From my underwear drawer I removed a bulky wad of tissue paper, which I brought to my bed as well. It was the same tissue paper I'd found in Tilly's drawer, but it had since grown crumpled and voluminous; I parted the folds, like petals of an unruly white flower, flattened the paper, and sorted the contents: a spool of fishing line, a simple metal clasp, eight tiny red beads, and a necklace I'd won in a grab bag in fifth grade. The necklace was made of rough wooden kernels, like nuts or seed pods. They'd been strung on a waxed thread that resembled nothing so much as dental floss; I had been disappointed when I drew it as my gift, but now I was glad I'd saved it.

I suspended it before my face on one finger. It dangled like a pendulum. With my other hand I picked up the scissors and snipped through the floss, right near the top. The necklace flopped open, gutted; beads rained onto the tissue and across the spread. Some rolled under my crotch and some fell to the floor.

After I spoiled Hy's mood at supper, Tilly had turned sweet, bringing to the table bowls of soup for all of us, and saying that the social sounded like fun. It's this Friday, said Hy. The night before my birthday, said Tilly. Hy had smiled and squeezed Tilly's shoulder. I looked from one to the other. They did not look at me. I did not eat my soup. I brought it to the stove and dumped it back in the pot, and then went to the pantry and got the scissors and concealed them under my shirt and went upstairs.

Here, feeling deeply sorry for myself, I fashioned Tilly's birthday present. I was making her a new bracelet from the old, homelier but sturdier, with her fine red beads interspersed among my knobby wooden ones. I made the task harder than it was, gritted my teeth while I threaded each bead, huffed wisps of hair up out of my eyes as I hunched over my hands on the bed. Outside, it got dark very slowly. I didn't turn on a light. I pretended I was doing penance: for not telling Hy about Bill Rouen at the cove; for telling Norah and Isobel our parents had gotten drunk; for not telling Tilly to leave alone the story of their death; for telling Hy she looked silly when she'd been happy tonight. But it was not a pure, heartfelt penance; it was complicated by bitterness. I felt wronged and abandoned by Tilly and Hy, probably still downstairs, sharing tomato rice soup. It made me sorry to think I'd been mean to Hy, yet part of me wished to inflict more hurt.

I thought of a thing Hy had once said, one time years ago when Tilly and I had had a bad fight. She said that people get hurt so much in the world, by all kinds of things beyond their control, earthquakes and floods and fires and storms, cancer and heart attacks and plane crashes and everything, and so, she said, it was especially important to be gentle and careful about the things, the kinds of damage, you *could* control, like being mean to each other. And at the time, it had the effect of making Tilly and me sorry we'd fought, and I had decided that from then on I would be vigilant about being gentle; I would be a kind of soldier of carefulness.

But now, sitting cross-legged on my bed, frowning at the nearly invisible fishing line—I had finished stringing the bracelet and now tied the ends to the loops in the metal clasp, made tiny knots, and pulled them tight with my teeth—with my stomach growling because I hadn't gotten enough to eat, I thought about that moment at the supper table—Hy with her eyes soft and dancing over the hanging pots and pans; Tilly bent, stiff and silent, over the soup—and it seemed like a perfect fact that I couldn't have controlled what I felt and said, that it had been as urgent and natural as an earthquake or a heart attack. The kinds of damage people did to one another seemed no more avoidable than the kinds caused by nature. This struck me as a very sad and grown-up thought to have.

I cried then, and afterward fell asleep fully dressed, with Tilly's completed birthday present fastened around my wrist. I dreamed that I surprised Hy standing naked in front of her dresser, just about to step into a wet sealskin.

Dr. Rouen went over the ridge by herself in the morning.

I awoke cramped and stale, with my head at the foot of the bed and my clothes tight and twisted, and something pricking my leg when I shifted; I sent down an exploratory hand and retrieved the pair of scissors. Sitting up then, I saw Dr. Rouen, cardiganed, alone, striding through the vivid slats of light that calibrated dawn on Ice Cart Road.

My wrist itched. I scratched at it vigorously for one second and froze: the bracelet. But it was intact. I unclasped it gently and laid it on the bed, the alternating pattern of red and brown, fine and sturdy, in a straight and simple line on the spread. I would find a little box for it, and a bed of cotton, but for now I just blinked at it, pleased by my design, and yawned and raked my fingernails luxuriantly along my wrist; the bracelet had left neat, regular indentations in the night.

Delia Rouen. Her oddly pretty name floated into my sleepy head, and I glanced back down at the road. She had gone.

I had slept badly, yet felt strangely refreshed. Already being dressed from the night before, I was efficient about leaving. I wrapped the bracelet back in tissue and hid it in my drawer, went to the bathroom and peed, thought of putting shoes on and then thought better, went down past the snow roses and through the bluish morning hall, running lightly, but my lungs and heart ballooning in my chest with sourceless urgency.

Leaving the front porch was like stepping into a great glass bowl. The air held dew and a chill, and light pinwheeled through churning tree branches. It was funny to veer left instead of right on Ice Cart Road, away from the dead house, from the beach, from town; it was like waking up with my head at the foot of the bed: not altogether unpleasant, but lopsided in a fresh and daring way. Soon I came to a barrier—a rusted chain between two concrete blocks—that marked the fork where part of the road snaked down over the ridge, and beyond which cars could not go. I stepped around one of the concrete blocks and immediately the road narrowed and sank into the woods. I was entirely in the shade now, so thick and close grew the canopy of trees, and walking toe-to-heel.

After a bit, the tree cover receded and I saw that this part of the road had been cut or blasted right into the hill. It was bordered on one side by a wall of jagged pink-and-bone-colored rock, and on the other by a grassy slope that fell away sharply hundreds of feet; at the bottom wound a narrow band of shore interrupted only in one place, where a pocket of salt marsh curved into the land. Beyond that lay the Kittiwake, flat this morning and blue-sky blue.

It was a benignly pretty walk down this river road. The pavement was even, the brush dotted with chicory and goldenrod and some variety of brilliant red berry. Birds were singing familiar songs. At one sharp bend there was even a guardrail in place— everything orderly, safe, and tended, I was surprised to see. I knew the way even though Tilly and I never came here. My vision of the river was ever from above, from the old graveyard on top of the hill, or the bowl-shaped meadows at Bluefields, or the high roads that connected the towns all built to look down on the river valley. When Tilly and I wanted water for swimming or sand castles or skipping stones, we had always gone to the lake. And although no rule enforced this, no reason even, really, kept us from the riverbank, I felt a little brazen as I ventured there now, passing toe-to-heel through the very early shadows with the chill like an alertness in my arms and legs. The incline propelled me forward faster than I meant to go. I opened my mouth to breathe and as the air swept over my molars, thistle-sharp, the old story, too, came breezing through. And the sharpness of the morning was like a fine, hooked tool, like a nutpick, prying at the corners of the story, dislodging the body from its tight and wrinkled casing.

In the story, the mother is standing in the graveyard on top of the hill, and then she goes down to the house. She goes down to the house, to the phone, the house that is the dead house, the phone that only crackles and spits. Then the mother and the father leave the house, leave the baby girls who are Tilly and me, and go back up the hill. But they don't go straight back up the hill, surely: there is no way to the river from the top of the hill. The graveyard edges out to sheer rocky drop. To get to the river the mother and the father must go down the steep fork of Ice Cart Road. They must leave the dead house and walk past the house that is Hy's house (stopping, knocking, agreeing the aunt will go stay with the babies while the other two go down), and then follow the road beyond the house, past the rusted-chain barrier and down the steep, the rainy, the slippery slant where the road cuts so narrowly into the hill. The incline propels them a little faster than they want to go: the mother out in front, smiling, her mouth open to the rain; the father just behind, using his calf muscles to slow himself to a controllable gait, yet at the same time trying to keep up with the mother, and he's anxious now and maybe even angry as thunder claps close by and he blinks, half blind, against the teeming rain, wondering if she hasn't brought them a little too eagerly into danger.

I emerged at the bottom of the road breathless, halting myself where the pavement ran out. My bare feet stood on fine, silty sand, shot through in patches with spiky reeds. To my right a jetty, not visible from the graveyard above, extended its tapered finger into the water, and it was in a small way jarring, because I had not known of its existence, and it did not figure in any of my mental pictures of the story; I stared at it for a moment now, making the necessary adjustments. To my left began the marshy pocket that had attracted the Rouens here this summer. Up close, it was more diversely detailed than I had imagined, with dense lanky rushes in gold and green, and opaque pools dark as oil, and occasional bald spots of clayey mud that glistened with a kind of lunar gloss.

I stood in the spot where the mother and the father must, too, have emerged. For them the sky would've been dark, greenish or plumlike from the storm. They would've stepped out from under a partial shelter of rock face and trees into slicing rain, like liquid pebbles breaking against their bodies. I looked out along the jetty, placed the boaters somewhere there; actually, that worked well: the mother and the father would've climbed out on the jetty, navigating along the slippery rock top. Waves charging across it, swirling back, sucking at their ankles. I saw the mother barefoot. I saw her still smiling. The father behind her a little still, noticing how the mossy jetty was slick as ice, noticing the way he had to parry his weight against the wind and the water crashing over the top, noticing how craggy and sharp were the rocks that bowed out from the jetty under the water. The mother, blind to these considerations, only batting her lashes furiously to try to make out the boat again between lightning flashes. Drawn here for reasons she could not express: the pull as out of her control as a heart attack or plane crash; she's as little to blame as the storm itself.

I waited for something to happen, now that I stood here at last at the actual scene, the physical place where they had drowned. I waited for a click, a realization, a wave of grief or profundity. The morning was not yet warm. I crossed my arms around my middle and awaited sensation. The sky was blue and peach, the air stiff and clean, like a sheet just unfolded. The jetty was a staid, well-made breakwater, the river a placid mirror. That was all. It was quiet except for birds. A wash of sunlight deepened across the shore and I felt its thin warmth on my forehead and cheeks. To my surprise, then, I yawned, hugely.

There at the edge of the river, in the span of a single exhale, my anger toward Tilly cleared. I don't mean my anger went away: I mean it became clear, slid into focus. The way she had usurped our story, messed it about, tailored it to suit her own ends: all at once, that did not matter. It was not what she had done to the story that offended me—the violation of a few details we'd never been sure of in the first place; it wasn't the words themselves that were of consequence. How stupidly literal I'd been! All those quotes and names and facts meticulously copied, verbatim, onto recipe cards, vigilantly stored beneath my underwear, as if they themselves were inherently of value, would someday fall together in the marvelous shape of a key. As if I were their guardian.

I looked out on the water where my parents had drowned, trying to conjure up a sense of importance, of personal connection to the place. I kept thinking of Tilly instead. I saw her standing in the bathroom, a blue pajama strap across her sunburned arm, saying with gentle but utter closure, "You were the one who decided not to stay," and I swallowed, remembering that with violent frustration. She had said it as if it were a fact, but it was not a fact; it was not true. I stared, swallowing, at the idle, vapid river, which offered me nothing, not even ghosts.

I had been trailing the story of our parents' death as if that were the way back to Tilly, but it was a false pursuit: the tracks led nowhere, froze halfway. The story itself was vaporous; its few hard facts could be stirred into any number of solutions, each one equally subjective and insubstantial. I was tired of the story, sick to death of it, I realized with something like relief—sick of trying to establish a connection with what could never be had.

And then I saw Dr. Rouen, working not far from me but crouched, so that it took me a moment to recognize her figure. She was wearing rubber boots and one of her sundresses, the magenta, and the tops of her shoulders showed very round and speckled, the color of toast. She seemed busy and complete, inspecting some minute thing in her palm. The skin of her shoulders looked as if it would be warm to touch. I stood and watched her for a little bit, as though I hadn't yet decided whether I wanted her to notice me. After a few moments passed and she didn't, I said hello.

Dr. Rouen looked up and searched for the source of the intrusion, then said, "Oh, my goodness!" in a not-unpleasant way. "Mole," she added a moment later, as though it had taken her exactly that long to think of my name.

"I just, came down," I said.

The marsh lay basking, reeling in the pale sunshine, collecting warmth and light in its silvery tufts. Pieces of it shimmered and stilled, and it smelled alive, unprettily but interestingly so. I could not tell whether Dr. Rouen felt intruded upon. It seemed to me I was seeing her for the first time as she meant herself to be.

"Out for a walk?" she said.

I shrugged and nodded, sort of.

"You're up early."

"I always get up early. I like it."

"Like me." She turned and bent her face back over the thing in her palm, in a way that was inviting rather than off-putting; she meant for me to come have a look.

It was mucky getting there; I misstepped once and splashed and said, "Uh!" but she didn't look around, just waited for me to arrive by her, and when at last I did, she lowered her hand some so that I could look into it, too. Then we were both looking into her hand.

A tangle of mussels sat there, ridgy, thicker than mine from Pillow Lake, all snarled up in their own beards of fine, glistening, worm-colored threads. Dr. Rouen prodded them a little, nudged one fingertip gently into the clump. "There, see the baby?"

It was infinitesimal, and no-color, just pearly. She nudged the clump again so that the mass of hairs rose and the sun stroked over the baby mussel, the tiny, translucent ellipse. I wanted it instantly for my mussel house; I would make a crib, petal-lined, for it, so small.

"Is it alive?"

"No."

It was the size of a grain, a half a grain of rice.

"What happened to it?"

"I don't know. I found this whole bunch on dry ground. You can see animals have eaten out some of the insides." She turned over a larger shell within the clump, and it was open along its hinge, and empty inside.

"What kind of animals?"

"Birds, most likely." She said it just plainly, not as if it were something happy or sad, the birds good or bad. She looked at me for a minute, squinting up so that two stubby lines formed vertically between her brows, and her very keen dark eyes clicked back and forth as she studied my own eyes, first one and then the other, as if gauging my interest, measuring something. I noticed again the discoloration in the whites of her eyes: a clotty yellowness and a pale, pale blue. It was a slight kind of ugliness that was not unappealing, but it made my stomach feel funny to notice. I became aware of a thick kind of odor clinging around us, and at the same time imagined Bill Rouen looking into those eyes, being in love with them.

"You see these threads?" she asked, and prodded at the clump with her fingertip once more. They were vaguely awful-looking, so hairy and damp and fine, like some part of the body you were supposed to pretend you didn't know about. "These are the byssal threads. I think you were asking about them?"

A smile leaked over my lips; she had remembered the talk from Bluefields, back when none us of knew about each other. I nodded—my chin dipping a shadow across her hand as if something had flown over us—and put a finger down, lightly stroked the silky snarl.

"They're formed by, the mussel has this little, it's called a pseudopod, it's like a foot, this one foot it extends. And it secretes a—the foot has a groove in it—and it secretes this fluid down the groove, and then when the fluid hits the water, it hardens into this thread. It makes dozens of these. It attaches itself."

It wasn't the words I was loving so much as it was the sound of her voice, its gravelly city timbre, and the way she seemed to be inside of what she was saying, as if her voice were a lasso twirling, marking a space, and catching me in it. She didn't look at me but pored delicately over the mass in her hand, pointing things out with the tip of her pinkie, while I divided my attention between the mussels and her, her teeth showing between her lips on certain words and disappearing behind a pucker on others, her round, freckled shoulders, and her serious, unpretty eyes. The queer odor again asserted itself, some warm, rank element lingering heavily around us.

"What *is* that smell?"

"Oh—sulfur, that's sulfur." And she handed me, as though it were nothing special, the whole pile of beard and shells; she entrusted me with them; I cupped them in two hands. Dr. Rouen squatted and inserted the fingers of both of her hands in the marsh, worming them intimately around. "I don't know if right in this spot . . . yeah." She withdrew them and they were coated in black, rich globby black. She held one set of fingers up toward my face, and I bent to her gingerly.

"Uck!" I jerked back, smiling.

"Like rotten eggs, yeah?"

"Yeah," I agreed softly, although I did not think I had ever smelled a rotten egg. It was recognizable, though . . . hot egginess . . . Bill Rouen clicked into my brain, the odd, stumbly Bill Rouen of yesterday afternoon, with the white webby deposits at the corners of his lips, the sulfur smell on him mixed with sweat and complicated breath—whatever had been in his metal canteen. I saw him stripping off his scorpion belt, bearing himself into the water.

"This is the most productive land on earth," said Dr. Rouen, rubbing her fingers together.

"This right here?" I asked doubtfully, gesturing across the little patch of marsh bordering the Kittiwake.

"Yes—marshes. More than the rain forest or the ocean. By biomass, marshes are more productive than any other place on the earth."

I did not know what biomass was; she might have been talking about vacuums and gold, or frogs and half jumps, but her great ordinariness, her firm delivery of facts, was like a lullaby, and I wanted her to go on explaining things to me. I didn't care what things—it was her manner of exposition; it held such ballast it was cozy. I listened and was entranced by the mottled whites of her eyes, and abruptly had a thought, or at any rate wondered, if perhaps she didn't like Tilly. It seemed a disloyal and unaccountable thing to wonder, and I felt myself blush.

"Is it soft?" I asked.

"The sulfur? Feel it."

I squatted beside her, shyly, and dipped my pointer into the muck, which was surprisingly warm, warmer than the air, and then withdrew it and passed my thumb across the black silt. It was soft and incredibly smelly; it smelled deeply, deeply personal. A smile that I couldn't prevent crept back and I stood up, self-conscious. Dr. Rouen stayed low. I saw the hem of her dress was darker pink from being wet, and it had some mud or muck on it. I could see down the top of her dress, too, just a little bit, where the tops of her breasts came together and the skin started to be white like chicken meat. She was poking at something down there and her breasts jostled a little bit and I thought of a child in a rocker, rocking.

Dr. Rouen kept talking, showing me things, the way the marsh grasses spread their runner roots, and she named things, called the grass spartina and another plant (an almost comical stubby tube) salicornia, and I said the names after her, shifted my own tongue along their sounds, that later I might write them down. The salicornia she snapped a piece from, and crunched on it, and then offered me the other half. "Delicious in salads," she said seriously, and I laughed. It tasted like salt. It was as if I had been looking forward to this for a very long time.

"You study all this whole marsh?"

"Well, in segments," she answered, "like, look," and lifted from the ground what I had not noticed, a piece of nylon line weighted at the ends by pellet-sized lead sinkers.

It jarred me for a moment into the memory of the sad white soles of Bill Rouen's feet (him bending by the dresser, in the dim bedroom, looking for fishing line), and he seemed to have so little to do with any of this here, with the blue-and-peach morning and the sulfurous marsh, and with Dr. Rouen, squatting solidly in muddy boots, translating the items she held in her hands. *"Delia delia delia delia."* I didn't want the memory of his voice saying that, but it came explicitly to me, the low, suffering sound of his voice, each *delia* cast out like a byssal thread, a strong gripper; and then the memory of the not-pained cries, the little womanly sob-breaths that meant something other than sorrow, something self-concerned, and the voice: ". . . the children . . . foolish . . ."—those words that were not words for a mother to say.

"This," Dr. Rouen was saying, "is a study plot," and ran her fingers over the ground by the lead sinker and picked up another line, attached perpendicular to the first. "These map out square meters, our specific areas of study."

I envisioned the lines spread out across the whole marsh, over all of Pillow Lake, a secret grid below the soil, mapping town and cemetery, rushes and sand, past and present, with all that it contained capable of being counted and fixed. I asked her how far it went.

"There's just these six plots here. Two each in the low-lying, middle, and high marsh areas. See that line there? It's pretty hard to see, but you can tell by its—kind of orangish—marker." I looked to where she pointed—"Around waist level, see there?"— and did spot what she meant, a thread running down the whole length of the marsh, from the tree line to the river. It was attached at intervals to thick wooden stakes I'd not noticed, and from the top of each stake fluttered a length of vivid orange tape. The string itself was colorless and clear, like a spiderweb, visible only in places where it caught and spat back light.

"And that one there." Dr. Rouen pointed out another, parallel, several yards away. "Those are called transect lines."

"They've always been here?"

"No." She smiled.

"But do they, I mean, do they just exist? In science?" I thought of the lines on a globe, netting it, holding and dividing it into invisible but understood lots.

"No." She saw exactly what I was getting at. "It's nothing to do with longitude and latitude. We just put them up when we got here, to help confine, to organize, our study."

We. It was the first time she had alluded at all to her husband. It was odd to insert him in this picture, in the slow peacefulness of the marsh, with its fine silvers and golds, its smelly black muck making little sucking noises as we moved around in it, its odor frank and basic and running together with light and river and air. If Bill Rouen were here, he'd be making jokes, teetering unsurely over the uneven, unfirm ground, speaking odd phrases in fake accents, wandering, in his silly way, toward the fringes of the marsh, lakeward.

"Where is *he?*" I asked.

She rubbed her dirty fingers together. "Bill? Home. At the house." I blinked. Her voice was light and cold and shut everything down. Her whole manner, and face, and body—just shifted. It was like Hy last night, when her gaze came down from the pots and hardened on her melon rind.

"Is he sick?" I offered.

Muscles formed neat little packs on either side of her mouth. "That's right."

"He seemed a little sick, I think."

She turned to me.

"Yesterday, at the lake."

"Where?"

"Yesterday. I was down in our cove, Tilly's and my—well, really just my cove. And Bill R—your husband came down there. I think he was looking for you," I decided to add.

"What makes you think that?" Something about the way she asked made me sorry I'd lied.

"I don't know. He asked if I'd seen you."

She regarded me intently.

"And then, he seemed a little dizzy. So I guess maybe he was coming down with it yesterday."

She didn't say anything for a few moments. "What do you mean, he seemed dizzy?"

I didn't know how much truth to tell. "He just kept losing his balance. And he kind of fell in the lake."

Her face just had no light in it. It looked like it had turned into a piece of wood. "I'm sorry," she said.

"That's okay." I was surprised. "You don't have to be sorry."

"Well, I am." Her words were heavy and tight. She didn't sound sorry. And she wasn't looking at me when she said it. I thought of his black eye.

"Did you two get in a fight with each other?"

Now she did turn to me, with a definite frown between her eyes. "That's rude," she snapped.

I blinked.

"You don't ask personal questions," she said, with hard, staccato emphasis. After a moment she breathed heavily, once, through her nose, reached into the large side pocket of her dress, took out a small green notebook, flipped it open, and began reading that page. I gazed at the side of her face, the lowered lashes, the whitened bridge of her nose, the flat, shut mouth, the bit of soft fullness under her chin. Not looking up from her book, she moved her body a few steps away from me, lakeward, and then a few steps more. Her ponytail, long and dark, fell straight down her spine, but all around her head escaped wisps of hair were backlit by the sun, still lowish, across the Kittiwake, whose surface was slightly choppy and blinding. The magenta dress swung in loose folds as she continued, oddly haloed, away from me in her heavy boots through the marsh, toward the mica-bright river.

My stomach growled. My heart seemed to thicken, grow sluggish in my chest, and I became aware of the small, damp mass still cupped in my hand. "Here!" I darted after her, leaping barefoot through the marsh—"Here!"—and caught up, held out the clump of dead mussels, panting. "Your shells."

She glanced over her shoulder—"Oh. That's okay, I don't need them"—and glanced away again as coldly.

I spread apart the hairs, poked through their damp snarls till I turned up the baby, the fraction of a grain of rice, clinging to the slippery mess. I wished that I would cut myself, start to bleed, get a splinter. "Can I have it, then?"

"What?" She looked over her shoulder again. "Mm."

I kept my head down, squeezing warm muck between my bare toes. The fragile tangle blurred in my palm. "But how *can* I save it?"

"What? I can't hear you. What's the matter?"

I sniffed with a loud snotty rattle. "I don't know how to save it so the little one won't break in my pocket."

Slowly, the book got slipped back into her dress. She came a step toward me, bent. My head was still bowed, eyes still blurry, but I could feel the solid weight of her leaning over my hand. "The what one?"

I touched it with my pinkie. "The baby. For the cradle." And then I sniffed again and wiped my nose on my shoulder and I told her about my mussel houses. I told her about the rooms and the blankets and the toilet and the chair, and about the hail and the spiderwebs and people stepping on them, and how I kept building new ones all summer. And while I told her, she took a small plastic envelope from her other pocket and took the whole mussel bundle gently from me and slid it, threads and all, into the envelope, and it was a real scientist's envelope, with a space to write information on the outside in a special pen that would write on plastic, and she had such a pen and wrote, "Mussels—Study Plot #4—August 11," and put the bag right into the pocket of my shorts, in a delicate way, so that I barely felt her fingers. And it was kind of a trick on my part, because now she was not gone off anymore.

Then she began to tell me what she knew about mussels. She said mussels were important to a marsh. She said they helped extend the marshland and hold it together, that they helped the marsh plants have a place to grow, to take hold. She said mussel shells got used for making buttons. She said also they were delicious: she liked them dipped in beer and melted butter. Her manner was flat and almost brusque, and it lulled and comforted me; I wiped my nose a final time on the front of my shirt. There was something in it of Cal when he was explaining about the history of Pillow Lake, when he told of the fire of '26—particularly when he had told us about the lady with the bananas. To know magnificent things and state them so plainly. It reminded me of him saying, "She was thrilled by their bravery."

Dr. Rouen resumed walking while she talked, and I followed at her side, occasionally brushing against the magenta or a warm, toast-colored arm. We looped back in the other direction, toward what she explained were middle and high marsh, and visited different study plots, Dr. Rouen squelching in her boots, me with my bare feet making whispery sucks. We stopped talking. We walked carefully, noticing things. When she squatted, I did, too. Neither of us had anything to say. She let me watch what she was doing. She seemed to count things with her fingers, put a hand into the water and count shells, or shoots of spartina. She ran her fingers along a runner root, then drew a picture of it in her notebook. She wrote things with numbers. Her handwriting was messy. Spots of water dripped onto the pages.

Even though she'd said there were only six study plots, I couldn't help envisioning a fuller grid just the same, a whole giant checkerboard underneath us, divvying up the land into precise squares of scientific data. There was something reassuring about such a concept, and the idea of Dr. Rouen, with great intimacy and exactitude, deciphering the contents of each block. After a while she stood, and her knees cracked. She wiped her sulfury fingers thoroughly on her dress and then, squinting, eyed the marsh, whether scientifically or dreamily, I could not say. The sun had risen high, basted all the golden reeds. Dr. Rouen stood wholly apart from me, not acknowledging my presence and not ignoring it either. I was glad I'd stayed with her all morning, had put an hour of silence together between the talk of Bill Rouen and now.

I asked, "Are you near to finding out what you came to find out?" I interrupted her mind when I asked her that.

"Pardon?" She wiped her forehead with the inside of her wrist.

"This summer," I said. "Didn't you . . . you came here, right? to find out why—something. Why the mussels are polluted?"

"No . . ."

"But you said that, at Bluefields, about a shoe factory."

"A shoe factory? Did I?"

"Dumping chemicals into the river." It was lonely always having the best memory.

"A shoe factory, I said?"

"Yes. It was, I think, an example."

"Well." She brightened. "Yes, okay. I think I know what I was saying." And at last she turned to me again in such a way, like when her own little children had wondered at the mystery of hang gliders, and her lips began to work now in neat, earnest movements over her teeth, and my stomach filled up with the feeling of being her audience. "It's true that mussels are what we call filter feeders—they take in everything, slurping up the water around them, and filter what they can use. And what they can't use often builds up inside them—it doesn't kill them, they're pretty tough, but it builds up—so that we can sometimes, by studying the mussels, learn a lot about what pollutants are floating around in the food supply."

"And so then you can fix it?"

"Well, you see, but . . . 'fix it.'" She smiled, faintly, at her boots. "You know, some mussels *themselves* are considered pollutants. The zebra mussel, in parts of the country, goes and clogs intake pipes. It's not written in stone what needs fixing, what's good and what's bad. We're not trying to answer any specific question, solve any specific problem, not in this study here, anyway. We're sort of mapping out, generally, the overall environment for this particular mussel population. We're counting waves, and measuring tide lines, and, oh, counting the number of byssal threads per square whatever. We're looking for many, many small things."

"Why?"

"Why?"

"I mean, what is that good for? What will that do?"

"Maybe nothing," said Dr. Rouen.

Far out on the Kittiwake, someone was motorboating; the fat sound of its engine seemed to signal noon.

"Maybe over time," she continued, "it'll get combined with other studies, become part of a bigger picture."

"Do you hope it does?"

"Well. Sure." She said this quite complaisantly.

"But it might not? Doesn't that bug you?"

She laughed. "It's sort of the nature, at least of the kind of research we do, that it's slow, and small, and for many, many years after completing a study it may not seem to mean anything at all." Cheerful was actually how she sounded. "You publish a little paper, and, much later on, some other guy might look at your paper and a bunch of other little papers, and see a pattern or a picture emerge—like figuring out they're all a piece of one big jigsaw puzzle—and then he announces it and everybody gets very excited about it. Or not," she added.

"You mean you don't even know if what you're studying now is even going to tell you anything?"

"Well, it is telling me things. But I don't know if they're going to be useful things . . . or, or, I don't know if I'm ever going to *understand* the usefulness of the things they're telling me. Will I ever understand it entirely? No, I think not." And she sounded, explaining this, so happy, so delighted; it was clear she loved the thought. The wind blew her wisps. A streak of dried muck smudged her forehead.

"If those threads of mussels are so strong, what makes them let go?" I asked.

"A storm could do it," she said. "A strong enough storm." The sun made copper in her hair.

"I wish you didn't have to go away," I said.

She looked at me with surprise, and began to smile, but then without any words it went the other way and her face turned slowly, quietly sad.

CHAPTER ✦ ELEVEN

I SAT ON Hy's bed Friday evening and watched her comb her hair. She had good hair to watch being combed, so springy was it coming through the teeth. I wasn't used to watching her get ready for things, to watching her watch herself in the mirror. Her mirror face was lopsided, almost not like Hy at all, but someone who merely bore a great resemblance to her. She wore a slip with lace on it across the chest. Even though Tilly and I would be going with her, it gave me the homesick feeling in my stomach to watch her getting ready to go out.

"Is Cal going to be there?" I asked.

"As far as I know, yes."

"Will he play his trombone?"

"Trumpet. And no, I don't think. I don't even know if he has it anymore."

"What would he have done with it?"

"Oh—given it away. Lost it."

"How could you lose a trumpet?"

A pipe shuddered and clanked: Tilly shutting off the shower. Hy shrugged at the mirror and picked copper earrings out of a wooden box on her dresser. "Or, I don't know, sold it." I watched her thread the wires through her ears. She bent forward a bit toward the glass, wholly absorbed, concentrating on finding the tiny holes in her reflection. The curtains in her room were closed, but not the shades, and the beginning of sunset was gilding the cloth, making the room look old-fashioned. I rocked myself petulantly at the edge of Hy's bed, swung my heels against the coverlet. The feeling in my stomach churned in hot bursts. I wondered whether there might be such a thing as medicine for the homesick feeling.

Hy got both earrings in and smiled at herself. It was not the kind of smile that starts inside the body and journeys to the surface; the life of this smile existed only on the face. She took a tiny glass pot from the top dresser drawer, unscrewed the lid, which was the palest jade green, dipped her pinkie in, and wiped it behind each ear and in the center of her chest. I knew, from years of reconnoiters, that the contents of this pot were creamy and translucent and smelled like lily of the valley, but I had never known what one did with them. As Hy recapped the pot, her lashes grew heavy and a real smile curled itself upon her mouth.

"What?" I said.

"Mm?" I hated it that she always responded with the tiniest sound possible, not even a whole syllable. She put the perfume back in her drawer and closed it. "I didn't say anything."

"What were you thinking?"

"I don't know. I think a mixture of things. Whether we have enough eggs for Tilly's cake tomorrow." She pulled the comb once more, slowly, through her hair.

"How many do we need?"

"Oh, two."

"For chocolate?"

"Mm."

"Bill Rouen said he would have thought Tilly would have an angel food cake." She didn't respond. I flopped backward on her bed. It creaked heavily, just once. The sound made flames of recognition spurt through my stomach. I sat up and flopped back again, harder. The bed creaked against the wall. It came to me the smell from Bill Rouen's mouth after he'd drunk from the dented metal canteen, and the smell from Dr. Rouen's slippery fingers, coated with sulfury muck from the marsh—not the memory of these smells, but the smells themselves, warm and rank and actual. And the image of Bill Rouen's purple eye came to me, and Dr. Rouen inside the black car, and Isobel's wilted bloom slipping down the neck of her dress. I creaked the bed and creaked the bed, a nasty, rhythmic sound.

"What are you doing?" Hy turned, amused.

"Nothing." I supported myself on my elbows. Her nipples showed through the slip, dark and flat. I tried to think of something to say that would shift my discomfort to her. "You're not planning on dancing tonight, are you?"

She cocked her head, baffled. "Why do you say that?"

"It would just be embarrassing."

The words had no effect. She went to the wardrobe and reached in and moved hangers; their wire sang against the rod. "You are a real pill tonight, Mole," she said lightly. It was all golden molasses-light in that corner of the room beside the curtained window, and Hy in her ivory slip moving through it looked distant, evocative of her own memories.

"My stomach hurts," I said. I picked at a loose thread in her coverlet. I tried to break it off and it unraveled several inches along a seam instead.

Hy removed a tan dress from its hanger.

"It kills," I said. I wished I were sick enough to throw up.

"Why don't you get yourself a glass of milk?"

"But it really *hurts*."

"Milk may help settle it," she answered mildly.

I sighed and rolled off her bed. "I hate socials," I said as I went through the doorway.

"While you're in the kitchen, you could check on the number of eggs," called Hy.

In the hallway I met Tilly on her way from the bathroom. Her hair was wet. She wore her blue-and-white robe.

"You know you're bleeding?"

She followed my eyes down to the trickle on her shin, then wiped it upward with her finger and sucked her finger clean. "I nicked myself shaving." She sounded a little proud.

"Tilly?" I followed her to her room. "Can I come in while you get ready?"

"I'm not dressed."

"I won't look," I promised, crossing into the room and sitting on her bed. The heat was flashing through my stomach like a trapped firefly.

"Mole!"

"I have something important to tell you."

"What?"

But I didn't know which thing to say. I flopped back on her bed. Her bed was silent.

"Mole, I have to get dressed."

"But, Tilly—" I sat up. "Bill Rouen said he thought I tasted like a nut." Sort of, he had.

"When?"

"A few days ago."

"I told you not to go around him."

"I didn't! I couldn't help it, he came down to the lake."

"What did you do?"

"Nothing!"

"Well, what did he mean?"

"How should I know?"

"Well, don't go around him."

"But I just told you—"

"Mole, I have to change." She held her bathrobe tight around her and raised her eyebrows a little apologetically.

"But wait!" I flopped backward fiercely against her bed. It didn't make the creaky sound. "Wait." I did it again, harder.

"What are you doing?" She glanced at the little clock on her bedside table.

"Wait, listen." I tried again. "What's this sound?" I kept trying to make it, but her bed wouldn't creak.

"Please go now so I can change."

"But I wanted to ask you, I heard this sound . . ."

"You can tell me about it later." She glanced at the clock again. "Come on. Out." She took my elbow and ushered me to the door, which closed inevitably behind me. I stood alone in the hall with my helpless rage. I had wanted to ask: was it a sound people made only when they were fighting, or could it be if they loved each other?

I waited in the kitchen, chipping bits of paint off the radiator.

Hy came in, in her tawny dress and copper earrings. She had put on shoes I didn't know, strappy ones with little heels. She smelled sweet. "How's your stomach? Did you get some milk?"

"No."

"Oh, did you check the eggs?"

I shook my head.

She swung open the refrigerator and counted the eggs under her breath. I remembered unpacking them the night we did jam, conveying them myself from the cardboard carton to their smooth individual nests in the fridge door.

"Hy?"

"Mm?"

"I feel sick."

She shut the fridge and came to me where I leaned against the cool slats of the radiator, and felt my forehead with her broad palm. "Your temp seems okay."

I used her hand as a support and burrowed into it. She got the idea and put her other arm around me, drew me against the front of her dress. "Poor Mole."

I sighed raspily against the dark wall of her body.

"Sad Mole." She patted my back.

"What's wrong with her?" Tilly had come into the room.

"She doesn't know," Hy answered for me. Then she turned and her body pulled away from me some. "How nice you look!" she exclaimed warmly. I looked up.

Tilly was wearing her red culottes, a white halter top, white anklets and sandals. She had done her hair up in an awkward way: plaited, wet, into a single French braid—but it was too short for the style; the bangs wouldn't go back; limp crescents of hair hung along her brow, and every other strand was pulled so tightly it made her forehead seem high and strained.

"Thanks," said Tilly, smiling shyly. She reached up self-consciously to poke in a stray piece, and fastened around her wrist was a little gold chain I'd never seen before, fine as a transect line.

"Where'd you get that?" I said to her in the car while we were still in the driveway, leaning over the front seat.

"Walter." She held her wrist in the concentrated light of sunset flooding across the dash. The chain glistened in the light like a string of gold saliva. "Early birthday present."

"It'll turn your wrist green."

"Don't be so ignorant."

"Guess what?" Out the window I could see Hy coming from the house. She had skipped a kerchief tonight, and her hair stood out, crinkly and full, around her face. The heels she'd put on made her hips swing foolishly as she walked. I lowered my voice and spoke quickly before she came around and climbed in. This was still something Tilly liked about me, the secrets I'd shared with her. "I found a little baby mussel for the mussel house. Dr. Rouen the mother gave it to me."

"Can you not whisper on my neck?" said Tilly at normal volume, and wiped it off with her hand.

*   *   *

As we neared the dead house, I watched to see whether Tilly would turn her head. I watched the naked back of her neck, the glossy knot of hair, still damp, fastened thick and messy with countless bobby pins poking out, the fine design of short black wisps that lay loose against her skin. The skin of her neck was incredibly pale and fragile-looking, with parts of it pulled fiercely taut by the pins. I thought if I barely scratched it, it would bleed.

Tilly turned her head to the right. I turned mine. The dead house was dark, the car gone. Bikes up on the porch, leaning against the side of the house. Their spokes catching fire in the last slants of direct light. Blaze striking every window in turn as our angle changed, making a hot mirror of each pane of glass, as inscrutable, as inflexible, as ever.

What did Tilly look for when she turned her head? Signs of the Rouens? Signs of something else? Or was it only reflexive? I wanted badly to forgive her, to have us be thinking the same things, but when I turned back toward the front of the car, there was only the back of her head, impassive, facing forward, with her neck so regal, her braid so tight.

I looked once more at the dead house before it slipped from sight. I wanted to pitch a rock, smash the windows, see the glass panes explode.

At the firehouse there were a million cars. They filled up the Lefferts Engine Company lot and also the gas station across the street. People were walking from all directions toward the door to the meeting room, the men wearing fresh shirts that buttoned, the women wearing skirts that swished from side to side with each step, the kids all noticeably scrubbed. Some men—firemen,

I supposed—were standing in front of the garage, whose giant door had been flung open; the company's sole engine gleamed hugely, peacefully dormant, inside. The men held silver cans of beer, and the cans looked small inside their big grips. One of them would shout occasionally, teasingly, to the group of women clustered over on the steps, and the women, their wives and girl-friends, would crack up and retort. Between the men and the women, on their own patch of sidewalk, some little kids were pretending they knew how to tap-dance.

Hy had to circle three times before she managed to find a spot for our car, way down in the vacant lot opposite Day's Auto Parts, and even then she had to turn around once more to get on the right side of the street.

"Am I okay on your side, girls?" she asked midway through the U-turn, leaning forward and peering left.

"There's a brown car coming," I told her.

Tilly snorted.

"What's wrong with that?"

"She doesn't care what color it is."

"So?"

"Forget it."

"Girls!" Hy snapped. "You both be still and let me concentrate."

It was that time of evening when some cars were driving with their headlights on and some were not, and they were all milling slowly, confusedly, like groggy, end-of-summer yellow jackets. The people in the cars and walking amongst them appeared, by con-trast, snappily alert and punchy. I saw a woman in the passenger seat of a pickup lean over and toot the horn, then wave crazily at the occupants of a little orange sedan. Groups of people crossed the street with easy recklessness, winding between traffic, laying their hands on the hoods of cars as if against the flanks of sweet-tempered horses. A teenage boy yelled, "Rhoda Fisher!" out the window of his car, and a girl on her way up the firehouse steps swiveled, so sharply that her skirt flared, and shook her fist at him. And my stomach writhed, recoiling from all the queer, brilliant energy.

Hy maneuvered us finally into a space in the vacant lot and shut the engine. I opened my door and stepped immediately into garbage: a paper bag of rotted zucchini. The plump lengths of squash gave way beneath my sandal and, not knowing what it was at first, whether vegetable or animal, some small body I had perhaps crushed, I started and had to catch myself by gripping the door handle. The vacant lot was strewn with litter: tiny empty liquor bottles, and paper bags, and plastic wrappers from packaged cupcakes and chips. I was angry with Hy for not having gotten us a better spot, for parking in rubbish. She should have known to leave the house earlier.

"Hy . . ." The zucchini had splashed on both my sandal and my foot, and it smelled bad. Balancing myself with one hand against the side of the car, I hopped around to show her.

"What'd you do there?"

"There was something—*you* parked so that right when I got out, I had to step in this!"

Hy inspected my foot, which I was holding up toward her face as high as I could, and I saw her mouth twitch. "In the firehouse," she said, "we'll get you some paper towels."

"Paper towels aren't going to get it off; I need to wash. It smells. I need soap."

"Well, okay. We'll get you that. In the bathroom when we get inside."

"I have to go in like this?"

"Mole, I don't have soap and water for you here." She turned up her palms and made a show of looking in either direction across the lot, jammed full of parked cars and high weeds and broken things, hunks of metal and cardboard and glass. She was amused, on her way to being irritated. The last traces of sun had receded fast, all the gold in the air exhausted, blown out like candles on a cake.

Hy and Tilly picked their graceful, long-legged way through weeds and trash to the sidewalk. I limped behind them, placing my foul foot gingerly, as though I had been injured.

What did I own? I found myself wondering as I trailed them along the sidewalk to the social; what did I own that I could ruin?

There were people on the sidewalk, more of them converging from across the street as we drew nearer the firehouse, women with sweater sleeves tied over their shoulders, men with their hands on the small of the women's backs. All of them seemed to be humming, not from their throats but from their skin, a silent, collective hum, a shimmer in the air, a kind of base excitement that made even the strict, bald men, even the solid, grayed women, seem in on a secret, frivolous plan. It was the feeling of anticipation, palpable and self-interested and radiating from each person, that made me disgusted in the tight back of my gullet, and the way that Tilly was walking out in front, her hair so black and fretted over. The caged bulb over the firehouse entrance buzzed on as we approached, cast its cone of thin yellow light down on the people.

I walked behind them all, limping on the ball of my zucchini foot. I saw all their grown-up backs, saw the hairpins and the necklace clasps, the white collars stiff against red-brown necks, and all the arms placed around those backs, pressing one another forward toward the entrance. I heard their sounds of greeting, so high and bright and exactly alike, they might have all been mimicking one another, mocking. Even the familiar faces seemed different tonight, uncertain, unsafe, as if they wanted something for themselves. I felt sick to be in the presence of so much anticipation and desire, embarrassed to recognize it. I did not share it; that thought was my peace. I wondered methodically what I could wreck, what was mine to ruin.

In the bathroom, I didn't bother taking my sandal off, but hiked my leg up, my foot brought all the way into the bowl of the sink, and washed off the rotten vegetable that way. I let water soak into my sock and sandal, drench the cloth, turn the dun leather chocolate. This seemed mildly destructive. When I had finished washing, I went to work with several paper towels, but my foot still squelched when I set it on the floor.

The women's bathroom was small and neat and oddly feminine for a firehouse, with a can of chicory someone had picked on the windowsill, and a tube of hand lotion beside the sink, and yellow curtains. On the other side of the door, music and voices slid around and knocked against each other like toy boats on stormy water. I tried to imagine the firehouse women, sunburned and rowdy and wisecracking, tending this place, this little room within the firehouse that was theirs only, thinking to pick the wildflowers, to bring in that tube of lotion. I tried the lotion, squirted a little on my hand: it smelled like cake. I dabbed some behind my ears, and down the front of my T-shirt.

In the mirror I locked eyes with myself. My reflection grew more and more serious, until it didn't seem to be me, but someone older and sterner and more comprehending, and it chilled me, but I could not break away. The more I stared, the less I could see what I looked like. The licorice librarian had said like my mother. I gazed and gazed into the starkly somber eyes in the glass, and stayed so long the bathroom seemed to grow light and floating, and the laughter and music lobbed and broke against the door, and I stayed focused on the grave face before me, feeling I'd lost myself to that stranger in the glass. I did not want to go off. But I was stuck at the mirror, frozen, locked outside myself.

Then some ladies came in to use the toilet. That broke the spell and I went out.

The meeting room was dimly lit, with streamers crisscrossing the ceiling; also, it was packed, with far more people than ever came to a Monday-night movie. There were tables with food, and tables with huge bowls of red beverage (kid punch and grown-up punch), and a table with a stereo system and milk crates full of records. Searching for Tilly and Hy, my eyes found Cal. He stood against one of the metal filing cabinets, not talking with anyone; neither was he smiling. I thought we were the only two people in the room who did not seem glazed, candied with gaiety.

I had to touch his sleeve before he noticed me, so dim and noisy was the room, and then he edged a half step away before dipping me a slow nod and saying, "Mole," in a voice like crumpled paper. He said he had a cold and was keeping a little distance from everybody because of germs. He was sucking a cough drop and the tail of a cloth handkerchief poked from his large fist.

"Why did you come?" I asked, but before he could answer he sneezed, and then shivered. "Want me to get you a chair?" He started to wave off the offer. "No, yeah, let me get a chair."

They'd been stacked up on dollies against the back wall to make room for dancing. A man had to help me. First he needed to hand a woman his punch in a plastic cup, and then he reached to the top of the stack and swung down one of the slatted wooden folding chairs. "Where do you want it, sweetheart?" he said, muscles standing out along his arms.

"That's all right, I got it." I carried it upright with two hands back over to Cal and opened it for him. This was the good self I'd meant to be with Norah and Isobel, advising them how long to digest their grapes before swimming, teaching them how to get to tensies in jacks.

"Thank you." Cal sat and coughed. I stepped back a bit when he did, so he would know I was being responsible. From there, half ensconced behind Cal, I let myself look out around the room, skimming faces, seeking ones that were familiar. I had to admit I was a little sorry to see no Rouens.

Tilly stood by the refreshment table with some other girls. One of them bent down to cuff her anklets in a way that made cuffing your anklets look like an extremely interesting thing to do. The anklets were blue. Each girl had a cup of red punch. The girls were moving parts of their bodies—shoulders, necks, knees—in a slight, tentative fashion to the music, which was the sort of music that plays on the middle of the radio dial, and all sounds similar and tired after a very short time. Tilly was doing it, too. She was bobbing her chin the smallest degree.

"Cal," I said, standing close to his ear.

He cocked his head back toward me.

"Do I look like my mother?"

"Yuh."

"I do?"

He nodded.

"Does Tilly?"

"Less so."

"But she's very pretty, right?"

He nodded. He wasn't being uncommunicative, it was just that the sounds in the room were very loud and congested, and he had a sore throat, so it would be hard for him to shout. For me, I liked speaking loudly into his ear and having no one else hear it. I felt at peculiar liberty, shouting in the noisy room.

"Cal, how did that fire start, back when you were little?"

He cupped a hand to his ear and I repeated the question into it. Then he shook his head. "Don't know."

"Did anybody die in it?"

He shook his head again with a kind of uncomprehending grimace to show it was a strain to hear, and, maybe emboldened by this, I asked him something I'd been wondering. "What's fella-tio? A kind of pasta?"

But then he was not even trying to listen, because Hy had come to us and was standing there with her dimple in place, looking down at Cal, so that her wild hair tipped forward around her face, framing it like an electron cloud. It looked like someone had been rubbing balloons against it.

"Hello, Hyacinth," said Cal. I looked at him quickly to see how he meant it, but couldn't tell. Of course no one ever called her that, but he said it with the ring of something resurrected. Hy smiled at the greeting, not with surprise. I looked from one to the other, excluded from the weight of their history.

"I have a cold," Cal said quickly now, but she was already leaning in, and went ahead and kissed him on his hair.

"I was telling Mole about your trumpet," she said, casting a twinkling glance around the room. "Kind of like old times, this."

Cal grunted. "Hardly," he said, and used his handkerchief. Then he looked up at Hy. "You look a picture," he said begrudgingly, or maybe it was just his cold.

The tan dress hung from her lean body in folds like molten metal in the dim light; it was just a cheap fabric, but it looked touched with gold, and her hair, loose, was like a fairy's. She was taller than ever because of the shoes, and she smiled richly down at him, wide enough to reveal for a moment the silver cap in the back of her mouth. It had a cool, impish shine. Seeing her like this roused the homesick feeling back into fiery orbit. I pressed myself against the back of Cal's chair. He coughed again, this time with a fair amount of wheeze in it.

Hy said, "You smoked today."

"This is a cold," he replied. "And as a matter of fact, I didn't."

"Oh, Cal," said Hy, and kissed him on the top of his head, and I was embarrassed because she'd kissed him twice and he didn't want anyone catching his germs. I wondered why she couldn't understand that, why she wouldn't behave responsibly.

I slipped among the thickets of grown-up legs and elbows, through the alternately darker and lighter pockets of people and sweat and smells, of bright, bright voices and jostling arms and drops of punch raining on the old firehouse floor, and was gripped by the need to keep walking, to continue walking straight through it, outside and beyond all the strange laughter and clasped waists, the bodies propelling one another in tight circles, shaking in undignified and meaningful motions. I wanted to go off away from it, out where I could breathe and the strength of the night air would fill up my lungs and stomach and nose.

Describing a circle around the circumference of the room, straying slowly in the direction of the door, I got shoved against the wall by a man dancing with his bottom lip between his teeth. He didn't even notice. I'd bumped my head, and reaching up to rub it, my hand came into contact with the cool surface of glass. I turned and saw what I'd hit up against: the story of the fire, the old newspaper clipping. It was without deliberation that I reached up then and gingerly pulled the frame forward. The wire lifted easily off its hook. I looked over my shoulder and met no one's eyes, just shadowy torsos throbbing hot and close together, abandoning themselves to a kind of willed blindness. I turned back, invisible in my sobriety, and took the story down from the wall.

The front steps were crowded with a few people still arriving and many others already slipping out for snatches of cool air or cigarettes, all of them sidestepping one another and holding high their beer or cup of punch so as not to spill any, and it was easy for me to get out that way, shuffling along with the current of bodies, as if I were one of them, the picture frame sandwiched between my shirt and skin. The air was velvety and moist and tasted of rain; as I passed the garage I heard one of the firemen say, "It looks like we're going to get some weather." Men smoked next to a high bush, their cigarette ends glowing as they got sucked, dimming as they were lowered. I hurried past them, conscious of the hard glass pressed against my stomach, feeling brave and giddy, the illicit guardian of this stolen good.

I did keep expecting someone to stop and question me, at least to notice me, a small girl hurrying from the firehouse with arms gripped around a strangely chunky middle, but I traveled down the sidewalk and left the light of the firehouse bulb without being spoken to. And then there was nothing to do but continue: past the gas station and The Sleeping Dog and the liquor store, where I slowed down a little; and the *birrrrrup* of crickets was loud and pulsing, like a heart, like the strongest muscle, singing in dark, empty grass lots that fell away on either side of the street. And still I continued walking, just now uneasy. The night seemed very huge, more like a night in a dream than a night in real life. It felt as though someone had lifted the lid off the sky.

By Steve Day's Auto Parts was where I stopped, under the high, mounted security light that shone all night on the spent shells of cars retired in gray rows. The light, feeble as it was, marked a kind of civilized harbor before the road ran out into the dark lake and woods. So I stopped here and took myself back between two cars, one with no wheels and one with no doors. I climbed into the driver's side of the one with no doors, so I was hidden from the street, and perched sideways there so some light fell across my lap. The seat was damp and cool. When I adjusted my position, my thighs came off the vinyl with a moist, sticking sound.

I extracted the frame from under my shirt and tilted it so that the security light washed wanly across the article. For the first time, I was able to read it without having to crane my neck, and without missing the uppermost third. I bent over the text and devoted myself to it with self-consciously pursed lips, self-consciously furrowed brow.

I had stolen it from the firehouse on a whim, an irrational internal dare, fueled more by contempt for the frivolity of my surroundings than by any intention of obtaining information—it was like my trip to the library, undertaken only to spite Tilly, and which had fizzled under my inability to probe the librarian for any real news; so, too, was my piracy this evening a thin act, an invention for me to infuse with importance and heroics. So it was with surprise that I came, at the top of the last column, to a paragraph that stirred me:

Guests at Short Clove Lodge cheered the firemen on in the final hours of the blaze. Countess Watari, summering for the third year in a row at Pillow Lake, supplied the men with bananas and declared she was "thrilled by the fire and their bravery."

It was queer; for just a moment I thought I was glad, that I had received a confirmation I had been waiting for. Then a collapsing feeling of humiliation gusted through me, because instead of receiving something, I had been robbed. Cal hadn't known, hadn't sensed or divined the fine reasoning of the lady with the bananas. He hadn't plucked it accurately, surely, from his own memory, from his own clear understanding of what her motive must have been.

I thought of him sitting there in the firehouse on a movie night, adjusting a cough drop into his cheek, thinking for a moment before he delivered the sentence, as if to give himself that time to be sure, to put himself in her shoes, understand what she had meant. That had been the beauty of his pronouncement: my faith in his ability to get it right, to intuit purely the sensibility of another human being. When he'd said, "She was thrilled by their bravery," in my mind it had struck a blow against the terrible loneliness of the inexpressible. It had countered the prospect of never being able to know just what another meant, what another thought. I had loved him saying it: it was a kind of rescue mission he performed, an act of heroic devotion, disintering the meaning of the story. And I had copied them, his words, onto a recipe card. As if they counted for something.

But he hadn't known the meaning of the bananas at all. It had just been something he'd read, somebody else's stale sentence that had lodged in his brain. Humiliation gave way to something else as I thought of Cal, Hy, the librarian, teachers, the Rouen parents, even Walter and Tilly: all in the business of dispensing so much data—and all so casual about getting it wrong. It was their casualness that made it unbearable, their blithe oblivion to the importance of their own words. Which I kept, which I tended. I was the guardian of their words. Which were nothing.

Fine pricks of moisture struck my face. The car in which I sat had been stripped of more than its doors: it was additionally missing the steering wheel and a large portion of dashboard, and the misting night wind blew freely through its body, crisscrossing in and out the four bare doorways and the entire space where a windshield might have been. I imagined fixing it up, building a secret hideaway. I could see me coming back here with a blanket, a sandwich, a bottle of Queen Anne's lace. A book. A cut-up apple. Some colored rocks for the dash. No.

I would do no more refurbishing. I didn't want any more things of my own invention. The impulse for violence came into my mouth like a taste. If I'd had my recipe cards with me then, I would have ripped them, scrunched and wrung and torn them to bits. If it had been my mussel houses, I would have ground them to pieces, pounded them to dust. As it was, I took up the one thing in my lap and with both hands flung it as hard as I could against the vacant hull of the next car. The picture frame smashed against the metal. I heard glass break, and pieces skitter down the door and rain against asphalt. Then it was extremely quiet: I had frightened the crickets.

The sugary tonic of vandalism scurried through my blood, exhilarating and a little nauseating. I wanted to laugh, and I covered my mouth with my fingers and thought of my teeth hidden behind them, little and white and mean, and I was scaring myself.

A car door slammed. Not one of the ghost cars in the lot, a real car, out on the street. An engine shut, and I heard voices and footsteps. I thought: *I'm caught. Someone noticed the missing picture frame and they've sent people out to find the thief.* But the footsteps receded across the street. The voices fell away. *It's only some people arriving late to the social,* I told myself. Then I heard singing, a woman's sandpapery voice and a song possibly familiar, although I could not place it, I could not place it—and concentrated, leaned my mind forward.

Dr. Rouen. I hopped from the driver's seat with strange relief. Bits of glass crackled under my sandals. I made my way out toward the sidewalk but caught myself up short. She stood a few yards down from me, in the direction of the lake, not alone. Bill Rouen was with her.

This was the first time I'd seen him since that afternoon at the cove, and whereas when I'd thought it was just his wife I'd been all set to burst out and greet her, now I found myself pulling back into the shadow of a gutted car. I watched them. In the shadows cast by their own hair and features, both their faces might have been all-over bruised. I wondered about their children, where they were, who was with them. Dr. Rouen had stopped singing. She was facing the car lot and he was facing her, looking at her as though waiting for her to speak. I viewed them from the darkness of the auto parts. They looked frozen and flat, just outside the direct spill of the security bulb. If not for the insects cutting swerving paths in the light, and the steady descent of fine moisture illuminated by it, they might have been trapped inside a black-and-white still.

The father spoke. "Stay," he said.

The mother didn't move.

"Promise," said the father. "You know you will." He seemed to be asking.

The mother said nothing.

Then he lifted his open hand to her face and touched it. His thumb was on her mouth. She wore a black sleeveless dress and didn't look at him. He moved his thumb over her top lip and over her bottom lip. Then he moved apart her lips and put his thumb right in her mouth. This all happened slowly. Then she shut her eyes or lowered them and, not roughly, took his wrist and moved his hand off her face. For one more moment they looked like a photograph. Then the father turned and walked away, in the direction of the firehouse. In a moment, a bright whistled melody carried back over his fading footsteps. The sound persisted on its own after the figure disappeared, and then it went away, too.

Dr. Rouen, alone, moved to the black car parked beside Day's lot. Shadows deepened over her as she left the spill of the security light. She opened the driver's-side door and paused, looking off down the street in the direction of the lake, her hand lingering on the door handle. I stepped out on the sidewalk and made a sound like a cough.

She shut the door and swiveled, saw me. "Oh!"

"Hi."

I stood within the milk-cool glow of the light. Moths and mosquitoes flew between us. "You scared me," she said, seeming to size up where I might have come from.

"Sorry."

"What're you doing out this way? Where's your aunt and Tilly?"

"At the social. I came out for a walk."

She regarded me speechlessly from the darkness.

"What about all the rest of *you?*" I asked. "Are the others here? Are you here for the social?"

She hesitated a little before saying, distractedly, "Yeah. Yeah, they're there," and again before adding, "I just had to come back to the car for something." Her voice sounded filtered, remote, like a person talking from out of a dream.

"Oh."

Her fingers still wrapped around the door handle, playing with the smooth metal of it.

"What?" I asked.

"What what?"

"What did you have to come back for?"

"Oh. Nothing. I want to leave my sweater," she said. "It's such a warm night."

"It's kind of raining," I said.

She didn't answer. She seemed a different person from the one at the river. She looked off again through the silvery-specked air, away from the social, toward the lake.

"Well." I moved toward where she was. "Do you want to go?"

She looked at me sharply. "What do you mean?"

"To the social." I tried her hand and she let me take it. It was cold. "We can walk together, okay?"

We started toward the firehouse together at a slow pace. Soon, shapes of people emerged from the smoky-looking mist. They stood clustered and alone in half shadows outside the firehouse. Some families with small children were already leaving. I wondered where Dr. Rouen would have gone had I not been there. I stole a look up at her. Her cheek was damp with the rain that was not raining but only accumulating in the air. "It's kind of late to just be getting here," I observed cautiously.

She said nothing.

"How come you're so late?"

"We got a late start leaving the house."

But their car had already been gone when we left.

"I don't really like this social," I told her, to make her know I would rather have driven off somewhere else, too. "All these grown-ups acting all silly," I went on, to show her she and I together were not like that. "All, you know, dressed, and dancing together, acting dumb." We were nearly at the stairs and she hadn't said anything. I wanted her to know I was like her, that I didn't want to be here either, that whatever was making her sad bothered me, too, and I went on quickly, with increased derision, mocking my aunt and sister to show her I understood. "You should see Hy, she's in this kind of dressed-up dress and these earrings. Everybody's all sweaty and fake inside. Tilly tried to change her hair—"

Dr. Rouen stopped walking and regarded me coldly. In the darkness, the imperfections of her eyes were not visible, only the shape of her strong, small body in the sleeveless dress, and she looked surprisingly elegant, with her ponytail fastened up in a twist and the curve of her neck smooth and precise and gleaming damply. "You don't cut people a lot of slack, do you?" she said, and removed her hand from mine.

I don't think I understood quite how much the Rouens were a family in the middle of trouble, not even by mid-August, when we'd gotten to see so much of them. In later years, other people and events I encountered would make me look back on that summer with little dawnings of recognition and apprehension. But at the time, I really didn't know. No grown-up around me offered any clear message or instruction. It seemed Hy or Cal or somebody should have been responsible for telling what he or she observed, for explaining what it meant. Maybe Hy never noticed the drinking, the remarks, the black eye; maybe she overlooked them because they were nothing amiss, simply acceptable adult behavior. There was a deficit of information that summer. I did the best I could.

CHAPTER ✦ TWELVE

FOR THE SECOND time that night, I entered the social, clean-footed now but with insides no less rotten. After Dr. Rouen's snub, I had pushed up after her through the clusters of smoking teenagers on the steps, furious and ashamed and trying to think how to tell her she had misunderstood me. But as soon as we stepped inside the firehouse, we were engulfed by a blaring pop song and air that had grown sultrier and more pungent. Further degeneration seemed evident in the flung-off cardigans, overshirts, and shoes piled on the floor along the wall; in the plastic cups and crumpled napkins strewn beneath the refreshment table; in the sight of the folding chair I'd gotten out for Cal—he was no longer in it. Someone had moved it, evidently, out of the way of the dancing, but something was amiss—it buckled forward now, crippled; its two front legs had been broken.

Who did that? I wondered angrily; who is responsible for doing that and then just leaving it there? But then I thought of the framed news article, stolen and smashed by me not fifteen minutes ago, abandoned and unaccounted for, in pieces amid the broken cars down the road. I was no longer a caretaker but a vandal. I had wrecked the picture and wrecked the walk back with Dr. Rouen. It was Tilly's fault, somehow: she had made me wreck things.

"Where did you go, Mommy?" said a piercing voice at my side: Gus, who must have been waiting immediately inside the door. He had stationed himself now rigidly before Dr. Rouen, looking straight up at her, blank-mouthed and severe.

She bent but did not touch him, looked him right in the eye. "I was coming, Gus. I was coming along behind you. Thanks for waiting for me."

Thoughts flickered visibly over his lips and brow, and he opened his mouth and breathed through it, laboring, I thought, to funnel some of them into speech. His mother continued to meet his eyes steadily, waiting for him to form what he wanted to tell her. She looked available, trustworthy. Watching them, I felt manipulated. Minutes ago she'd been on the verge of *not* coming; it was me who'd delivered her here, who was responsible for that. But her ingenuous gaze focused patiently on him and in the end Gus said only, "I was waiting for you, Mommy."

"Yes, I can see that. Thanks, old man." She stood up straight again. "Shall we look for something to drink?"

"I want juice."

"Okay. We might have to do soda, but let's see what they have." And they went off toward the refreshment table, not holding hands.

Maybe I should have understood that something was broken with their family, that Gus needed his mother, and perhaps she needed to be his mother right then. Maybe I should have felt sorry for them, had some distance and compassion. But in that moment when Dr. Rouen and Gus walked away from me, without a word or a glance, I felt only wronged. I wanted, vividly, to lash out, smash another stupid picture, hurl a handful of potato chips after them. Or better: injure myself, get a splinter—or much worse: something that would summon them back, not just them but Hy also, and Tilly and Walter and Bill Rouen and Cal, something that would demand everyone's best behavior.

I wanted Cal. I began to duck and navigate between the tall trunks of bodies, looking into the funny, false expressions on people's faces, their eyes half lidded, opaque with a peculiar intensity, their mouths held in poses, with lower lips either bitten inward or shoved out and droopy. From the sidelines came periodic laughter, fast and sharp as metal coils unsprung, and there was something frightening about the sound; it was not *noticing* laughter; it had a hollowness, a ring of omission. Once, someone danced backward right onto my foot. He stumbled, caught himself, turned, and panted, "Sorry." A bit of spit landed on my cheek.

I wanted something to make them all stop, to snap them all back fast into their bodies and responsible minds. I cupped my hands over my ears and tried to hum my own song against the tune of the dance music. Someone pulled one of my hands away from my ear.

"Mole!" It was Norah, and her voice was bright and sharp. Isobel was by her side. "Watchya doing?"

"Nothing." I dropped my other hand.

"We didn't know you were here. We just got here. We got here late."

"I know."

"Come with us to the bathroom, Isobel's going to wet her pants," she invited, and took my hand. I hadn't seen them since the day of the air-tea, when I had been rotten and made them upset, and I was a little surprised by how generously Norah included me now. She led us to the ladies' room. We had it to ourselves. Isobel went immediately to the first stall. She didn't bother shutting the door. She was wearing a green dress, which she pulled up around her waist, and flowered panties, which she pulled down to her ankles, and she hoisted herself onto the seat and began to wet. We could all hear it. I could see her listening to herself wetting. When it stopped, she stayed where she was, swinging her legs with the panties around her ankles, and said, "I thought we would never get here."

"How come?"

"Our parents," said Norah. "We had to wait while they had their argument."

"Where did you have to wait?"

"Nowhere, in the car—we—they had to get out and finish."

I pictured this. It sounded very strange and troubling. What did they look like when they fought? Did they get out of the car in order to shout, or hit? Or had I seen it? Was what Bill Rouen had done with his thumb fighting? "What were they having a fight about?" I asked. Norah's eyes slid away over the tiles and she began to pluck at her lower lip. I did feel a little low, mindful of how I'd bullied her with questions the other afternoon, and of how quiet and anxious she had become. But I was so curious to know.

"The dishes," said Isobel from the toilet.

"What?"

"Our mother says she can't let Daddy do the dishes," confirmed Norah, "because he only does one side of the plate, one side of the spoon."

"That's what they were fighting about?"

"I don't know, and then they came and dropped us off here so we wouldn't have to be sitting in the car while they finished having their talk." The words were punching out of her as though she were short of breath, with a loud chipperness, and her cheeks had pink rashes.

Isobel, who, it now struck me, had been arranging the same piece of toilet paper for quite some time, broke into a dreamy singsong: "One side of the plate, one side of the spoon." Something about the incantatory sound of this—in a voice you might use for telling stories to a doll—and the sight of her there— folding and refolding the fluttery white tissue, gazing at it with her head cocked and her underpants dangling around her ankles—gave me a dizzy, addled feeling. I stared at her, transfixed and disoriented, until it came to me why.

She reminded me of *me*, making too much of those words, salvaging the sound, working her tongue over the chosen phrase. I thought it probably meant nothing at all, this one-side-of-the-plate-one-side-of-the-spoon. I didn't suppose it was at the heart of any fight between Bill and Dr. Rouen, only something Norah had misheard or misunderstood, something trivial and out of context—but I could see how it would happen: how a little chain of words could settle in and take root, like Dr. Rouen's salicornia, runner roots that would spread beneath the surface and later send up shoots that would seem to blossom with significance.

"Hurry up, Isobel," commanded her sister.

Isobel sighed and disposed of the length of toilet paper, and finally slid off the seat. Then, still within the stall, she looked up at Norah. "When are we going to go home?"

"We just got here. Pull up your underwear."

"No, not tonight," she said, obeying. "I mean when are we going to go *home?*" Her face had suddenly taken on a pressurized fullness, as though she might sob.

"At the end of the summer."

"How many more weeks till the end of summer?"

"I don't know," said Norah quietly. "Two?"

"And then are we all going home together?"

"Of course. Come out of there now. Wash your hands."

Over at the sink, Isobel was too short to reach the water, so Norah boosted her up.

Cal had gone home sick, said Hy.

"How sick?"

"Well, he has a cold."

"I know."

"He wasn't feeling well." Hy was taking a break from dancing. She had a blue paper napkin, which she was wiping down her neck and across the top of her chest. Her bones and muscles showed clearly under the skin. With the low lights and gleaming sweat, everybody's underlying structures were highly defined. Hy looked sinewy and old. Tilly's braid looked labyrinthine.

She was standing a short distance away, with Walter. She had her fingers on the rim of a cup of punch, which she dangled up close to her collarbone but did not drink from; it looked like a prop there, high and idle, the liquid sloshing a little when she moved. The back of her head was turned toward us, and I could not keep from staring at the blue-black braid, which looked like a riddle in this light, like an optical illusion, one interlocking cable diving into itself again and again, each segment plump in the middle, tapered at either end, the shape reminding me of mussel shells, a clump of mussel shells knotted underneath by byssal threads.

Walter was drinking no punch. He had his hands down his front jeans pockets, kind of jammed into them so his shoulders rode up, and his gaze wasn't directed at Tilly so much as over her head, traveling restlessly around the room. His eyebrows tented faintly toward the middle of his forehead.

Dr. Rouen appeared beside him. She had Gus on her hip. A tight smile sprang to her lips as she glanced briefly at Tilly, then faded while she leaned her head near Walter's—I had never noticed how he was nearly her height—and spoke by his ear. He nodded several times without any expression on his face, just short jerks of the head. He looked different tonight, not only taller but something else, something around the mouth or eyes.

Bill Rouen came through the crowd and maneuvered himself to stand behind his wife. Walter, without looking at him, shifted his body away. I saw Bill Rouen's hand slip around his wife's Gus-less hip and rest there. Dr. Rouen looked down at the fingers with great concentration, as though working out a difficult math problem in her head, and then the muscles of her face softened, and slowly, she leaned her head back against Bill Rouen's chest and shut her eyes. Bill Rouen rested his chin on the crown of her head. His eyes then slid over to Walter and Tilly.

I don't what he said—his lips moved, his jaw worked open

and shut against his wife's skull—and I don't know whether his comment was addressed to Dr. Rouen or Walter or Gus or Tilly, only that Walter's neck and ears became dark pink, and when he spoke, his words were bitter and somehow also dark pink and they cut roughly through the amplified music to reach my ears. "You don't know anything about it."

Dr. Rouen opened her eyes and lifted her head, but Walter had already pushed away through the knots of people, with Tilly weaving neatly behind him.

"Hy," I said.

"Mm?" She glanced down from the dancers she'd been watching, her apple-seed eyes smiling happy-sad and far away. "Mm?" she said again.

"Nothing. When can we go?"

"Soon."

I looked back over at the three Rouens and they stood frozen now amid jostling bodies, a small still-life of a wreck, his hand off her hip and his chin off her crown, her eyes shut again, Gus intent on his knee.

"Tilly." I found her against the back wall, near the spot where the picture ought to have hung.

She managed to look down at me in a way that suggested she was more than a head taller. "Mm? Hi." I saw her lips move without hearing her voice, caught in crossfire from the speakers.

Walter, beside her, nodded hi at me in a polite, humorless way, then returned his gaze restlessly to the room at large. His fists were still shoved in his pockets, so that his shoulders stuck up by his ears, and there was something else, too, different.

"Can I taste that?" I shouted.

Tilly handed me her cup and I sipped red punch. When I went to hand it back, she shook her head and shoved her own fists deep in her pockets.

"I have to tell you something," I shouted.

"What?" She bent her ear to me. Wisps from her braid stuck out around it.

"I have to talk with you," I shouted again. "I really have to."

She rolled her eyes but said, "C'mere," and, pinching a piece of my shirt in her fingers, led me toward the door, shooting Walter a look to come on. He followed. We got out on the stoop. "What?" said Tilly. Walter stood a step above us, making himself skinny against the banister so people could get by. The banister was slick with mist. Already Tilly's hair was coated in it, a fine silver beading defining each wisp.

"I have something to tell you," I repeated.

"Yeah, so . . ." Tilly widened her eyes and jutted her chin forward impatiently.

"It's private."

Tilly sighed and again led me by the shirt, this time down the steps to a quieter patch of sidewalk. Walter trailed us still. I wanted to tell her what I saw Bill Rouen do with his thumb and Dr. Rouen's mouth. I wanted to see what she'd say, whether she'd be surprised or whether that was something she knew about, something grown-ups did, and then maybe she'd know if it was awful or not. I wanted to tell her that Dr. Rouen might leave, that she'd lied about going back for her sweater, that Bill Rouen had fallen down in the lake and that he washed only one side of the plates, that Isobel wanted to go home and Cal was sick and I'd stolen the newspaper article and smashed it among the auto parts. I wanted to tell her Hy wasn't so good to talk to, and the licorice librarian had said I looked like our mother, and Bill Rouen had licked my wrist and called me nut-brown, and also that her hair looked too silly and foreign like that and she had to be nice to me.

But Walter was standing there, hovering, fists in jeans, not looking at me, not in the conversation, but planting himself on the periphery, listening.

"I said it's private."

"Just tell me, Mole. Walter doesn't care."

"But, Tilly—" I said.

"Oh, well." Tilly, deciding my time was up, swiveled and started away.

"Fine," I spat after her, quickly, casting about for the most barbed remark. "Then we can tell Walter that it's all a game."

"I don't know what you're talking about," said Tilly, but she dropped her voice to say it, turning back to me so that she shielded Walter out some.

"Let's tell Walter how you've been lying to him about our parents. How you made up the whole story that there's something fishy just so you could impress him."

"You're the liar."

"You are. There's no information to find out."

"I don't know that."

"Yes, you know that."

We were both breathing with our mouths open.

"It's a game, Tilly. All right, I did it, too. It's fake. The whole library thing, and the cemetery. You weren't even trying to learn anything. If you want to know where they're buried, why don't you ask Hy?" She stared at me, and even in the dark I could see water trembling in her eyes. I stared back, not sorry. Well, a little sorry, but not enough not to add, "You know you could have asked her all along." A tear slipped out of one of her eyes. I had a terrible sense of relief.

But when she spoke, her voice sounded level and absolutely bored. "Are you done? If so, I'd like to get back to the social." She started to leave.

I was still holding her punch that she didn't want to drink anymore after I'd had one sip. I looked at the cup in my hand, then deliberately turned it upside down, shoving it forward a bit as I did so. The little bit left splashed Tilly up the backs of her legs.

She gasped and turned back, slowly. "Nice." She pulled the empty cup out of my hand. I reached for it and she jerked her hand away; I scratched her arm instead and she slapped me across the face. Quick as if she'd been prepared to do it. And cool. Her cheap little Walter-bracelet stinging my cheek. I punched her chest and then we were fighting as we did not ever fight, right there in the street with our hands balled, hitting and yanking and shoving, "brawling," as Bill Rouen would say, curling the word ironically around his mouth, so that it was as if he were laughing at us now.

Walter separated us. He was surprisingly strong. His fingers, clamped around my upper arm as he yanked me off Tilly, hurt more than her punches had. Tilly, her face ducked down, fumbled to tuck in strands that had come loose from her braid.

"See, you know I'm right," I said. My voice shook.

She faced me. "Fuck you, Mole. I hate you." She spoke softly, but a tremor passed over her face, as though the ugliness of her words was a shock to her, too. Then she walked away.

Walter and I met each other's eyes for one second; accidentally, it seemed, there being nothing in his gaze, neither sympathy nor reproof, and him glancing away again as inadvertently, catching up with Tilly in a matter of strides. It came to me the other thing that was different about him: he had left his eyeglasses home.

I lost track of everybody after that. I wandered up and down the sidewalk for a bit, reluctant to go back inside, and watched families thin out toward their cars and teenagers form and dissolve and re-form little clusters. A tussle broke out in the firehouse driveway. Two boys punched each other, silently: the sounds of their blows and their breaths carried through the wet air. Several other boys came to break it up. A car down the street revved loudly then, peeled out, and disappeared in the direction of the lake. Just down the block, a girl with big thighs and a short skirt was leaning on the hood of a car, her shoulders heaving. Another girl patted her over and over, listlessly, on the back. The mist turned almost imperceptibly to rain.

I stepped inside again just as the rows of overhead lights were being turned back on. People were blinking, ransacking piles of sweaters and shoes for their belongings. Bits of potato chips and pretzels crunched underfoot. Crumpled blue napkins dotted the floor like cornflowers. Cal was, of course, already gone; I didn't spot Tilly or Walter either; nor Hy, Dr. Rouen, Norah, Gus.

A single, unlikely couple remained on the dance floor: Isobel and Bill Rouen. She was standing on her father's feet, his brass scorpion buckle level with her mouth. She looked proud and intent, gripping his fingers—two from each hand—tightly in her fists, gripping her own tongue between her teeth.

But it was the sight of Bill Rouen that held my attention, Bill Rouen the strange, the wrist-licking, eye-winking, name-calling one, who hadn't spoken to me since the day he'd called me "nut-brown" and "little priss" and gone crashing idiotically out of the boat and into the lake. And just now his face pierced me; it appeared infinitely tender, a little haggard, and caught up in perfect fatherliness as he went riding his child carefully on the tops of his big shoes.

"Mole." Hy's big hands cupped my shoulders. I tilted my neck back and looked at her upside-down face. "Have you seen Tilly?"

I shook my head. Immediately into my mind came the last image of her, walking away from me, stiff-backed, into the heavy mist.

"Hm." Hy removed the solid pressure of her hands. My shoulders seemed to drift up without them. She walked away from me, clicking unaccustomedly in her heels. I turned and watched. She went to Dr. Rouen, standing over by the back wall, and they conferred inaudibly. I saw Bill Rouen notice them, too, and gently shake Isobel off his shoes in order to go join them. She drifted over to the refreshment table, where Norah and Gus already stood, licking their fingers and then pressing them into the potato chip bowl to get whatever crumbs were left. Their faces looked drawn, their eyes pink-rimmed with exhaustion. A fireman's wife had gotten out a push broom and was beginning to sweep the floor. Hy clicked back over to me. "Walter's not here either," she said. "Did either of them say anything to you about leaving?"

"No." Beyond Hy I could see Bill and Dr. Rouen in further conversation against the wall. He had his thumbs slung down behind his belt buckle and his head lowered so that his voice might travel more directly to her ear, and she was turned sideways to him, frowning and nodding. They appeared deep inside the same kind of communication as when I watched them go to the river from my bedroom window: serious, dependable. Now that their actual features were within view, I could see nothing in them to suggest what I would call warmth or affection, but still, I found something exemplary in the sight of them, something that was in a way even heightened by the lack of smiling, lack of touch: a kind of collaboration bred of necessity, of fact.

"Did either of them say anything to you that would give you some idea where they might have gone?" asked Hy.

I shook my head. I pictured them, in rapid succession, in the old cemetery at the top of the hill, at the mussel cove, winding down the steep arm of Ice Cart Road to the river. They might be anywhere back in behind the lake, entwined in joint moodiness, talking about science and parents and annoying younger siblings.

Hy straightened and crossed once more to the doctors Rouen. There was something in their manner now of evaluation and planning. Norah and Isobel and Gus looked up from their chips, greasy fingers poised midair, and watched. The room was nearly cleared out now, except for the woman sweeping and a man winding an extension cord around his elbow. I moved toward the Rouen kids and their eyes flicked to me and then back to the grown-ups. I could feel the energy accumulating, drawing all seven of us together.

Presently, the grown-ups broke their huddle. The Rouens

called their kids over to claim sweaters and things, and Hy came to me, taking car keys from her pocket as she walked and twirling them once with a little metallic shake. "Okay," she said. "Bill's going to drive straight home and put the little kids to bed. Delia's going to head back on foot, because we think they probably did the same. And I'm going to take our car and drive around town a little bit, see if I spot them, then catch up with Delia. You can go back now or come with me; you have your choice."

"Are you worried?"

"No."

"Are you mad?"

"I'm annoyed."

"I think I'll walk with Dr. Rouen."

"That's not really what I meant, Mole. I mean you can either come with me if you want or get a ride straight home with Bill."

"But why can't I go with Dr. Rouen? I feel like walking."

"Because it's late," began Hy, and then she frowned at her own illogic.

The Rouens were by now all rounded up and sort of hovering by the door, the children yawning and slack-faced, waiting to see whether I was coming or not. Bill Rouen held Gus. He had his eyes closed and his head down on his father's shoulder. Dr. Rouen reached up and smoothed a piece of hair off his small forehead, and it was almost like she was touching Bill.

Hy went to the door. "Mole would like to walk?"

"Sure." Dr. Rouen nodded crisply. We all went out.

Going down the street, heading all together toward our various destinations—two separate cars and Ice Cart Road—I was surprised to notice that I felt very good. Rain skimmed us lightly, coated us with its warm breath. The street, now dark and mostly emptied out, seemed unfunny, unfrivolous. And though we walked mutely, the little children draggy with fatigue, the grown-ups silent with whatever secret thoughts they harbored, and two of us missing altogether, I thought we were at our best then, the group of us making our way down the street. I thought we showed real promise, setting out to complete our agreed-upon tasks: some of us going to tuck children into bed, some of us going to gather in the others.

Not until we'd split up, the two cars driven off in the cushioned swish of wet tires, did I regret my decision to walk with Dr. Rouen. I began to have the tiny, unsettling impression that walking home was not anything she particularly intended to do. This did not derive from anything she said; in fact, she did not say anything. She only walked, rhythmically and unhurriedly, and barefoot, I noticed disapprovingly: her shoes dangled from two fingers against her thigh. Her black cotton shift grew sleek in the rain and pressed close to her body. Walking through the warmth and wetness was like swimming, and my head swam as we walked, and the rain gathered speed.

I raised my hand to my mouth, splayed the fingers across it, moved my thumb between my lips experimentally. Trying to see what it meant. *Stay*, he'd said. It was a little like hooking a fish. I stole a sideways glance at Dr. Rouen. She walked with her face tilted up toward the rain, and it broke over her brow and nose and teeth. Her mouth was open.

"Are you worried?" I asked, more as a suggestion than a true question.

She blinked, licked her lips, looked down at me. "About Walter, you mean? And your sister? Not really. They probably just got bored and went back to the house."

"Are you mad?"

"At them? I suppose I should be."

"But you don't really mind?"

She shook her head. She had her face slanted to the rain again.

We veered onto Ice Cart Road, where the darkness intensified, tucked itself in around us. Now her face, when I looked, became eerie, grotesquely featureless, except for a gleam of dark eye, wet nostril, tooth. The road before us began to climb, and we climbed for a long time and still there was no light coming through the trees to signal the dead house, and no sound of a car engine to signal Hy circling back to meet us. I thought it was about the place where Tilly had put her foot through infinity.

Dr. Rouen didn't speak, she just climbed and climbed in her rhythmic gait, her wet black dress, her bare feet, and then she began softly to sing, that song she always sang in a language I didn't know, and all that came from her was neither worried nor annoyed, but strangely content. She walked slowly through the dark as though she were alone and free, as though the rain coursing over her body were the most natural thing, as though she didn't belong to anybody or anybody to her, and I was afraid the road had been jinxed and we would never see the lights of the dead house, only pass it by and continue up over the hill. And it was not a way for a mother to act. *Stay*, he had said. Nothing you should have to say to a mother. *Sealskin*, Tilly had read. I looked at Dr. Rouen in her black shift, undulating featurelessly through the rain. I knew it was just a story Walter had brought us; I knew it was just made up, the things Tilly said about our parents' drowning, but it was so dark on Ice Cart Road, and Dr. Rouen so distant and barefoot and singing to herself.

Then there came two lights at once: from just ahead, house lights; from behind, headlights. Dr. Rouen stopped singing. We moved in unison to the side of the road. Hy's car slowed and came even with us just as we all rounded the bend, and then it stopped, idling loudly, illuminating the dead house and Bill Rouen, who was coming at a clip across the lawn.

Hy rolled down the window and leaned her head into the rain. "No sign?"

Dr. Rouen, who in the sudden presence of lights and adults seemed to have reentered her sensible, concrete self, shook her head briskly no.

"They're not at our house; I checked," said Hy. And both women, their faces undergoing minute changes as their thinking seemed plainly to escalate to new levels of urgency, exchanged glances of discreet but unmistakable unease.

Bill Rouen, jogging damply across the lawn, reached us then, his shoes skidding momentarily on the sopping weeds as he brought himself up short. The women looked at him with quiet concern gathering in their faces, and he, with voice strained by the opposing efforts of catching his breath and trying to sound casual, reported, "Walter's bike's not here."

The opposite of a sigh pricked the wet air around us. I did not know whether the intake of breath was traceable to Hy or Dr. Rouen or me or none of us; possibly it came from the trees: a sound of wind, or of the rain faltering, a tiny stoppage. And when everything resumed a moment later, a brand-new sense of

crisis had crystallized among the grown-ups. With terrible alertness and concentration, they turned to me, worry fairly singing
from their bodies, and issued a fast list of questions—"Are you
absolutely certain, Mole, they didn't mention anything? Where
were they headed? Were they together? Did they say what they
were intending to do?"—and up from my throat, while I looked
at this trio of tightly pursed mouths and narrowed eyes, came
one of those strange, misplaced laughs that cannot be helped.

"This is not a joke," said Hy.

"I know. I wasn't laughing—"

"What do you know about where they are?"

"No—I mean nothing—I don't know." It was just that these
were *my* questions; these were what *I* was always wondering,
about my mother and my father, about Dr. Rouen and Bill; these
were all the things I cared about knowing and no one could tell
me, and here now were the three of them, and it was all turned
around. *They* were turning to *me* for information, glaring at me
through rain as though I were the one withholding something of
importance, and really, I had nothing, knew nothing, and in spite
of myself, now emitted again a feeble, helpless kind of laugh. My
lips were wet with rain.

Hy considered me briefly, then turned away to face the adults,
and they talked then, just them three. I half listened. Lightning
flashed, and I jumped when the crack came a few seconds later.
I edged nearer Hy, touched her wet dress.

And from this position I gained within the triangle of their
bodies, I watched Dr. Rouen slip her shoes back on, and as she
did, steady herself with one hand reaching absently for her husband's forearm. This he held stiff and strong for her, a bar, a post

for her to lean against, and all the while each remained focused only on the rapid conversation, the talk of the missing children and what was to be done.

They made a plan. Hy and Dr. Rouen would drop me home. I was to get myself dry and put myself to bed. The two women would drive full around the lake with their eyes out for bikes and, if necessary, continue back through town. Bill would stay with the little children, already in bed. He would wait at the dead house, by the telephone. Thunder rumbled. The doors of the car got opened. "Mole, hurry in." I sat, my wet shorts puddling the vinyl backseat. The father jogged back over the lawn. The wipers began their metronomic lament.

"I wouldn't be worried," said the mother.

"I'm just not crazy about this lightning," said Hy as more came. We rolled to a stop in front of our house, large and hunched in the rain, with none but the porch light on.

"Okay, Mole?" said Hy. "I won't come in."

I hesitated.

"We'll be back soon, but go to bed, don't wait up," she said impatiently.

I opened my door, stuck one foot out. "But don't be mad at me, Hy."

"I'm not." She turned around in the driver's seat, spoke more gently. "Go on, Mole, get dry now and go to bed."

It thundered and I got out and they drove away, toward the fork where Dr. Rouen and Bill would normally veer left, go over the ridge, down to the Kittiwake and the marsh. But the sound of the engine fell away to the right tonight as they circled the lake, looking for Tilly and Walter on their bikes.

*   *   *

Lightning came again, and quick thunder, as I crossed the sopping grass toward our house, which looked very desolate, from its high peaked forehead to its cellar casement windows, a dark and closed box, bound up in itself. I clattered up the steps, out of the rain, and pushed open the door, which we never locked. Inside, I immediately clicked on the hall light. Then I stood frozen, one hand still on the doorknob, my heart skittering. I thought I heard the house breathing.

The fixture over my head dispensed a waxy yellow light over the grave emptiness of the hall, the immobile staircase and its silent banister, the dark windows, dark doorframes. I wished I were still in the car with Hy and Dr. Rouen. I waited a long moment, straining my ears for anything unnatural, before I relaxed and pushed shut the door—and froze again. Tangled up in the sound of the hinge and the lock I could have sworn I heard the house titter and shush itself. A voice floated thinly from the rear: "Is it just you, Mole?"

"Tilly!" I exclaimed, and headed, for some reason stealthily, through the dark living room doorway.

"Sh-sh-sh!" she cried out softly as I circled through the living room toward her voice, coming from the kitchen. "Walk carefully! Tiptoe!"

"What? Why aren't the lights on? Where are you?" I came to the kitchen doorway and paused, my eyes adjusting to darkness. The only glow inside the room came from the oven: not the light over the burners, but a rosy glow from the pilot light inside the oven itself, the door to which gaped partway open. A piece of cloth draped across its mouth. Across the room, by the pantry, I made out Tilly's legs, stretched out along the tile floor in a no-moon, no-stars kind of gray light; she was sitting with her back against the wall, beneath the side window. Beside her were boy legs, long and trousered. "You guys are in big trouble."

"Walter has done the best thing," Tilly crooned in a floaty, unbothered way. "Look."

"They're looking for you," I said. "How come the lights are off? They're worried. Your bikes are missing."

"Shhhh," said Tilly, and giggled.

I took a step into the room, reaching toward the cord that dangled from the light over the table.

"No—don't! Don't shake the table. Look," she urged again. Her voice sounded dislocated, pearly, and I wondered that it contained no edge of hardness from our fight outside the social less than an hour ago.

I drew back my hand, seeing just now what she meant. All of the eggs that Hy and I had bought early in the week, the full dozen, had been removed from their carton and placed around the kitchen: two on the table, one on a chair, one on top of the refrigerator, one on the windowsill, one on the toaster, one on the pile of cookbooks, one on the threshold to the pantry . . . everywhere I looked in the frail light of the kitchen, another pale matte ellipsoid seemed to emerge from the grainy rain-wavering shadows and assert itself: a cool white fact. The peculiar thing was that each egg lay not on its side, but pointed straight up, sitting tall on its rounded bottom.

"Magic," whispered Tilly. "Walter did it."

Fishing line, I thought, and passed my hand tentatively over the top of the egg nearest me on the table. But there was only air. The egg didn't even wobble, but remained preposterously, presumptuously upright.

"Is it the tides?" I whispered back. "Is it something with the moon?"

Tilly giggled again, something she was not normally wont to do, and I looked sharply at the space where the two of them sat on the floor beneath the window. Watery light passed over the tops of their heads, made them silver-haired. A kind of amber flicked weakly along their legs, from the gas stove. They seemed not like Walter and Tilly, but transformed versions of themselves, seal-like and reckless and capable of enchantment: *Walter and Tilly slipped away from the social and entered the darkness behind Pillow Lake, the rainy darkness where they gathered up eggs and made them point straight at the sky . . .*

"It's magic," Tilly repeated, and I could hear a foolish smug smile color her syllables.

Lightning again, almost greenish, outside. Somewhere on the loop of Ice Cart Road, two women were driving with anxious hearts, their party dresses soaking the seats, their eyes finally alert and attentive, straining past darkness and windshield wipers. And down the road a man, finally shaken free of irony, was sitting by the phone. Thunder followed. Panes rattled. There had been enough pretend.

"There is no such thing," I said, low and level, as if speaking to a guilty puppy, and I brought the flat of my hand down hard on the table. The two eggs tumbled over obediently on their sides, returned to their normal selves, and lay there rocking to and fro.

"It's salt," said Walter, and burped in a moist and sprawling way.

Tilly laughed.

I looked at them more closely, my eyes having grown better accustomed to the gray. "Why is Walter wearing no shirt?"

He passed a listless hand over his bare chest, thinner than Bill Rouen's, hairless and flat. Thin as he was, you could see tiny pleats of flesh at his stomach, and the contour of muscles, the apparatus beneath the skin.

"Got wet," he said, only the words were misshapen, dull, as if their corners had been knocked off with a mallet.

"It's drying," added Tilly, nodding more or less at the oven, and I saw now that the cloth draped across the open door was indeed Walter's shirt, lit a soft orange from the glow of the pilot light inside.

"What's the matter with you both? You're in trouble. They're worried about you." I looked round the room, taking in all the eggs again, furious at them in their whimsy, their insolent erectness. "These are for your birthday cake, Tilly. You don't play with them." The words came out in tightly furious bunches I could not help; I was suddenly vibrating with rage. "Get up. Get up!" I demanded, and moved toward them and kicked something over: a can, silver and empty. It rolled hollowly across tiles into the pantry.

"Oops," said Tilly. I noticed an identical can by her side, and next to Walter a cluster of others.

"What are those?"

"Don't tell," said Tilly.

"It's beer?"

"Duh."

"*Tilly.*" I felt righteous, but her name came out sounding more like a plea.

"I only had one and a half," she said, but suddenly there was more Tilly in her voice, the big-sister variety, with reassurance and authority tucked in around each other, and now she got to her feet, using the sill behind her for leverage. She stood with her back to the window, a head taller than me and lovely, with her French braid entirely unraveled, hanging in black spikes across her pale face and neck; her damp blouse molded against her strong shoulders and what I could see had become actual breasts, small but shaped like the real thing, like little meringues; and her face for once was gentle and unguarded, stripped to soft uncertainty and concern. We held gazes for a moment; I thought she might tell me something important. I thought she was glad I'd come and found them. But she had no words.

"What about him?" I asked, looking at Walter, who appeared to have gone to sleep with his mouth a tiny bit open, his head back against the wall. "He had more?"

"Uh, four? And a half?"

We both looked at him. Tilly prodded his hip with her toe. His eyes came right open. "Yeah?"

"You have to go," said Tilly. "Walter, you have to go home right now."

He obliged, groggily getting to his feet, knocking over a few of the cans beside him, and began to follow as she led him through toward the front hall. I brought up the rear. When he suddenly pivoted around, he stepped on my toe.

"No, Walter, come on! This way," said Tilly.

"My bike," he mumbled.

"Leave it; you can get it tomorrow."

"No, no. I need my bike." And he navigated himself back through the kitchen, with all its strange eggs and empty silver cans and the red glow from the oven, and through the pantry, where he fumbled for a moment with the door before flinging it open. Rain sprinkled the soaked dirt and pebbles of our drive. It appeared to be letting up. I noticed the moon now over the stable, a wan lump beyond the clouds, but showing through. Tilly and I stood inside the pantry and watched Walter pick his bicycle up off the ground, sling his leg over it, and pedal, jerkily at first, so that I was reminded of Bill Rouen struggling into and out of the rowboat. But then he evened out and disappeared down the drive.

Tilly's bike remained there, also lying unnaturally on its side instead of propped on its kickstand. She said in her normal voice, "It'll rust," and stepped out to retrieve it. I kept her company through the lessening rain as she walked it around the side of the house to the dry front porch and leaned it there against the side of the house, next to mine. We were set to head back through the front door when, from down the road, we heard the screech of wet tires and the crisp, metallic ring of a sickeningly light crash.

CHAPTER ✦ THIRTEEN

BILL ROUEN HAD a drink in a short, heavy glass. The liquid was pale amber and there were ice cubes in it and they made a quiet, hard sound from time to time. He sat in the cane-backed chair on the porch of the dead house. I sat on the first step with my knees pressed together and my palms pressed together between my knees. I was very tired; the night had been too long already, but it wasn't yet possible to go to sleep. Tilly sat on the porch railing facing in, toward the house and toward Bill. Her hair hung in loose damp clumps. They curved forward across her cheek and chin. The dark striations against the pale were all I could see of her face.

Walter had slammed into Hy's car as she and Dr. Rouen had swept around the bend on their way back to the dead house. They had given up on finding Tilly and Walter in the rain, and decided to head back to update Bill and call the police. Coming around the blind curve, they had seen the figure coming toward them on a bike. Hy braked and Walter continued, sailing into the bumper of the car and flipping over the handlebars. He had landed on his back and not answered to his name.

This was the story Tilly and I pieced together from what Dr. Rouen and Hy were saying when we reached them, out of breath and full of dread. The car motor was still on. They were kneeling side by side in the road, Dr. Rouen feeling tenderly and professionally all along her son's body, and they were talking to each other in quick, low voices, and then to Tilly and me, asking with terrible efficiency and calmness why Walter's shirt was missing, what he had been doing, what that smell was—alcohol?—on his breath. Tilly's own breath came raspingly and did not form speech. Spillover from the white beams of Hy's car bathed us in harsh, mist-stippled light; the rain had backed off almost completely now. I could see Dr. Rouen's hands working swiftly, thoroughly, over scratched torso and freckled limb. Then Walter began to make small sounds and Dr. Rouen's voice changed, became so soft I wanted to cry, and she said, "What hurts, Walt, besides the shoulder?" I couldn't understand his response.

There followed some quiet talking between the two women; of it, all I understood was Hy asking whether Dr. Rouen wanted her to get Bill. But she didn't; they lifted Walter together into the backseat of Hy's car. Dr. Rouen slid in after him and Hy got up front. She said, not to Tilly but to me, out of her rolled-down window, "Mole, go into the house and tell Bill. We'll call from the hospital." Then the car did a U-turn, lights swinging giddily through the pines (with a piece of my mind I registered the green, as though it were important, something needing noticing), and disappeared back down the road.

Beside me, Tilly swayed. I turned my head to her quickly.

"I'm okay." She was looking straight ahead. The dead house showed lights on both up and down. It looked crazily inviting, fairy-tale cozy. Neither of us moved toward it. I tried to scrape from my mind the picture of Walter on the road, his white back crossed with scratches, his hands big and limp at the ends of his wrists. I thought of him in our kitchen, leaning back against the shadowy wall beside the cluster of silver cans, swaddled in heavy silence.

"What were you guys doing?" I asked.

A sigh. "Just, nothing."

"But, Tilly—"

No more rain was falling on us. We could hear it dripping still off the leaves of trees.

"But tell me," I insisted, and was surprised by the authority in my own voice. "I want to know."

And her resistance must have been used up, or maybe she wanted to tell, because she obliged. From her stunned and tired mouth came the events, in pieces: how Walter had been angry with his parents and she had been angry with me, and they had left the social and walked back to the dead house, and how Walter had gotten the six-pack of beer from the fridge, and Tilly had held it in her arms while he rode her on his handlebars to our house, to pick up her bike, and how they had been going to ride down over the ridge to the Kittiwake for once and go skinny-dipping there, because Walter said the water always feels warmest when it's raining, only then the lightning had begun, and they had been that sensible, at least, to change the plan and come inside, and then Walter had said they should dry their shirts out, and Tilly had said she didn't think she would hers, but she had lit the oven for Walter and he'd stripped his off and hung his there to dry, and how then they had cracked open the beers and spread out on the kitchen floor and he had leaned over and Tilly had thought he might be about to try to kiss her, but instead he had gotten up and taken all the eggs out of the fridge, and the salt shaker, and told her it was something he'd learned in science about the nature of crystals, and he wanted to do it for her, and he had made this whole egg-thing all around the room and then come and lain back down beside her and they had just watched it, the wonderful eggs in the flashes of lightning, like they were watching TV or something, until I came in.

Unmistakably, it was nice to be told. But even as I listened I could sense how it wasn't the same thing as really knowing how it had been. I looked at Tilly. She was still facing straight ahead. She had a clear tiredness about her, as though she had woken from a particularly exhausting dream. What I liked best about the story was the part where they decided not to go to the Kittiwake when the lightning began. I thought about saying that, but then Tilly took a breath and said, "Come on. We have to tell Bill," and started across the lawn. At first I thought she meant tell him about her and Walter and the beer and the trick with the eggs and everything she had just told me, but then I realized she just meant the message about Walter being hurt and going to the hospital. I had followed her over wet crabgrass and thistles and up the porch steps and we knocked and Bill had come very quickly to the door.

And now, twenty minutes, a half hour, an hour later—I could not judge—we sat on the porch still, the two of us and Bill Rouen, and waited for the phone to ring. The little Rouens had all stayed fast asleep upstairs. The citronella candle burned, and it made that same song come into my head, "*What can you do, Citronella,*

Citronella? What can you do, Citronella little girl?" I thought about singing it for Tilly, asking if she recognized it, but I did not. I suddenly ached to tell her what I'd done with the framed news article out in Steve Day's lot. And I wished I had told her about the disturbing afternoon when Bill Rouen had stumbled down to the rocky cove and landed on my mussel houses and uttered those strange words out to the lake. I looked over to where she sat on the rail on the other side of the steps: a profile feathered black, a candlelit shin and knee. She seemed all right now, quiet, but steady as herself. I realized how little of her was not unknown to me.

Bill Rouen had appeared full of concern when he first came to the door, but when we told him what had happened to Walter, and that Dr. Rouen and Hy had taken him straight to the hospital and sent us along to deliver the message, his concern seemed to give way to anger, and this anger to grow more bitter and silent as the minutes passed and the phone did not ring. He did not ask us in, but sat with us on the porch, saying nothing except once, when he went to refill his glass and did the queer thing of offering, in a brusque, sarcastic way, to get one for Tilly. She said no, of course, sounding aghast and almost shaken. I wondered if he knew or suspected about the beer. He treated me no special way at all, and I didn't know whether I minded or was glad of the absence of any reference to his earlier strangeness at the lake. When he returned with his fresh drink, he seemed more relaxed, pleasanter—offering to bring out chairs for me and Tilly while we waited (we declined) and making an odd remark about the rains "rejuvenating the lands and leaving them pure and fertile"— but it was hard to tell with him.

After what seemed ages, the telephone rang. Bill Rouen stood; ice clinked. He brought his drink inside the house, picked up on the third ring. The profile and bit of leg that was Tilly moved; she slid off the railing and shifted slightly toward the door, in order to overhear more clearly. But through the screen we could make out only the low rumble of his voice, no words; then the sound of the receiver set heavily back in its cradle; then glass on wood, a cabinet hinge, liquid being poured. He came back through the house at a leisurely-sounding pace. Tilly stepped away from the door. He creaked with his glass onto the porch, paused, and with his fingers guided the door to a gentle close.

"Well," said Bill Rouen, "he is okay." Although Tilly had positioned herself before him, he addressed the bushes just past the railing, with precision. "Nothing broken. A sprained shoulder and a bruised xiphoid process. From the handlebar, apparently. They're on their way home." Either his hand was unsteady or he kept toasting the bushes with tiny gestures as he spoke.

"What's a xiphoid process?" asked Tilly, with her hands behind her back and no lisp at all. Her voice sounded cracked and thin; it must've been about an hour since she'd last used it.

Bill swiveled to her and paused consideringly before he answered. A muscle tightened near his eye. It was as though he was noticing her all over again, standing there in her still-damp blouse, exhausted and pale. "It is the point at the tip of your sternum," he said with measured interest.

"What's your sternum?" asked Tilly.

A wind blew and the citronella flame lowered and rose up again in the interval before he responded: "Your breastbone," and with the hand that held the drink, brought his middle finger to

the center of his own chest and touched it lightly there. Ice
clinked against glass. Then his voice took on a falsely suave edge;
he leaned toward her confidentially, cocked his head. "If you were
any older, I'd show you myself."

Tilly was still.

"You know," said Bill Rouen into that silence, straightening,
regaining a quiet deliberateness of tone, "this is my birthday."
The ice chinked. His voice flattened, reminding me exactly of fur
on the back of an animal's neck. "If you were any older, I'd have
to ask you for a kiss."

Still Tilly made no response. He stared at her, waiting. She
neither spoke nor laughed. In the face of her unsmiling silence,
the import of his words seemed to grow heavy and imposing.

"Little nymph," he said, unkindly. Did he mean like a water
nymph, a sea maiden, like that? But the word was ugly in his
mouth.

I slid my palm lightly over the wooden porch, courting a
splinter. Tilly stood rigidly before him, oddly silent, letting him
go on. *She's very tired*, I thought. *And must feel bad about Walter.*
I passed my palm more roughly over the ends of the floorboards.

"Nymph with beer-breath." Even more unkindly. And he
smiled after that, with one half of his mouth only.

I saw him rock, almost imperceptibly, onto the balls of his
feet, then steady back on his heels. Ice knocking against glass.
His eyes looked at her body. Her shirt was not so wet anymore,
but it still rested damply in such a way as to broadcast her small
mounds, and tiny peaks of nipples, with candlelight dancing
across her front.

"Beer-breath birthday biss. Kiss. Of course, you *are* older, are you not?" His voice had a hint of playfulness; his pale eyes, trained back on her face, had none. "It is past midnight," he continued quietly, not consulting any watch. "How old are you, prithee tell?"

The phrase sickened me. It was as though I'd heard it before in another context, and it went through me now like a wave of nausea, coming from him on this night: an embittered echo of something that had once been truly light, truly playful. The ice was a constant clicking now, as though the glass were being swirled, but the two of them, face-to-face above me on the porch, looked immobile, frozen. But I could see Tilly gripping one wrist behind her back, fingers visibly depressing the flesh. And when she finally spoke, it was my favorite Tilly: "If it's past midnight"— her voice neat and pointed as scissors—"then it's not your birthday anymore."

Relief broke through me. I thought, *He will give in now, laugh in appreciation of her cleverness, sit once more in the cane-backed chair, and soon Hy will pull up and we'll go home and to bed.* But it did not happen. Her words did not break the spell this time; if anything, they wound it tighter. The same muscle tightened near his eye. "Ah, then," he said in a low voice. "It must be yours."

The pail of citronella was burning near me on the porch. I reached over and laid it quietly on its side. Wax spilled out; I remembered Isobel another night dipping her fingers in hot liquid, saying *Ouch ouch ouch.* Which had been too little to give him pause. I remembered also my splinter, Bill's yellow-jacket sting, the hang glider's accident at Bluefields that first day. Tonight I should have thought Walter's accident would be enough, would do the trick, make him remember how he was supposed to be.

But tonight was long past—the clock had trespassed into the following day; the accident had grown remote; that same little glass had been filled or topped off more times than I could say; he seemed angry tonight in a way I hadn't seen him; and Tilly was not his child. Was barely a child.

"In which case," Bill went on after a pause, "I guess you have to ask *me* for a kiss."

Tilly continued to say nothing. She seemed to be made of stone. I thought I understood what she was doing. Wild animals, evil spirits, bullies—any child knows the advice for handling each is much the same: show fear and you lose. If Tilly could keep mastery over her composure, she would have mastery over herself.

Now he launched softly into song. "Happy birthday to you . . ." easing the notes out slowly, dragging them up from his throat, pausing between lines with a terrible teasing kind of suspense.

I gave the citronella pail a push with my fingers. It rolled up against one leg of the cane-backed chair. A section of newspaper lay on the seat. I eyed smoke from the sideways flame writhe sootily up toward it.

"Happy birthday to you . . . happy birthday, dear Tilly . . ."

Behind his back, the smoke seemed to be licking a hole clear through the newsprint, yet without any flames. I boosted myself up a step, slid a foot over toward the chair, and moved the paper, gently, closer to the flailing candle flame.

"Happy birthday to you . . ."

The smoke increased, roiled grayly around the paper. But it remained slow, actually, to catch fire. I pushed it so it dipped a notch lower over the side of the chair. It caught; a tongue of orange fled up the page.

"And now you get a kiss," said Bill Rouen. "Or is it a spank?"

Fire, freed at last roamed heartily all the length of the paper, crackling now like candy wrappers. Bill Rouen heard the noise and spun around. "What the hell are you doing?" He snatched the paper from me. I drew back, pressing myself against the porch railing. "Ow—shit!" He dropped the burning sheets; a few pieces, charred and holey, twinkling with red sparks, rose tranquilly to the ceiling and snuffed out there, succumbing quietly to ash. The rest he stamped out with his big brown shoes, those upon which Isobel had earlier danced, and then he used the toe of one to kick out the flame in the center of the candle. The porch sank further into darkness. He surveyed the blackened papers, panting, and dribbled a little of his drink on them. They sighed under the drops, released a short hiss of steam. Then, almost as an after-thought, he drank what was left in the glass.

"Stupid," he muttered. "Playing with fire." But he didn't scold me directly, didn't even look at me. He rattled the ice cubes sharply in his empty glass, then turned abruptly back to Tilly, as though a thought had just occurred to him with great force. "That's what you're doing, missy," he told her, his voice suddenly virulent, hoarse with contempt.

She remained impassive.

Still holding the glass, he pointed his middle finger at her. "Playing with fire." He stepped toward her, right close to her, finger out, until it touched her face. She blinked and her lips stiffened, but her body did not budge. He looked confused. His finger, very slowly, as if of its own volition, traced up the side of her cheek to her temple. It was terrible to see her frozen. I hated to see her not move. The glass must've been cold against her face.

Through the screen door, then, Isobel appeared, like a little phantom, wearing pastel pajamas and half crying in a drowsy, distraught way, two hands cupped over the lower part of her face. Through this web of her own fingers she wailed, "Daddy!"

As he turned from Tilly, his hand dropping away from her face, Isobel dropped her own. Blood poured down her face. "Oh, no!" she cried; it was a voice tinged with sleep-muddled terror.

The drink went aside; Bill thrust it at Tilly without looking at her, without even realizing, I thought, that he did so, and she, turning also to see Isobel, accepted it as reflexively, like a surgeon being handed clamps. But it was Bill who was the doctor, who, in the second it took to rid himself of the glass and wheel back to the door, made the switch to doctor, to father, with an alacrity that made his previous behavior seem not possible, imagined. He pulled the screen open and knelt to his daughter.

"It's just a nosebleed, Isobel." His voice was solid and unworried. "We'll take care of that." The hall light skimmed the top of Isobel's head and her father's hands as he cupped one behind her neck and used the other to smooth hair from her face. He felt in his pant pocket and then, not finding what he wanted there, yanked his whole white undershirt over his head, bunched up a corner, and held it to her face. "Tip your head back, Iz, and pinch that part up near the bridge of your nose," he directed, in spite of his words pinching it there himself. His back was wide and luminous. He stood, lifting Isobel in the same motion, without any word to us, and carried her through the hallway. The screen fell shut after them.

"Tilly?" I said. She might have been a statue.

His footsteps landed, sure and powerful, on each wooden tread as he ascended the stairs to take care of his daughter. He rose out of sight.

"Tilly?"

She remained where he had left her, her body turned to look through the door after them, his squat drink glass balanced stiffly on her palm, black wings of hair obscuring her face.

"Till!"

She didn't answer still, so I went to her, went around the front of her to see what was in her face, and it was tears, streaming down, perfectly soundless and abundant, coursing down her contorted features, the rest of her rigid except for her shoulders shuddering in spasms, so that although I'd lost her I could have her still, and I took the glass away and set it on the porch and with both arms comforted her then, Tilly who never, never cried.

The two of us going back down Ice Cart Road, light-headed from no sleep, and raw, spent, from all the events of that night, spotted the strange light and kept walking forward, I, for one, trying to make coherent sense of it, that dancing reddish glow coming through the trees. Disbelief goes a long way; neither of us said anything until we were fifty yards from the blaze, and then Tilly, with no expression, said, "Our house is on fire."

We stood where we were, as if trying to relate the fact of what we were seeing to what she had just said. By now the rain had ended completely, or anyway, moved on: far to the east, lightning rippled the sky but made no sound.

Then I spoke. "Should we go back and ask to use their

phone?" And Tilly hesitated; I think she would have said no. I think maybe she would have had us just wait there, watching it burn, rather than ever return to the dead house. But then came headlights, and Hy, back from the hospital, and then we were in the car, where we waited while she phoned, and then listening for sirens which did not come, only red flashing lights and the engines themselves, two of them—the one from Lefferts and one from somewhere else, another town in cooperation. The massive vehicles rushed out of the blackness with an almost eerie lack of noise. We watched numbly from the car. And we stayed there, Tilly and me, in the front seat, watching through the windshield the flashing lights and the blurry figures of firemen and hoses and the mesmerizing twitch of firelight within our house. Because the fire was slow-burning and contained within the kitchen and pantry, Hy was allowed to make trips in and out of the house, rescuing pieces of furniture and things from water-and-smoke damage, and so we watched her as well, moving with surreal tranquility to and fro across the lawn, piling chairs and pictures and things on the grass. In fact, not just Hy but all the firemen, too, seemed bizarrely calm, reacting not to a crisis but to a natural, if unanticipated, event: everyone going about his task with methodical grace. Beyond them all, the far-off lightning continued to shimmer soundlessly, no more than a prospect now on some distant horizon.

At some point just before I fell asleep against Tilly's shoulder, I remember gazing through the broad frame of the windshield and thinking I would like to do something for them, for Hy and the firemen, all concentrating so hard and so truly on their labors, that I would like to go around the lawn with warm drinks, a plate of food, a hand to stroke softly each one's back. Thinking I would like to pass out cocoa and toast, that I would like to deliver to each one some small, good thing. Not so much to comfort or even praise them as to instruct them: that they should be this way always, this responsible and wise and strong.

CHAPTER ✦ FOURTEEN

WALTER'S SHIRT, HUNG over the oven door to dry, had burned up in the fire it caused, but the beer cans remained on the kitchen floor, and the story came out the next morning. I think Tilly would have told, anyway.

The house was not so badly damaged that we were barred entry; it was weeks before the kitchen was back in full working order, but we slept in our own beds that night. At least, Hy and I did; Tilly, whose room lay directly over the kitchen and sustained most of the smoke damage, climbed in with me.

We laid our heads down shortly before dawn and awoke sometime the next afternoon. Tilly and I, pajamaed, drifted through the altered house in a sort of dismal awe. Hy we found already downstairs, airing and scrubbing and throwing away, filling a giant cardboard box with the scorched remains of cookbooks, dishtowels, spice jars, cereal boxes. The rubber spatula. The transistor radio. The wooden salad bowl. Burned fruit. Some, but not all, of Hy's jam jars had burst; shards of glass littered the pantry, and the preserves had bubbled and hardened onto walls and shelves. The eggs were even more difficult to get up; these had exploded and cooked onto the surfaces where Walter had balanced them. One had fused right into the plastic cutting board, like some kind of art project or science experiment.

Tilly and I began silently to help, the air tense with guilt and morbid anticipation until Hy, surveying the blackened stove where she was to have baked Tilly's birthday cake, said dryly, "It's just as well—we're out of eggs." Tilly and I exchanged glances, and then watched as Hy plucked off the melted burner switches and chucked them rather gaily into the garbage. It was sort of funny, all of this. A little. Tilly and I joined in the spirit, tentatively at first, picking up the misshapen cocker spaniel salt and pepper shakers, the napkin holder, the drying rack, saying, "This, Hy? How about this? This, too?" and when she nodded, pitching them across the room into the box of junk. Then Hy got out a screwdriver and began prying the really badly burned doors off the cupboards, and we ran out of room in the cardboard box and began throwing things out of the pantry door, and we three went a little mad that afternoon, got silly, gasping with giggles. It was the first time we'd gotten like that since the start of the summer.

Later we went as a threesome to inspect Tilly's room. Along the rear wall, the baseboard and plaster were stained sooty black, as were the curtains on that window. Hy took these off their rod, and Tilly and I stripped her bed. A unicorn poster, blackened, got put in the garbage. We all three carried the mattress onto the front lawn, then spread the braided rug there as well. The garbage bag of mothballed sweaters had melted in one spot. All but one of the sweaters were all right, though, just smelly; they also went on the lawn. The magazines stacked under the bed got tossed. Tilly, on her knees, dragged the cookie tin out last. "The cover wasn't put back on tight," she said, with a look at me. She removed it. The dozen Violet and David pictures were stuck together, their images, when she peeled them apart, smoked over, ruined. "Well," said Tilly, looking in her lap. No one spoke. Then, quickly, she dumped the tin upside down in the garbage. After a moment, she looked up at Hy, standing over the bare bed frame, and Hy looked back at the two of us. The sun was going down already, outside the curtainless window.

That is what I remember of Tilly's thirteenth birthday.

We didn't see the Rouens again. Hy might have, I don't know, or maybe there was only a phone call, explaining that they had decided to pack up a week or so earlier than originally intended. They realized they had collected enough data, was how Hy transmitted their message later. We didn't question her.

We never told her about that last night on the porch with Bill Rouen. As Tilly said, what would we have told? That he sang "Happy Birthday"? Asked for a birthday kiss? Touched his finger for a moment to her cheek?

Tilly said, with what seemed to me dangerous confidence, that he wouldn't have done anything more, even if I had not set fire to the newspaper, even if Isobel hadn't made her entrance just then. She said that he was all posture, all pretend. But I wondered, how could she know this for sure?

The Rouens left that weekend. Tilly didn't seem grieved by their departure, not even Walter's. Possibly she was relieved; she did not ask special permission to visit him to say good-bye. She would have needed special permission because Hy had grounded her to the house for two weeks. But she showed neither surprise nor disappointment at news of their early departure. She was keeping busy scrubbing her bedroom walls white again, as well as those of the kitchen and pantry, and reading library books Hy and I brought her, and experimenting with plucking her eyebrows.

The night the Rouens left, Hy brought a pizza and store-bought cupcakes home, and we ate them out on the back step and gave Tilly her presents. Cal, still suffering from his chest cold, had sent via Hy a pale green strongbox with its own tiny padlock. From Hy there was a real grown-up present, a slim black camera with automatic focus and flash, and two rolls of film. My present was the bracelet I'd secretly assembled in my room, of the tiny red beads and chunky wooden ones. Tilly opened this last and scrutinized it for a minute. "Are these my beads?" she finally queried. "Did you get them out of my room?"

"I fixed it for you," I explained, I hoped winningly.

She shot me a wry look but did not comment, only extended her arm so I could fasten the clasp, which I gratefully did. We sat three abreast on the stone step, hip to hip and barely fitting, so that I could not help but notice how Tilly and I had grown. Colored paper and ribbons lay in the dust at our feet, and the sun went down and the air blued. "Do you like it?" I could not refrain from asking.

"Don't push it, kid," she said, but held her arm out before her. The bracelet dangled from the flat bone of her wrist. "It's nice."

I did not see her wear it again, though, and some months later, going through her drawers, was unable to find it, although I did come across, in the pewter pig that held ticket stubs, the little gold chain from Walter, which had indeed gone green. By then I couldn't quite remember what it was I had been trying to do by giving her back those red beads, and was embarrassed by what then seemed to me the forced importance I had bestowed upon the gift. It was to be an even longer time before I could recall the same act with compassion for myself, for whatever thing, now lost or forgotten, I'd been trying to do.

As for me, I wasn't sure how I felt about the Rouens' sudden departure. Relieved. Also sad, I thought, but was unsure what exactly about. With Tilly grounded, I was left by myself to wander down the road in the days after they left, to consider alone the empty house, the spot in front where their black car did not sit, the front porch voided of bicycles and candle pail and cane-backed chair. I thought, *It is odd when you don't realize you are seeing a person for the last time.* And standing there, I tried to locate and cement in my mind each last: the little children pressing saliva-dampened fingers into potato chip crumbs; Walter steering muzzily down our driveway on his bike; Dr. Rouen in a wet dress lifting her injured son into our car; Bill Rouen turned away from us, his bare back and heavy shoes ascending the stairs, himself attentive only to the bloody-nosed child in his arms.

Already I could feel myself squirreling away chosen details, fitting them into a kind of mental time capsule with splinters and belt buckles, cemeteries and marshes, mussels and sardines. Only they didn't fit quite neatly, didn't organize themselves according to anything that might readily have made sense to me, so that what they yielded was less a coherent picture than a jumble of jigsaw pieces whose collective meaning remained as yet unclear. Like Dr. Rouen and the marsh, I thought. All right. I would try, like her, to be happy with exactly that.

CHAPTER ✦ FIFTEEN

WE BOUGHT NEW shoes before we went, and Hy didn't tell us she was taking us there until we were back in the car with our new shoes on. They were school shoes, brown lace-ups for me, black-and-white saddles for Tilly, and we both wore them out of the store, carrying our old sandals in the fresh cardboard boxes under our arms. Hy got to the car ahead of us, then turned to appraise our admittedly slow progress.

"Why are you girls limping?"

"We're not." We giggled. "We're trying to admire our feet."

She frowned at this, though, and ran her keys slowly, almost dreamily, along her cheek.

We had just been shopping also for barrettes and socks and spiral notebooks, and although the air was not yet crisp, neither was it muggy, and the stores all had plaid things on display and paper leaf decorations in their windows, and as Tilly and I reached the car in our stiff, shining shoes, I found myself dreaming the smell of hard, tart apples, and asked, "Can we have grilled cheese and mustard for lunch?" Our new stove had finally arrived.

"Maybe," said Hy. "I suppose. But I wasn't going to go straight home."

"Where were you going to go?"

She sounded elaborately neutral. "I was thinking of taking you two somewhere."

And Tilly and I noticeably did not ask her what she meant; we all just went a little bit formal then, and got in the car quietly, each of us pensive and alert.

The drive was spiced with warm air billowing in the windows, the smell of end-of-summer, a parched, sweet stock. I sat in back, conscious of new shoes, and of the feeling of being driven somewhere. I felt myself bask in the luxury of being taken. We had left town, curved around by the lake road, and now branched off north, in the direction of Bluefields.

"Are we going to Bluefields?" asked Tilly.

"No."

Again neither of us asked for any more. Sunlight played in leaf-relief across the back of the front seat, and on my shoes, and after a bit we veered onto a side road, and then another, this one narrower and shady, and the air still smelled sweet and dry, though pinier, here in the denseness of firs. I was barely curious, or else my curiosity was counterbalanced by an unnameable certainty or faith in our destination, although I could not guess what that might be, when Hy slowed the car and turned in under a stone and wrought-iron arch that read, beneath curlicues of ivy, "Quashpeake Cemetery." We bumped over a length of unpaved ground before Hy cut the engine, and then we all got out, as easily as if we were home. Tilly and I, our smart new shoes receiving their first dust, followed our aunt down an earthen alley, the soil caked hard with August dryness, the grass pale yellow, matted close to the ground.

Their two stones: simple rectangles with rounded tops, the color, I thought, of cold cooked meat. They said only "David Grummer" and "Violet Moore Grummer" and the dates, not a thing else, but even that was almost moot by now, besides the point.

The fact of Hy's bringing us here was what meant anything to me—just now I realized this, standing before the two gray slabs and feeling little if anything for them—it was her gesture that suddenly interested me, itself a sign of something new or changing, and for the first time I sensed, with a real sharpness that almost hurt when I breathed, that I was in it, my life, that it was happening and I was in it, not as an observer, a careful collector of artifact and event, but as its chief participant, its architect and mason.

Beside me, Tilly pulled up her socks, new white anklets, and folded down the tops.

Hy said, "I was thinking I should have brought you before."

She pointed out then our grandparents' gravestones, right nearby, and some great-aunts and -uncles and second cousins and things. We all paused to listen to a bird.

"What's that?" asked Tilly.

"Meadowlark," said Hy.

We didn't have other questions for her. Of course there were things we did not know. But it was nearly September: Tilly had become a teenager; the Rouens had left; our kitchen had caught fire; and Tilly and I had grown out of the need for that particular mystery.

We wandered a little then in the piney sun and shade, admiring other graves, also wildflowers and birdsong, unimpatient, but when Hy said, "Lunch?" we were ready and went straight to the car.

Down at the lake after lunch, I gathered up my mussels.

Hy had gone to the shopping center to spend some of the insurance money on a new toaster and timer, and Tilly, who had finished serving her sentence only a few days earlier and was still savoring the novelty of any excursion, had decided to accompany her. I had switched back into my old sandals and brought the glossy cardboard shoebox down the zigzag path to the lake.

Now I reached my hand in under the root-roof, slid the shells out one by one. The kitchen and the bathroom, with their pearly linoleum bottoms. The moss-carpeted living room with its twig table and lamp, its pebble easy chair. The bedroom, its two valves laid with lichen and butterflied open on their hinge. The cradle, in whose hollow nestled the tiny translucent baby mussel Dr. Rouen had found.

Water slapped at the aluminum boat. I looked up and it nodded at me, sun winking off its side. The public beach across the lake was packed: families enjoying a last vacation day before school began. I watched them for a while, kids splashing off the dock, tiny lifeguards watching from their high white chairs. Over their heads passed a ragged V of Canadian geese, honking.

I blew each shell lightly free of sand and lowered them side by side into the new shoebox. Then I stood and, holding the box carefully level, made my way up the path. I had not yet decided whether to save the shells. Until I did, I would keep them here.